Joan shook her head, l[...]
warn you—!"

"Warn me? Why?" Nathaniel asked, pulling her hands so that she had to step a little closer to him. Why indeed? If she were not attempting to lash out at him for being the Cavalier, nor just to retain her cousins' flawless reputations, then why warn him of their plans at all?

"Because . . . because wagers are a very silly reason to do anything so important as to marry."

She did not want him to marry one of her cousins. There, that thought brought on that feeling again, that warmth, so different from the tingling the woman of the masquerade had filled him with, and yet it inspired the same response: he wanted to kiss her.

He pulled her closer yet, so that the toes of their shoes met, eliciting a small sound from her. Not a sound of denial, but the kind of noise that meant both surprise and reluctant pleasure. "Joan," he said, looking down into her face, "say you will not run away again, not just yet."

"Why would I run?" she asked, but the idea of flight lay in her eyes. Still, he almost smiled to note that she did not pull away, did not put any distance between them.

He held her gaze a moment longer, and then slowly, very slowly, he lowered his face toward hers. She did not step back, did not turn her face, and even in the dim light that came into the alcove from the corridor, he would swear she lifted her chin, just a little, as though to offer her mouth to his.

ZEBRA'S REGENCY ROMANCES
DAZZLE AND DELIGHT

A BEGUILING INTRIGUE (4441, $3.99)
by Olivia Sumner

Pretty as a picture Justine Riggs cared nothing for propriety. She dressed as a boy, sat on her horse like a jockey, and pondered the stars like a scientist. But when she tried to best the handsome Quenton Fletcher, Marquess of Devon, by proving that she was the better equestrian, he would try to prove Justine's antics were pure folly. The game he had in mind was seduction — never imagining that he might lose his heart in the process!

AN INCONVENIENT ENGAGEMENT (4442, $3.99)
by Joy Reed

Rebecca Wentworth was furious when she saw her betrothed waltzing with another. So she decides to make him jealous by flirting with the handsomest man at the ball, John Collinwood, Earl of Stanford. The "wicked" nobleman knew exactly what the enticing miss was up to — and he was only too happy to play along. But as Rebecca gazed into his magnificent eyes, her errant fiancé was soon utterly forgotten!

SCANDAL'S LADY (4472, $3.99)
by Mary Kingsley

Cassandra was shocked to learn that the new Earl of Lynton was her childhood friend, Nicholas St. John. After years at sea and mixed feelings Nicholas had come home to take the family title. And although Cassandra knew her place as a governess, she could not help the thrill that went through her each time he was near. Nicholas was pleased to find that his old friend Cassandra was his new next door neighbor, but after being near her, he wondered if mere friendship would be enough . . .

HIS LORDSHIP'S REWARD (4473, $3.99)
by Carola Dunn

As the daughter of a seasoned soldier, Fanny Ingram was accustomed to the vagaries of military life and cared not a whit about matters of rank and social standing. So she certainly never foresaw her *tendre* for handsome Viscount Roworth of Kent with whom she was forced to share lodgings, while he carried out his clandestine activities on behalf of the British Army. And though good sense told Roworth to keep his distance, he couldn't stop from taking Fanny in his arms for a kiss that made all hearts equal!

Available wherever paperbacks are sold, or order direct from the Publisher. Send cover price plus 50¢ per copy for mailing and handling to Penguin USA, P.O. Box 999, c/o Dept. 17109, Bergenfield, NJ 07621. Residents of New York and Tennessee must include sales tax. DO NOT SEND CASH.

Teresa DesJardien

Borrowed Kisses

ZEBRA BOOKS
KENSINGTON PUBLISHING CORP.

To Morgan Teresa Donaldson

*Because I love you, and because
you are my favorite kind of person:
the amusingly pushy kind who let
it be known when a book has yet to be
dedicated to you.*

Author's Note

In America, a building's ground level is called the first story. In England, the first story refers to what in America is called the second story. For purposes of authenticity, I have employed the English usage for this tale. Therefore, Joan's room is referred to as being three stories up—or, in American usage, on the fourth story, a space usually reserved for servants or storage.

Prologue

March, 1814

Miss Joan Galloway giggled as yet another pair of lips were briefly pressed to her own. She reached up blindly in the blackness of the unlit corridor, her hands finding the fabric of a man's evening coat, a sleeve. She pressed against the fabric, levering herself away from the cobwebby feel of arms trying to encircle her waist.

"One kiss is quite enough," she reprimanded, a laugh still coloring her words.

"I believe the only person I have kissed twice tonight is the old butler," a man's mock-petulant voice came out of the darkness.

Joan laughed again, moving away so that the unknown fellow might not too easily follow her voice and catch her once again. That was the spirit of the game, of course, to keep moving, to be kissed in the dark by many different pairs of lips. It was a rather wicked game, but harmless enough, and everyone was playing. It could not last long; soon Mr. Field's mother would be informed exactly what manner of entertainment her son had contrived during her masquerade, and that lady could be counted upon to put an end to such a thing as a Kissing Game. For now, while it lasted, Joan played as eagerly as anyone. Even as she was seized by another pair of male arms, she thought indeed how very much to her taste this cork-brained game was, for she had to admit she was not the most beautiful woman in London. A sightless game was an equal game—in the dark she was as beautiful as this or any Season's crop of "Incomparables." To the mouth now pressing hers, she could be no less than Aphrodite. Not that she was a quiz, of course, not by any means, and indeed two gentlemen in last year's Season had cared to beg a kiss from her—but she was equally aware that no offers of marriage had followed those kisses.

True, she had not received an offer in her first Season, but she was hardly daunted as to her matrimonial prospects. Perhaps the unidentified man breathing a wine-perfumed whisper of appreciation against her lips would one day, perhaps even soon, turn out to be her husband. Perhaps they would compare notes and realize they had kissed unknowingly "that night at the masquerade." Or perhaps this kiss, like the others she'd had tonight, would remain just a little secret she would forever keep to herself.

Either way, she had certainly made a wide acquaintance in the ton, enjoying many invitations. Being the daughter of a viscount, she had every hope she would receive an offer this year. After all, Mr. Mallington came each week to call upon her, and Lord Brackett had claimed over a dozen dances with her already this Season, and she did not feel it prideful to think she might even deem the handsome Lord Crowell as a beau. No, despite her somewhat advanced age of twenty, Miss Joan Galloway could not yet be described as being on the shelf.

As she moved away from the fellow who had last detained her, feeling her way along the wall with her fingertips, she added up the number of times she had been stopped and kissed in the lightless corridors at the back of the Field home. Seven times, so far, she giggled to herself and knew with an eager appreciation that other kisses waited in the maze of midnight-dark hallways.

Joan bumped into someone, who immediately felt her

shoulders, a feminine voice then saying, "Oh, a girl. Excuse me." The someone moved past her.

Perhaps the voice had belonged to Miss Atcheson, but Joan could not say for a certainty. Even had she seen the other woman's face, she might not have known her. Miss Atcheson might still be wearing her mask, even as Joan did, on the small chance that someone might see through the ink-thick gloom. Little enough likelihood of that, however, for the curtains were drawn, doors closed, and the lamps snuffed out. There was no hint of candle or moonlight to alleviate the cloak of night.

Another hand brushed her sleeve, accompanied by a whispered lisp of, "Lucinda?" Unmistakably, it was Sir Perry speaking.

"Not at all," Joan replied, her skirt brushing against him in a sigh of silk as she slipped farther down the hall, away from him. So, perhaps Lucinda Hilbert was not so wrong in thinking Sir Perry was sweet upon her! Joan giggled again to herself, storing the tidbit away to share later with Lucinda.

A flicker of light caught her eye just then, and she could not help but feel like the proverbial moth, for she was drawn to the light without hesitation. Someone had obviously bumped into a curtain on an exterior wall, revealing for a moment the soft, dull glow from the fairy lamps situated down below in the yard behind the house.

She stopped, the light gone now, and just as she thought she might have imagined it, a chuckle split the darkness and an arm snaked around her waist. She gave a gasp followed at once by a giggle as she was pulled up against a hard male chest.

"What a trick, sir!" she cried, staring up to where his mask would be revealed if only she could see it.

"No one said it was against the rules," came the reply in a deep, well-modulated voice.

She ought to know that voice, but the identity of its owner escaped her. "True," she conceded, but got no further, for two fingers touched her face, tipping up her chin, and then his mouth covered hers.

She kissed him back, as she had the others, but then the kiss went on a moment longer than any of the others had. His lips were neither too wet nor too dry, but warm and supple, inviting her hesitation there against them.

He did not press her lips into her teeth, nor was his mouth a soft thing that fluttered over hers too faintly. His arms did not pin her to him—she could have easily moved away—but were just steady enough to promise to support her should she choose to lean back into them. There were short feathers attached to his mask; they tickled her cheek, in a way that did not detract from the kiss. Another moment passed, and with a little shock of wonder she knew it was an altogether different kiss than any other she had received today—indeed, in her entire life.

She could not decide whether to be mortified at this prolonged embrace—it was he who moved away first—or chagrined that the kiss ended before she was quite sure she wished it to. Her indecision paralyzed her body as well as her tongue, and they stood blindly silent for a moment, only the shrieks and giggles of others farther down the hallway coming to their ears.

His hand came up, touching her face again in the darkness. There was a rustle, and she knew from the sound, despite the darkness, that he had pulled free whatever mask he wore. A moment more, and he had pulled free her mask as well.

She did not utter a word when he pulled her back for another kiss.

A searing kiss. A kiss that reached inside her, made her bones seem hollow, made her feel she would float upward were he not holding her to the earth within the circle of his arms. A kiss that made her gasp and open her mouth to him, an action that had never occurred to her before but now seemed natural, for he opened his to her as well. A meeting of tongues, exploring, savoring. An intimacy beyond her imagination, but not beyond a sudden facility to appreciate, to seek, to want it to go on.

Then his lips were against her throat, somehow more intimate yet. That she allowed his kiss there was no less than an acquiescence, an agreement to something primitive, an offer of vulnerability in exchange for a silent pledge of protection, although she was not really quite sure whose role was whose, or if they shared both alike.

His lips traveled along her collarbone, stopping at the fabric of the small puff sleeve just at the corner of her shoulder, then returned unerringly once again to her mouth. She felt herself tremble, felt a warmth flow through every muscle, every sinew, and wished he might go on kissing her until the sun came up to match the glow that spread inside her.

He lifted his mouth at last, not far, their faces close together still, so that her breath met and mingled with his. His hands moved to her upper arms, and he gave a sound rather like a gasp.

"What is your name?" he asked, his voice raspy.

The timbre of his voice made her smile and blush at once, for it was filled with a warmth that sounded much like eagerness.

Her smile slipped a little as she wondered if his question would have been so eagerly asked if they had kissed in the light? Would he notice that she wore simple jewels and an uncomplicated dress, so that her average face might not be eclipsed by material grandeur? Would the fineness of the silk she wore, the glistening of the expensive pearl bobs and choker be seen, or would he, like others before him, mistake simplicity for drabness? Would a man, any man, care to see past the finery of peacocks to the everyday plumage of a brown wren?

Yet, something had happened here, something she swore he had responded to as well. "My name?" she echoed, giving herself another moment to think.

"Your name. I must know it."

"But that is not how the game is played."

"Is it still a game?" he asked, his voice dropping, the change making her believe his question was both serious and sincere.

Her heart began to pound, and her decision was made: he would know her name when he knew her face, not before.

She moved out of his arms with no effort, and appreciated him all the more for letting her easily choose not to remain there, just as his touch had promised. She moved back against the curtain, gathering a handful of fabric in one hand.

"No name?" he asked, sounding disappointed.

"Not yet."

"Then when? How shall I know you? We must meet again."

She pulled back the curtain, exterior light coming through the window to slice through the utter darkness. She noted in the back of her mind that dawn could not be very far off, for there was an added grey quality to the light that had not been there just a few minutes earlier. The light of imminent dawn blended with the dim golden light of fairy lamps below—certainly abrupt enough, coming as it did out of total darkness, to surely obscure his vision of her. However, with her back to it, it provided just enough to expose to her astonished eyes a familiar face, now freed from the black mask dangling by its tie from the gentleman's wrist: the man was Lord Price.

"What a trick, madam," he said, a hand shading his eyes. He blinked and began to move toward her.

She released the curtain, her breathing uneven, and plunged them back into darkness as she moved aside, reaching with her fingers until she found the wall in the renewed blackness. "No one said it was against the rules."

He laughed softly. "Touché. But you have not answered my question."

"You have my mask, sir," she said, her rapid breathing accenting her words. Nathaniel Vaughn, Lord Price! Simon's handsome friend. Had she known it was him, she would have hurried in the opposite direction, for there was nothing so disconcerting as sharing a kiss with someone whose embrace one has already secretly imagined a hundred times.

She heard him move, no doubt toward her voice, so she danced away from the wall to the other side of the corridor, wishing her silk skirts did not rustle so. No, no, not Lord Price! Not the very man who had been ever polite and cordial—and all that was lukewarm in a suitor. Well, never a suitor. A caller. Not that he had ever called on "her," but rather had come to be with his friend, her cousin Simon. Oh, of all the men in the world, why did the giver of tingling, rapturous kisses have to be the one man she already knew had no interest in her? Why this man who had been so agreeable and yet clearly also would never be more than a face for her daydreams? The only good thing she could find in the situation was the knowledge that he gave no evidence of knowing who she was in return.

"Madam," he said, sounding more amused than exasperated. "If you insist on moving I shall not easily be able to return your mask to you."

"But that is my point, sir. You are only to return it when I ask for it. Later. When we might see one another in truth," she said, the words tumbling from her lips.

"So I am to carry the mask about with me? Hang it on my sleeve perhaps?" He chortled.

"Of course not."

"Good. I presume you now know my face?"

"I do."

He sighed. "I cannot like to leave it to such a pass, but I suppose I must await your approach, later. You have but to ask for your mask, and I shall know it is you."

She made no answer, belatedly realizing how difficult it would be to approach him later. Kisses in the dark were one thing, a direct flirtation in the light something else. It might be simpler if he did not already know her, had not ever looked upon her as only Simon's cousin. Just Simon's cousin, already made known to him a hundred times, and each time dismissed a few moments later from his thoughts, however kindly so.

"Madam?" he asked.

Again she made no answer, not moving from where she pressed back against the wall.

"Madam?" he repeated.

The following silence rang in Joan's ears, causing her to hold her breath, not daring to make the slightest sound. Perhaps he would think she had slipped away. She prayed it would be so.

"Sly creature," he murmured, then gave a low chuckle.

He whistled as he moved away, down the corridor, and she gave a smothered sigh. This was followed by a moment's pleasure at the thought of him whistling to warn other ladies of his approach. He could not mean to catch and kiss others, not if he forewarned them with a whistle.

Yes, perhaps the kisses they had just shared meant something to Lord Price as well.

Joan put a hand to her too-warm cheek, flushed anew by a sudden acknowledgment to herself that she would never quite convince herself of the boldness necessary to ask that he return her mask. He might not look disappointed to find it was only Simon's cousin who had kissed him, but she did not think she could bear it if he did. She could not throw away the slim chance that he might one day find her charming or witty or gay, not all on one precarious gamble. Their borrowed kisses would remain nothing more than a fond memory—for her as well as for him.

Yes, that was surely quite the best thing.

Joan went to the curtain again, lifting it just long enough to show her the way out of the corridors. It was time to go home, time to put tonight behind her, forever.

Mrs. Lyle stretched in her corner of the coach, her eyelids fluttering open. "I shall be that glad to see my bed, Miss," the chaperone announced after settling opposite Joan.

Joan gave a lopsided smile, amused as always by the

woman's inclination toward slumber. The woman could sleep at any time, in any place. The propensity made Mrs. Lyle a wonderful chaperone for a young miss, or at least for the kind of young miss who enjoyed an unobserved kiss or two. While Joan had dallied in the dark, Mrs. Lyle had slumbered in a comfortable soft chair in the front parlor of the Field home, never the wiser to the partygoers' antics.

"Here now, what's Morse doing, coming here and all?" Mrs. Lyle wondered aloud, staring out the glass pane of the coach door.

Joan leaned to look out the window for herself. Her papa's head footman certainly was riding their way, one hand on the reins of his horse, the other grasping the handle of a large, seemingly heavy bag. "He is carrying my valise. Curious!" She sat back, sharing a frown of confusion with Mrs. Lyle.

Morse dismounted, handing the reins of his horse to one of Lord Field's grooms. He crossed to the carriage, said something up to their driver, and then the door was pulled open. Instead of his usual cheery face the dawning light revealed a drawn and worried countenance.

"Merciful heavens! Is something wrong, Morse?" Joan cried, stretching out her hand that he might help her down.

"Miss Joan," he acknowledged her, ignoring her hand. He reached up instead to remove his cap, nodding a greeting. "Yer not to come home, Miss Joan. Yer pa has said as yer to go on to yer aunt and uncle in Hanover Square," he announced.

"Is Papa injured? Ill?" she demanded, knowing Papa would never send her away for any less a reason, particularly following a late night's entertainment. Indeed, it must be something quite dreadful for him to send her to her aunt's so late into the night. It was nearly dawn, and Joan would be utterly unexpected there.

"Don't come to the house, he says, not even fer yer things," the footman declared.

"I am not going anywhere until you explain why I should."

Morse looked down at his cap, avoiding her gaze. " 'Tis the constabulary, miss. They're there," he said in a lowered voice. "Mr. Kendall has paid ter have yer pa brought in against the matter o' outstanding debts. Lord Stanmore, he's already explained to 'em he can't pay, yer see." His eyes flickered up momentarily, then lowered again in embarrassment. "He's more than bankrupt. I heard him meself when he said as how there'd be a finding by the court that he's a debtor in truth, and there's no manner o' paying the notes hanging over his head. So's they're taking him in, Miss Joan. They're closing up the house, to get it ready to sell the contents, you see. Oh, Miss Joan, it's that sorry I am!"

"Debtor's Prison?" Mrs. Lyle gasped, her tone as full of astonishment as Joan felt.

"Why, this is all wrong," Joan said through lips made stiff by shock. "I mean to say . . . Debtor's Prison? Selling our belongings?" She frowned terribly, and when she spoke again, her voice was stronger. "I cannot imagine Papa letting an account go into such arrears that it comes to this. There is obviously a mistake here. This Mr. Kendall—"

"A pastry chef," Morse supplied, looking miserable.

"Whoever he is, he must be made to prove his claim, for then it will be clear there is some error," Joan stated firmly.

"Even so," Morse said, shifting from one foot to the other, "if he's proved mistook, there're a dozen more what wouldn't be, Miss. It was only a matter of time."

Joan stared, persuaded it was true even though she had not known any such reality only five minutes earlier. Yet, how could she not have foreseen it was coming to this? How could she not have seen the signs of overpowering debt?

But she could only think of a few small things, small changes that now seemed suspicious—*objets d'art* sold, linens mended instead of replaced—yet all were measures that made perfect sense, that did not necessarily reflect a shrinking purse. Perhaps the debts were not too substantial. Perhaps things would be amended shortly and swiftly settled.

The knowing distress on Morse's face promised otherwise.

"You can't go home, Miss Joan," Morse said sadly. "Lord Stanmore, he wants yer to stay clear o' the house, just in case they decides to get ugly and take yer in, too. I don't think they'd dare, but we've all heard tale of whole families being thrown into Old Jug, so it's truly best yer go on to yer uncle now, Miss."

"I see," she said, not seeing at all, and not quite sure she said the words aloud, so cold and numb did she feel inside.

"Here's yer valise then, with some o' yer things inside. Annie packed it fer yer. They wouldn't let her take none of yer mother's jewels, though she tried her best, Miss." Morse lowered his gaze again, the action reflecting the shadow that passed through Joan at the thought of the loss of Mama's jewels. Oh, surely not! Surely all this would not end with such a loss, the legacy her mother had left her.

Morse looked up sheepishly. "I hate to ask and all, Miss Joan, but some o' us were wondering if'n you'd be good enough to write references fer us, now we gots to find new employment."

"Of course," she said, staring at his face, reading the uncertainty of the future there. Her hands balled into fists, and she pressed them to her collar, as though to ward off a blow. "Of course I will. You must come to Uncle Newland's home tomorrow night, and I will have them ready for you. For Annie, and yourself, and Hobbs, and . . . and Mrs. Lyle—Oh, Mrs. Lyle! Morse! This cannot be happening!" she cried, willing the two servants to tell her otherwise.

Mrs. Lyle just shook her head, pressing a kerchief to her mouth.

"I wish it weren't, Miss." Morse set the valise on the seat beside her. Joan stared at it with a dawning awareness that her whole world had been reduced in minutes to nothing more than that, the contents of a valise. "I've told yer driver, Hawkins there, to drive on to Hanover Square," Morse said sadly, stepping back to get out of the way of the carriage wheels.

Joan took a deep breath, nodding slowly. But then she sat forward. "I want to go past the house first. Tell Hawkins."

"Oh, Miss, I don't know as that's wise and all—"

"Tell him. I have to see it for myself. Just for a moment," Joan insisted.

Morse bobbed his head, his unhappy expression showing he understood her need. "Yes, Miss." He shut the door, and a moment later the carriage began to roll, turning to take the street home rather than toward Uncle Newland's house.

Dawn was breaking as the coach came to a halt on a side street. The driver dare not take them closer than that, Joan knew, so she did not lean out the coach to insist that he must. She had to look down the line of familiar frontages, past the homes of neighbors she had known for years, to where a black, windowless coach sat before her own home. There ought to have been some lamp-light coming from the windows, for the dawning day was yet too young to light the interior, but her home's façade was dark.

She began to rap on the ceiling, to let the driver know to go on, thinking Papa was already gone, but she had waited a moment too long. For she looked at her home again just in time to see two large men "escorting" her papa to the windowless, waiting carriage. It was the way Papa hung his head, chin to chest, that finally allowed her to fully accept that no mistake had been made, to know without doubt that her life of comfort and privilege had just been irrevocably altered.

One

The door opened, allowing for a moment the raucous sounds from the crowded public room beyond to reach into the private chamber. Nathaniel looked up at the sudden noise, hoping to see Simon enter this sanctum bespoken every Tuesday night for the members of their driving club. Instead, it was only the serving maid, returned with a tray filled with mugs of ale.

Nathaniel lowered his gaze once more to the thick, pitted tavern table before him, trying to ignore the niggling sense that tugged at him. Perhaps it was just that he looked for Simon . . . but, no, he knew better. The thought niggling him was of "The Woman." The one he had kissed at the masquerade, the one who had kissed him back. It was "That Kiss" that constantly tugged at his attention, that made him look into every female face he encountered, made him wonder: *is this the one?*

Six weeks. It had been six weeks since he shared That Kiss with the mysterious lady. Six weeks in which she had never come forward. Six weeks in which he had failed to discover who she was.

He had asked Charles Field for a copy of the guest list from the night of the masquerade.

"Ask my mother for the list? I think not!" Charles had declared. "She was never one bit pleased with me once she found out how I had added that kissing game to her party.

My ear smarts yet from the scolding I had that night, let me tell you that!"

The best Charles could do was to mention a name or two of some young ladies who he was sure had attended. But it was scarcely a moment after Charles finished listing them that Nathaniel knew none of them could be the slender, witty, engaging young lady he had shared a very special kiss with that night. He knew them all, and none of them could be The Woman.

Pushing his mug of ale about between his two hands, Nathaniel sighed, restless and not quite able to engage in the banter that went on around him. Most of the ten fellows who made up Price's Princes—the coach-and-four driving club, of which Nathaniel was captain—were here tonight, reviewing the race they had run just this afternoon. Normally the topic of challenging their arch rivals, the Devil's Drivers, would be all that he found riveting, especially since Lord Crowell's coach had cut a corner, thereby allowing Crowell to win the race, but Nathaniel had no stomach for controversy tonight.

Perhaps he should make his excuses and just go home. Still, if he stayed on a bit Simon might come and find some manner of conversation which would supersede this unsettling sense that beleaguered Nathaniel.

"Will your coach be ready to run on Sunday?" Jacob asked, sliding onto a bench opposite his.

"I think so. The coach builder said the new axle will be stronger and more flexible," Nathaniel answered. He did not sigh aloud, but he did wish the topic might turn to something other than racing. Something more important, or closer to the heart perhaps. Yes, tonight was a night for serious, thought-provoking conversation, the kind at which Simon excelled. But Simon was not here.

"Are you having both axles replaced then, or just the broken one?" Jacob went on.

"I told him to do both."

"Good show!"

Jacob was the younger of them, twenty to Nathaniel's five-and-twenty years. *True, Jacob is young,* Nathaniel had the sudden thought, but Jacob had an extensive history already with the gentler sex. For the first time all evening, Nathaniel sat forward to engage someone in direct conversation. "Say, Jacob, now you have sat a moment, let me ask you a question."

"My pleasure."

Yes, Jacob was the very one to ask, for he had proclaimed his great love for at least a dozen females, and consequently had reported just as many broken hearts. "What I want to know is this: what is the thing about women?"

"Women?" Jacob laughed. "What's what about 'em, Cap'n?"

"I mean, why do we fancy one over another, do you suppose?"

"Should have something to do with the size of their, er, charms, I should think." Jacob laughed again, but then he leapt to his feet, his attention already turned as he fell in step with Sir Francis. "Francis, did you know Nathaniel here has ordered two new axles?" he asked as he moved with the taller man to join where two others sat tossing dice.

Nathaniel started to stand, to cross and join the lively discussion this news touched off, but ended by leaning his back against the wall of his corner. He didn't want raillery; he needed commiseration.

Wherever is Simon tonight? he thought as he watched the serving maid leave the chamber. If Simon were here, Nathaniel would have someone to talk to about something other than the four-in-hand racing his club practiced, someone who would not mind overmuch if "good old Cap'n Nate" was the one to pour out his woes of the heart for once.

Troubles. Of course, his troubles were nothing compared to Simon's, but . . . all the same. . . .

Nathaniel picked up his mug of ale, taking a large swallow rather than his usual sip. He was not one to drown his sorrows, in fact he seldom drank at all, for his was a head not made for drinking. He had shaped that opinion long since. But he felt like indulging himself for once, felt as though he deserved the right to sit and drink a little and coddle a case of his own melancholia for once.

It was ironic, That Kiss. For the very first time in his life he had felt something larger than a simple carnal desire for a woman, and he could not find again the unparalleled woman who had shared it with him. The magic of something more than mere attraction had touched him, and had slipped immediately from his grasp.

If I do not watch myself, I shall grow positively maudlin tonight, he thought, frowning at his mug as if to blame it for the fact that, after all, he had no real appetite to drain it of its contents.

He began to contemplate which was more trouble, taking his leave or forcing himself to a companionable cheeriness to share with the others, when Lawrence sat down beside him.

"Laffy," Nathaniel greeted his friend morosely.

Laffy's face was arranged in its usual somber lines. Early acquaintances were never quite sure if the fellow were making sport of them or not, for he would say something witty or pithy, but the expression on his face remained ever sober. It took a few months' familiarity before Nathaniel had seen the face did not go with the clever tongue, and to understand the drollery that had long since changed "Larry" into "Laffy."

Laffy moved now like a man well aware of his own insobriety, smelling of Blue Ruin and ale, a combination that made Nathaniel wince to think of what the morning would bring for his friend.

"You've a long face, Cap'n Nate," Laffy said by way of a greeting, running a hand over his own long-faced features to indicate he was well aware he had made a pun at his own expense.

"Have I?"

"Yes, you have. Is something wrong?" Laffy looked mildly concerned as he took a draw at his mug. "Simon ain't dead, is he?" he questioned, solemn as ever, only the light in his eyes reflecting the fact he was jesting.

"No. Just my soul," Nathaniel sighed, then flushed scarlet at the silly, melodramatic phrasing. He pushed his mostly-full mug away, silently blaming the few swallows he'd had for the mawkish looseness of his tongue tonight.

Laffy evidently thought little of it, but then he was surrounded by like sentiments every time he came to one of their meetings. He'd been known to dip into an emotional diatribe against life's woes himself. Indeed, low spirits could only be expected this evening, as the team's sole coach that had raced this afternoon had lost to the cheating Lord Crowell and his Devil's Drivers.

"Dead soul, eh?" Laffy asked, much as he might have asked about a ruined cravat.

" 'Fraid so."

"Shame."

"I daresay so," Nathaniel said, then repeated it, louder, with the kind of silly righteousness too much drink brought out in others, "I daresay so." But even as a kind of piety that he had as much right as any other to bemoan his woes invaded his voice, the thought passed through his mind that, yes, his mates loudly and frequently mourned their broken hearts—but at least they'd had the good sense to first fall in love.

"But that is my very problem," he said his thought aloud, warming up to this new and personal experience of lamenting out loud.

"How's that?" Laffy inquired, planting his elbow on the table and his chin on his palm.

"Falling in love," Nathaniel said, urged on by Laffy's apparent interest. "Me. In love! I ought to have fallen in love at least once by now, but I have not. Not even one single time."

"Never?" Laffy sounded sad. "Never fallen in love?"

"Never. Not once in my whole life."

"Not even in your salad days?"

"He is still in his salad days," Sir Francis interrupted as he sat down at Nathaniel's side. "But what is this that Nate's never done?"

"Fallen in love," Laffy answered, looking pleased he had followed the conversation despite his inebriation.

"Stuff!" Francis snorted into his mug, but when he lowered it there was a contemplative gleam in his eyes. "But that cannot be true, surely? Let me think. There's been some pretty bit somewhere along the line, certainly. There was . . . well now. Hmmm. That Cynthia girl! But no, Simon fancied her. Hmmm." Francis frowned.

Russell—long since known as Rusty because of his red hair—sat down at the table as well, instantly joining the conversation. "I declare I cannot recall you ever speaking some fair maiden's name, Nathaniel. Imagine! But then, you are circumspect. Not one to carry tales. So surely there's been one somebody, a somebody we've not heard tell of?"

Nathaniel shook his head, beginning to feel just a trifle foolish as the room's focus shifted to him, as one by one his fellows turned to his table with considering expressions on their faces.

"I've kissed my share," he said, raising a finger like a schoolmaster making a point, for Rusty was looking at him with something too close to pity. "And I've ogled a fair sight more, I daresay, but no one lady has ever caught my heart." There, he'd said his piece; time to move on to another topic.

"No one's caught his heart," Rusty sighed.

"No one's caught his heart," Francis repeated, rolling his eyes. "Next he will be telling us he's a virgin."

"He ain't, you know!" Jacob pressed forward to assert. "Why, Simon told me about this one bawdy house in Berkshire—"

"Of course he ain't," Rusty interrupted with a disgusted

look. "But that don't mean he's ever gone and lost his heart, now does it?"

"I have not," Nathaniel assured them, suspecting this discussion had become more awkward than purgative, as it had once been meant to be. He cleared his throat. "But, now, this is all to no purpose. I mean to say—"

"Not even an opera dancer?" Laffy asked, looking worried, but then again, that was the way he always looked when he'd had too much to drink.

"No—"

"Lust and love are two different dishes, you looby," Rusty declared. Jacob nodded gloomily at this proclamation, and Laffy thought about it with a hand to his chin, taking no insult.

"But that is a discussion for another day," Nathaniel announced, sitting forward on his bench in preparation of standing, desiring to put an end to this evaluation of his lovelife.

"What will it take for our friend to experience *l'amour?*" Rusty cried. "Think, boys, think! We must help the poor creature."

"Leave him be. Love's a common, lowly state," Jacob muttered. "Better he should never know its sting."

" 'Better to have loved and lost than never to have loved at all'," quoted Rusty. "Besides, if your Miranda sent you on your way, it's no more than you ought to have expected with her married and all."

"Oh, please! Let us not speak of Merciless Miranda again!" Francis declared with a grimace.

"Gentlemen, gentlemen, this is all to no purpose. 'Tis Nathaniel we must aid," Rusty insisted.

Nathaniel stood. "I do not require any assistance, thank you very much. I am perfectly capable of handling my own affairs."

"How so, old fellow? Seems evident to me you are not capable, as you yourself have declared your heart utterly untouched."

Nathaniel stared at Francis for a long moment, a direct result of having no reply to that piece of logic. "Well, not untouched exactly," he managed to get out at last.

"Ah! So there has been someone who's caught your fancy!" Rusty leaned forward eagerly. "Was it Lady Langford? Or the Incomparable Miss Alstead? Or—" Rusty's eyes danced with amusement, "—could it have been Merciless Miranda?"

"I say!" an offended Jacob cried.

"No, no," Nathaniel said, shaking his head. "I merely meant that although there have been times when I was moved to admire a woman's beauty, to delight in her laugh, or to long to gaze into her eyes—"

"Well, that's love, all right," Laffy declared.

"—That the moment I'm away from whomever the lovely lady is, I have no inclination to write a poem to her beauty, nor strive to recreate her tinkling laugh in my mind, nor to moan and weep because she is not at hand so that I might gaze into her eyes. I cannot even remember what color her eyes are. Surely that's not love?" Nathaniel inquired, raising his eyes to gaze into the faces about him.

They each shook their heads sadly.

"I am afraid pining is a bit of the whole package," Laffy pronounced. "If you don't pine, you ain't in love." He looked down at the tabletop for a moment, as if pausing to remember an old lost love of his own.

Now everyone nodded. Even Sir Francis, who scoffed at all sentimentality, inclined his head at the truth of this.

"You see what I mean then," Nathaniel said, tugging his waistcoat neatly into place, and reaching for his hat.

" 'Tis just a matter of time," Rusty said, reaching up to give Nathaniel a pat on the back. "Someone special is just on the horizon, I have no doubt."

More nods all around.

"Perhaps you don't court them enough," someone muttered from the back of the group.

"What?"

"It could be," Jacob said. "I mean to say, perhaps you are not the courtly sort. A bit of flowery praise and a small gift or two can go a long way toward softening a lady's gaze, you know."

"I know that," Nathaniel replied crisply, firmly setting his hat on his head.

"And tending to her needs, that makes a lady look in your direction, too," Rusty put in. "The old handing-her-down-from-her-carriage routine, or putting one's cape over a puddle."

"Yes, aping a footman or ruining a perfectly good cape is always the best way to win a lady's heart," Francis returned in a sarcastic drawl. He rapped his cane head on the table to secure Nathaniel's attention. "No, Nate, what you want is to call on a lady's parents. Win the parents over, and the girl will follow every time, mark my words."

"No, 'tis flowers that win her."

"Poetry," came another bit of advice, and "Comfits," and "Attending services at her church," until the air was filled with the raised voices of gentlemen hotly debating the various techniques for attaching a lady's regard.

Nathaniel picked up his mug and banged it against the table surface. The action served its purpose, for the group quieted.

"My dear gentlemen," he said firmly, "as well-meant as your advice no doubt is, may I point out that I do not have any problem with engaging the affections of young ladies. My problem lies with the fact that *I* am the one who does not feel affection toward any one of them."

"Well, now, that is rather the point," Rusty said sheepishly, an agreeing murmur running through the group.

"Thank you," Nathaniel acknowledged the comment with a nod of his head. "So, you see, you cannot help me in any wise. I beg you do not even make an attempt to do so." He stopped a moment, frowning to himself, imagining a variety of stupid little acts his friends might attempt on his behalf should he allow them to think, even for a moment, that they might be aiding their friend somehow. Awkward introductions, forced dances, hired tarts—dash it! Certainly it was better to cut them cold, to put a stop to anything before their kind and misguided hearts could devise it.

"You know, there was that kissing game a few weeks back. Remember, the one at Field's home?" Laffy asked, his solemn face brightening a little at the remembrance.

Nathaniel at once shook his head. He shuddered—there was that tingly sense of discontent again, and all at the recollection of an unexpected kiss with an unknown lady. A lady who had never, later, in the light of day as she had promised, asked for her mask back, though six weeks had passed. A lady whose kiss had led him to the very sentiments he now rued speaking aloud. It was her fault, the blame of her kissable lips, that he had begun to experience a growing dissatisfaction with his lonesome state, his unengaged heart. What had once been the meat of youth and gaiety, was now the thin broth of a sharp and particular solitude. It seemed cruel that he could recall something special, with no way of knowing how to experience it again.

"I remember that!" Rusty cried. "The kissing game. Perhaps we could stage something like that for Cap'n Nate here."

"No," Nathaniel said emphatically. He sank back down to his seat. He would go nowhere until he was convinced no plans would be brewed behind his back. "No. No. No."

"But Cap'n—"

"No!"

"But—"

"I shall conduct my own love life, thank you. I hope that is sufficiently and emphatically clear to all."

"He's afraid to fail in front of us. I can understand that," Jacob said.

Perhaps the man meant well, but Nathaniel gave him a speaking look all the same. "It is not a matter of fearing to fail," Nathaniel said, speaking succinctly. "I care to conduct my private affairs privately—admittedly a concept many of you fail to comprehend."

"Could he be referring to the many moans we've had over Merciless Miranda?" someone whispered from the edge of the group.

Jacob colored. "Yes, well, I failed with that particular lady, 'tis true, but at least I have dared to love and lose."

"Are we back to that?" Francis cried, rolling his eyes. "Besides, you puppy, Nate Vaughn could have any of a dozen ladies in love with him at this very moment for all we know. He simply chooses not to love them back—though why, I fail to understand."

"There is a little matter of leading a lady down the primrose path," Nathaniel said. Really, the usual raillery was getting out of hand, slipping into snippishness. Too much imbibed ale all around, it would seem, the direct result of losing the race to the Devil's Drivers.

That was a pompous name for a driving club, Nathaniel thought yet again. Although, by accepting Kendrick Fitzhugh, Lord Crowell, as their captain, how could any group fail but be anything but pompous? "The Devil's Drivers" indeed! The name lacked that modicum of humor which Nathaniel hoped his own driving club had obtained by naming themselves "The Princes," for their driving gear was fashioned to keep out the weather, not to win any awards for beauty, whereas Crowell's cronies did their best to remain at the height of fashion in all endeavors, rain or shine. And certainly they drove any of their four available coaches like devils, whether in a race or no.

Laffy's coach had been out front for nearly the entire race, and would have won if Crowell himself had not cut his corner at the end of Rotten Row—though the man had denied the case emphatically despite the numerous witnesses who'd decried the fact. Tempers had flared, until Nathaniel had quietly bid his men accept the race standing as it was, to avoid a case of fisticuffs in Hyde Park. If Crowell were a consistent cheat, he would be done up by his own folly soon enough.

But perhaps some of the resentment from the event lingered; certainly everyone was in a testy mood tonight, and Nathaniel had to count himself among that number even though he had not been the man at the reins.

"Primrose path? That is not where I lead my ladies," Jacob continued the banter.

"See here, Jacob! Nate is only being noble. He will not engage a lady's heart unless he may offer his in return," Rusty pronounced.

"Yes, well, I say the ladies are put off by his ways," Jacob argued. "I say he ought not berate us for having love lives— howsoever misconceived they may have been—when he cannot form one himself."

Francis stretched out his long legs, looking bored. He told Jacob, "But he can."

"But I can," Nathaniel said at almost the same time. He sank back against the wall, suddenly tired. "I just have not wished to."

"Cannot!"

"Can." Francis sat up, raising his eyebrows, his interest once again captured. "You simply have not been a part of this coterie long enough to know Nathaniel can charm any lady when he chooses to exert himself."

"That is most certainly true, my good Sir Francis: I know no such thing. In fact, I am quite beginning to believe the opposite," Jacob pronounced.

"Whoa-ho! I smell a wager." Francis gave a feral grin.

"Indeed, sir!"

Nathaniel frowned. Jacob, normally a pleasant fellow, had his blood up tonight. It seemed he would not give way to any pronouncement by Francis.

"A wager on kisses," Francis proposed, laughter in his voice.

"Very well," Jacob replied, giving a firm nod of his head.

"No!" Nathaniel said yet again. He rose, hoping to put paid to the entire conversation.

" 'No' to what, good friend?" Francis asked, still smiling. " 'No' to a wager, or 'no' to your ability to fall in love? Or to win a kissing challenge?"

"I can!" Nathaniel cried, then paused, wondering for a moment which part of the question he had answered. He shook his head again. "No wagers," he pronounced instead. "Take my word, boys. I can kiss anyone I want, any time." As soon as the words were said, he realized how foolish and boastful they sounded. "I mean to say—"

"Oh, really?" Jacob asked archly, his eyebrows disappearing under a lock of hair that had fallen forward on his forehead. "Anyone, any time?"

Sir Francis laughed loudly, and exchanged a speaking look with Jacob.

"I can. So leave my business to me," Nathaniel said, frowning all the more, for there had been some manner of significance in that exchanged glance.

"Even the most beautiful woman in London?"

It was too late to retract his claim. "Even so."

"Oh, really?" Jacob repeated. He turned to Francis. "It is a wager then, sir."

"Even so," Francis echoed Nathaniel. "Twenty quid says he can kiss . . . oh, let us say six beautiful women, to be designated by us as a group, by the end of the month."

"Done!" Jacob cried.

"You will need a disguise, of course," Francis said, rising and turning to Nathaniel to gently tap him on the chest with the head of his cane.

"What?" Nathaniel felt a scowl spread across his face. "What's this you say? I'll be no part of—"

"Too late, old chap! The wager is set. You were the one who boasted he could do it."

"Do what?" Nathaniel growled.

"Why, kiss any beautiful woman in London, of course. No

backing out now. And no laying a wager on yourself! I declare you will have reward enough by stealing kisses from the six most beautiful women in London."

"I will not do any such thing! Taking kisses like some manner of highwayman in a poorly written drama! 'Tis not noble—"

"True enough. That is why you need a disguise, dear friend." Sir Francis, the taller of the two men, smiled down at Nathaniel.

The sight of that extremely amused smile put an end to Nathaniel's protests—he knew there was no turning back the wager. Through Jacob's high spirits, Francis's devilish humor, and his own folly, he had somehow pledged himself to kiss six women.

The persona of the Kissing Cavalier—a disguise intended to stave off society's wrath at having its daughters so summarily besieged—was invented by the others around him in the course of the remaining evening. For his part, Nathaniel sat, despondently listening and wishing he had never taken it into his head to speak his woes aloud. Or at least that Simon had been there to keep him from doing so in such an open and ill-chosen fashion.

Two

If only Simon had been there.

Nathaniel thought it yet again as he pulled his mount's head up from where the animal attempted to nibble the flowers lining this trail in Hyde Park. If Simon had been there to lend an ear the night of the wager, then the past two weeks of posing as the Kissing Cavalier would not have been necessary.

Nathaniel would never have had to pay some street urchin to place an anonymous advertisement on his behalf within the pages of all the daily news sheets. He would not have had to pretend at surprise and innocence when the article was mentioned, would not have had to listen to a dozen theories as to why someone would place an advertisement announcing an intention to kiss six beautiful women. He would not have had to bite his tongue when none of the theories came close to the real reason he had placed those articles: that he did not want to cope with screaming women, irately startled fathers, or over-zealous footmen. By letting the world know his intention, he had hoped to avoid giving anyone a severe shock—not least of all himself.

However, Nathaniel counted himself fortunate, for in the act of receiving the five kisses he had so far obtained, he'd had only one pistol waved in his face (the woman's brother, fortunately, had been as nonplused by Nathaniel's masked appearance as Nathaniel had been by the fellow's pistol, thereby allowing one precious minute in which to make good his escape); one mild abrasion (located on his person in a place polite society would never see but which his seat in the saddle reminded him of yet again); and one black eye from when a tree branch broke, sending him hurtling to a thankfully soft lawn below.

In fact, the whole affair, although distasteful, had gone past in a surprisingly swift and relatively painless manner. His only true disappointment had been confirming what he already suspected: that none of the women on the list he had been given was The Woman. He had thought as much, but the five kisses he had received had only confirmed the fact.

There it was again, that bothersome sense of discontent that came whenever he allowed his thoughts to roam back to the night of the masquerade. It seemed he would never come across The Woman again—perhaps she had gone to the country, or the Continent. Perhaps she was gone forever . . . or perhaps it was just a matter of time until they met again. Or had they met since already? Was she someone he knew, someone he did not suspect to be capable of the kind of unspoken charm he had so briefly known with her that night? If so, why did she keep her identity hidden from him? He would swear the kiss had left as much of an impression on her as on himself . . . could she be married? But why would a married woman have promised a later meeting, and then never arranged it? Discretion could be hers, should she wish it. And why did he choose to believe that, no, she was not married? Because his conscience would balk at daydreaming about a married woman? Or because he did not want her to have shared any similar experience with anyone else?

Such thoughts stopped Nathaniel as he rode within sight of where his friends had tied their horses under a large, spreading oak. He cast his eyes over the company as if he might find something other than the usual crowd of male faces, and sighed in something akin to disappointment. Of course, it was entirely possible his sense of discontent came from his task this night.

He was not supposed to bring his "proof" to this place

for himself. It was Simon's charge to bring the token here to the park, to where they had chosen to meet since the spring weather had turned fine, rather than at their usual inn. But Simon had not been at Hatchard's this afternoon as promised, had not come to retrieve the lock of hair Nathaniel took from the ladies he kissed, to prove to all and sundry that the kiss had indeed been obtained.

Nathaniel urged his horse forward. There were Sir Francis and Jeremy, engaged as usual in some manner of debate. And there, too, were Rusty and Jacob, Laffy, and Wiley, Trevor, Osgood, and Hugh. They made a lively gathering this evening, all dressed in their multi-caped driving coats to keep out the chill of a spring night.

And there, sitting against the oak, a bottle of wine in one hand, a cheroot in the other, was Simon—deep in his cups, Nathaniel saw at once, although few others would be able to know it at a glance. Nathaniel sighed as he dismounted.

A hail of greetings slanted his way. Nathaniel nodded to each man, stopping his advance toward Simon's side long enough to give a squeeze to Jeremy's shoulder. "Any more wagering?" he asked quietly, the words lost beneath the din of debate the two others had begun again as soon as Nathaniel's presence was noted.

Jeremy shook his head. "Learned my lesson, I did," he replied in a quiet voice. "Might risk a pound or two on quarter day, but elsewise I have sworn off the dice."

"Good man. Only a pound or two, mind."

"Never you fear," Jeremy said with an experienced shudder. He looked up from wide, youthful eyes. "I cannot say thank you enough for the loan. If m'father'd ever known—"

"I was very pleased to receive your payment Thursday last," Nathaniel assured him with a nod. Jeremy nodded in turn, looking pleased with his promptness.

Nathaniel greeted Wiley and Jacob, who clapped him on the back, and then moved to the base of the oak, stretching out his legs beside his long-time friend, Simon.

Simon greeted him with a lopsided smile. "Nate, m'boy."

"Simon. You are foxed. And you were not at Hatchard's."

"I was not, old friend. I apologize for that," Simon said, graceful in movement as always, with only the slightly slurred speech and mussed hair to reveal the secret of his inebriation. That and the fact he did not deny it.

Simon went on, flicking ashes from the tip of his cheroot, "I was called in to have an audience with The Newt."

Nathaniel did not smile at the nickname Simon used for his Uncle Newland. "An audience? Tell all."

"Not much to tell," Simon replied. He indicated the bottle with a movement of his head, not looking at all surprised when Nathaniel waved away the offer. Simon took a long draw from the bottle before going on. "Seems he has written a letter to my father," he said, his words too crisp, too clear.

Nathaniel waited, knowing more of the tale was to come.

"He read it to me. 'Tis a missive instructing my father to go ahead and purchase a commission in the army for me."

Nathaniel sucked in his breath, leaning his head back against the tree.

"He tells he is not quite ready to send it, however. I have one last chance to 'prove myself,' you see."

"What does that mean? One last chance?"

Simon shrugged. "Anything he wants it to mean. I do the slightest thing of which he does not approve, I suppose, and off goes the letter. Father will not hesitate then, you know. I shall be army-bound. And he would arrange it to be sooner than later."

Nathaniel lifted his head from the bark, surveying his friend's face. "What about America?"

"Or the Continent? Or India? The answer remains the same as the last time you suggested my removal from England: how am I to pay my way? That is ever the stumbling block, is it not? I have no sizable funds, and I have no knowledge of how to earn a living."

"I could—" Nathaniel began to offer, again.

"Lend me the money? And ruin a perfectly lovely friendship? Thank you, but no, emphatically no, old heart."

Simon had pride, of that there was a certainty. Perhaps too much.

"I loaned a pocket of the ready to Jeremy—" Nathaniel started to say, but a short, sharp look from Simon caused him to cut off the words. Simon was only too right, really: it would be unfortunate should Jeremy, through either circumstance or folly, prove unable to repay the debt. With Simon, it could only be a disastrous blow to their friendship, as much in Simon's eyes as anyone's.

Nathaniel did not mention returning to Oxford—that avenue had dried up after Simon was evicted for pinching the Head's robe and hanging it from a steeple, along with a vacantly grinning carved turnip for a head. That had led to his father's subsequent refusal to send Simon to Cambridge instead, or any other school for that matter. Waste of good money, he had claimed.

"No, it is the army or nothing for me, once Father decides I am not being a proper 'man about town.' I am not living up to his vision of what an eldest son should be, you see."

"Well, and what does he suppose town bronze to be? That was his stated purpose in sending you to your Uncle Newland, was it not?"

"Unfortunately, Uncle Newt is even less imaginative in his interpretation of 'town bronze' than Father. To my uncle, the phrase means I was sent here to marry an heiress, and nothing else will suit. I have been in his bad graces since the first moment I suggested I should like to consider whether or not I am ready to wed. And you may have noted I have failed to even become betrothed, despite my three whole months in London."

One corner of Nathaniel's mouth pulled up momentarily.

"And so you are being punished for being clever enough to avoid parson's mousetrap."

"Too clever." Simon's mouth turned up as well, but then

for just a moment his hands shook, just a little, and his Adam's apple worked in his throat. "Oh, Nate!" he said in a hoarse whisper, "What would I do in the army, tell me? I should be an utter failure at it, we both know it!"

Nathaniel blew out a puff of air, leaning back his head once more against the tree trunk. It was true: he had every reason to believe his friend would be either dishonorably decommissioned or dead inside six months. A spirit such as Simon's followed only its own internal orders, and that reliably independent nature was as likely to lead him down the path to disgrace as to a sudden foolhardiness. And during this war with France, foolhardiness on the battlefield was the same as a death warrant.

"In a life of nothing but taking orders, I am only one disagreement away from disaster," Simon murmured, his voice filled with disquiet and pain even as his mouth curved into a crooked smile at the truth of his own statement.

"You are too harsh in your opinion of yourself."

"Now is no time to take up telling me lies or pretty tales, Nathaniel Vaughn. We both know I cannot be a good soldier. 'Tis against my very nature."

Nathaniel nodded unhappily. "You make it sound a crime. But not everyone is cut out for a military career. You have other talents, other virtues. And you should ever remember you have a good heart," he assured his friend.

Simon laughed wryly. "But not an obedient one."

"No."

But how could Simon have learned obedience and still call himself a man? That was the crux of the problem between Simon and his father, of course. Too many lectures, too many canings had shaped a willful child into a defiant son. Sometimes Nathaniel thought that if Simon had not had a retreat, he would surely have become quite wicked or gone mad. Instead his increasingly frequent visits at Nathaniel's country home had shown Simon a household largely filled with harmony and tolerance. If his own father had had only dictates and rebukes for Simon, at least in Nathaniel's home he had known some peace, some appreciation of the person he was, not the one he was told he must be.

"I had thought when he sent you to London, that all would be better. The distance and all," Nathaniel murmured, staring at his boot tops.

"And so it was better, for I could be with you again, good fellow."

"But still he does not let you be your own man. He does not let you go despite your four-and-twenty years."

"He does not." Simon shuddered, lowering his head to rest his forehead on the knuckles of his hand, balled on his bent knee. "Do you know what makes it all the worse?" his low voice carried on the cool evening air. "Knowing Anthony and Wallace are with him still. If I went to America, or anywhere, I would have little enough hope of bringing my brothers to me. But if I go in the army, I have none. Thank God that at least they have their time away from him while they are at Eton."

Nathaniel clicked his tongue, narrowing his eyes, knowing it would do no good to request that Simon's younger brothers be sent to London during the holidays.

"Nathaniel!" someone called.

He looked up, seeing it was Sir Francis.

"Your friend there," Francis laughed, pointing at Simon, who sat up, his face at once rearranging into its usual pattern of *bonhomie,* "has failed to assure us that the token has been taken. Are we to assume the Cavalier has also failed?"

Several hisses of "shhh!" were raised, marking the passing of two other riders who had tarried in the park past the more fashionable hour.

Nathaniel shook his head. "We shall come to that in a minute," he said, then, in a softer voice toward Simon, "Now, as to this matter of the army—"

"Old news, old news," Simon cut him off with a seemingly

nonchalant wave of his hand. "I have been maudlin, and we shall have no more of that tonight."

Nathaniel bit back his words, knowing the effort it cost his friend to resume this mien of composure. They would talk more later, after the weekly gathering had ended for the night.

"What we want to know is this," Simon went on, arching a brow cockily for effect, "Did the Kissing Cavalier get his fifth token?"

Nathaniel glanced about, but no other riders drew near, so he pulled a paper packet from his coat pocket. He unfolded the paper, spreading the edges to reveal a ringlet of tawny brown hair lying thereon.

"Ha!" cried Francis in triumph, and the group's approving laughter filled the gathering twilight.

Nathaniel gave what he supposed to be a sheepish grin, even as he raised a finger to his lips. "Not so loudly!" he cautioned. "We shall draw attention our way."

The commotion subsided somewhat, but Rusty leapt up from his seat on the park grass, planting one foot on a tree root, his thumbs in his vestpockets, and demanded to know, "And the kiss? Let us have the tale. Was the lady willing?"

"But of course," Nathaniel said. He then rolled his eyes at their combined groans of envy and shouts of satisfaction. "I should never take an unwilling kiss from any lady," he explained. "But my fame precedes me, and so no lady objects to being kissed by a man who is known to kiss only the most beautiful of women."

Rusty turned to Jacob. "How did this fellow get the chance to be the Kissing Cavalier? I declare it is a duty I fancy for myself!"

"You may have it," Nathaniel offered at once, perfectly sincere.

"Oh no!" Francis interrupted, thrusting his hand between them, waving the offer away. " 'Twas Nate who boasted he could kiss all the beautiful women of London, so 'tis Nate who will prove himself or not. I for one, have twenty quid saying our captain will accomplish the task, and so we'll have no substitutes, thank you very much."

"You do not think I could do as well?" Rusty demanded with a grin.

"I know you could not. It requires charm to coax a kiss from a lady," Francis replied.

"Then you and I are both out of hope," Rusty declared in all good humor, laughing as a mock-insulted Sir Francis put his nose in the air.

Nathaniel shook his head at their raillery, folded the paper closed, and tucked it back in his jacket. "Too bad," he sighed. "I would have gladly relinquished the title and the duty." Nathaniel looked up to find Simon watching him, a quiet commiseration coming through light-colored eyes even despite the wine his friend had imbibed. Nathaniel knew a moment's gratitude that someone knew him well enough to believe he meant what he said. Simon, the only fellow here this night who was aware how misbegotten Nathaniel thought the wager to be, this silly business of taking kisses from beautiful ladies.

Nathaniel gave the slightest nod to his friend, warmed by the empathy he had seen in Simon's gaze. Then he looked away, wishing it took so little as a sympathetic gaze to solve all Simon's concerns.

"Oh, poor Nate! How terrible a thing to be made to spend one's time kissing beautiful women!" Jacob laughed in disbelief.

"It is terrible, old fellow," Nathaniel said to Jacob, allowing himself to grin. "As a result of so much kissing, I suffer horribly from chafed lips."

The group broke into renewed laughter, and even Simon had to smile despite the patent ridiculousness of five kisses causing any such malady.

Three

The members of Price's Princes turned their attention from considering Nathaniel's fate as the Cavalier, predictably and once again, to the serious matter of carriage racing. This left Nathaniel free to sit quietly beside Simon, who continued to drink, equally as quiet. In the manner of good friends, they did not need to talk idly merely to fill the silence between them. Simon was no doubt lost to thoughts of how he might best satisfy his Uncle Newland's exacting requirements, leaving Nathaniel free to think back on the past weeks.

Perhaps it was just as well he had not met again with The Woman. How could she possibly live up to the standard she had since acquired in his mind? They would, no doubt, prove a disappointment to each other should they ever in truth meet. Yes, there was more pleasure to be had in remembering that moment than in any attempt to recreate it, surely. But even as Nathaniel thought this, he knew he did not quite believe it.

And thank God this business of being the Cavalier was about to end! He had only one kiss left to obtain—and if Nathaniel could not take a kiss from Lydia Irving, then the rumormongers had the lady's reputation all wrong. The tattle was that the young lady was waiting on her balcony every night, openly desirous of being visited by the Cavalier and therefore firmly established as an Incomparable.

Yes, he need only one last time don the borrowed clothing and Francis's silly, large-brimmed hat (hence the "Cavalier," as Sir Francis had dubbed him.) Only one last time would he have to tie that ridiculous covering over his face. Only one last time would he have to try and keep the eye and mouth holes properly aligned. After one last appearance as the Cavalier, he would never have to climb another wall or waylay another carriage to obtain kisses from surprised young ladies—never have to invent another awkward system by which proof of the obtained kiss could be provided.

It was a simple system, really, once the group had agreed that the token he must bring back to them be a lock of the lady's hair. He was told to take the lock from a prominent place on her head, so that its absence might be easily noted by the interested parties.

The first young lady he had been instructed to approach, one Miss Cecily Halling-Smythe, was caught walking of an evening alone within the walls of her family's garden. Fortunately, she had read or heard of his advertisement, for she did not scream as one might expect her to do, given the fact he wore a mask and came unceremoniously over the wall to land before her feet. Quick words identifying himself as the Kissing Cavalier of the news sheets and explaining how she had come to be his chosen target—that is, glowing words of praise as to her great beauty—had proved to soothe any worries she might have harbored regarding his appearance. That, and convincing her he would go away and stay away only once he'd received the object of his quest.

He'd had his kiss, after which he had deftly taken his "token" by way of a small pair of scissors carried sheathed within his waistcoat pocket: a lock of the young lady's russet-colored curls, much to her extreme annoyance. In fact, she'd had quite enough of him by then, and so promptly kicked him in the shin and began to scream as if she were somehow managing to be skinned alive by those tiny little scissors.

He had never known before how swiftly one might go over a garden wall, even with a throbbing shin to hamper one's progress.

By the time he surprised the second young woman, the much-praised Miss Lucretia Alstead, she had obviously heard Miss Cecily Halling-Smythe had been the first to be visited by the kissing stranger. In fact, she told him as much.

"You are that fellow who kissed Cecily," she stated bluntly after he had guided his horse too closely to hers, causing the horse and curricle to turn sharply right, into a blind alley. Her maid had stared and moaned in fear at the sight of his masked face as he moved to block the only exit, but her mistress looked not so much frightened as annoyed as she gazed around the open carriage's side at him.

"Indeed, Miss Alstead," he had replied, his voice lowered in hopes of disguising it.

"Cecily was quite frightened by you, you know."

"Was she indeed?" he asked as he dismounted from his hired nag. He approached them swiftly, succeeding in going to her horse's head before Miss Alstead could think to back the animal and her carriage over him. "That is to my regret. I assure you, I mean no harm to anyone. I see I do not frighten *you,* however. Nor does driving home at the twilight hour with just your maid in attendance."

"I take it my habits have been observed?"

He could not tell if she was angered or amused by this fact. He nodded his head.

"It is quite true I have little fear of driving myself, at twilight or otherwise, sirrah!" she said with narrowed eyes. "Cecily Halling-Smythe is a simpering fool, but I assure you I am not."

"No one has ever said as much to me," Nathaniel replied, thinking to himself that a woman might be beautiful on the exterior, but rather less so in all other ways. Certainly for all her pretty face, Miss Alstead had a tongue well-versed in its ability to sting.

"And what is to stop me from simply driving away now from this attempt to accost me?" she asked crisply, allowing the driving whip she held to circle in his direction.

"Nothing, ma'am. I am dependent on your goodwill only."

"Well, that is a foolish way to win more kisses! And I assume it is a kiss you want? Or have you taken up stealing purses now?"

"No, ma'am. You were quite right in thinking it is but a kiss I want. I must, in fact, have one from each of the six most beautiful ladies in London."

"What schoolboy folly," she scoffed, but then she smiled, and he knew he had pleased her despite her feigned annoyance. "Very well," she went on. Her maid gasped, but Miss Alstead ignored the frightened creature. "You will have your kiss, but no lock of hair must be taken! Cecily might allow such a want-witted thing, but I shall have none of that!"

He put one foot on the curricle's step, swinging up to press his lips to hers, quickly, before she could voice second thoughts. The maid shrank back, groaning with apprehension, which served Nathaniel well enough. Her retreat gave him a little more room for his other foot, which he placed between maid and mistress just long enough to whip the scissors from his waistcoat and take a snip of blond hair from near Miss Alstead's temple. He turned and leapt down all at once, moving at once outside the reach of her driving whip.

"Oh, you rogue!" Miss Alstead cried, her hand springing up to feel where the lock had been snipped.

"I beg your pardon, ma'am, but I have no choice in the matter. And," he allowed himself to grin a little now, "I never promised I would not take my token."

Her eyes narrowed farther, and for a moment he thought she might come down from the carriage to pursue him with the whip, but then there was a reluctant amusement hiding there as well. "I ought to strike you . . . sir—? How was it you called yourself in that ludicrous advertisement, you evil creature?"

"The Kissing Cavalier, if it please my lady." He cut her an elegant leg, although he did not remove his large-brimmed hat, hoping it served to hide the color of his hair in the growing dimness. If not that, then hopefully at least the flush of color that sprang to his face at the ridiculous title his fellows had given him for use in this exploit.

"Kissing Cavalier!" She shook her head and made a derisive sound. She sat up, rearranging the reins in her hands. "Begone now, Cavalier Clod-pate. I only spare you my wrath because your actions have done me more good than harm."

He thought for a moment that she meant the kiss they had shared—certainly nothing special, nothing like another kiss he remembered all too well. He had known in an instant this was not that mysterious woman from the masquerade. "Indeed, ma'am. How can this be?"

She reached up again to where the lock of hair had been taken from her head. "I find it difficult to object overmuch to being marked as one of London's greatest beauties." She sniffed, a smile at last turning up the corners of her mouth. "Certainly far more so than Cecily Halling-Smythe."

"Indeed." He smiled in return, even if part of him sighed at the thought that, despite her beauty and a certain degree of wit, no adoring spark sprang to life in his breast. Why did he ever remain untouched by ardor? Perhaps he was not made for love? Certainly there were men who never married, who had presumably never been pierced by love's arrow. But did they ever wish to be pierced, or were they content with their lot?

He had bid her *adieu,* much to the maid's obvious relief— if less so the mistress's—and the next day had met Simon as prearranged to turn over the lock of blond hair. *If only she could have been that special woman,* he thought to himself now with a sigh as he looked down at the inebriated Simon leaning against the tree.

Their system had not worked today; Simon ought to have brought the fifth lock of hair—Lady Anne Graynolt's tawny brown ringlet—in Nathaniel's place, but since he had not come to collect the ringlet at the lending library as prearranged, Nathaniel had been forced to bring it to the meeting

himself. Their usual arrangement was for Simon to make a
point of being seen in a public place whenever Nathaniel told
him an attempt was to be made at obtaining a kiss and a
lock of hair, so that if Simon were later caught out with the
lock, he could easily and rightly claim he was but the mes-
senger, not the culprit, with dozens of witnesses to prove his
presence elsewhere during the execution of the "crime." True,
the eye of suspicion might still swing Nathaniel's way since
he and Simon were the closest of intimates, but Simon had
many friends—all of whom were far more likely to be suspected of such an escapade. Nathaniel Vaughn might be on
the list of suspects as the Kissing Cavalier, but he would be
low on the list. Heaven knew, he scarce believed it of himself.

It would have worked exactly to plan once more, if only
Simon's Uncle Newland had not called Simon in for that unfortunate lecture at exactly the wrong hour.

"Ah well," Nathaniel said aloud as he eyed his good friend,
now patently drunk. "Simon, you must be far gone to show
it so, my friend."

" 'Fraid so," Simon answered, with a slow, lopsided smile.

Nathaniel glanced at the darkening sky. "Time for home."

" 'Fraid so. If you c'n call m'uncle's house 'home.' "

"You can always come with me," Nathaniel offered, pulling
his friend's arm over his shoulder.

"No, Natey-boy. I mus' start getting used to living in Hades," Simon said, slurring his words despite an obvious effort
not to, "if I'm going to be joining the army soon."

Nathaniel counted to three, then stood, dragging Simon to
his feet as well. "Nonsense," he grunted.

"S'not nonsense, and we both know it. And b'sides, I've
got to return m'uncle's coach-and-four. Better to cast up my
accounts in his ve . . . vehi . . . vehicle than yours," he hic-
cuped.

"Difficult to argue with that," Nathaniel acknowledged
with an upward slant of his mouth.

Simon suddenly put up a hand, his signal that he required

a moment's pause to steady himself before they moved to find their carriages. In the pause, Nathaniel noticed that Francis and Jacob were caught up in yet another round of disagreement, and none too quietly.

" 'Tis blond, I tell you," Jacob insisted.

"Brown, you blind sheep!" Francis laughed.

"Blond!"

"Brown."

"Somewhere in the middle?" Rusty ventured, only to be ignored by the two other men.

"Blond!"

"Brown!"

Jacob whipped around to face Nathaniel. "You must produce the token again, so this nodcock can see the color for himself."

Nathaniel slid a significant glance toward Simon, cloaked about his shoulders.

Simon straightened his knees, wavered, and turned a ghastly shade of green about the mouth. "I should not mind sitting a moment," he managed to say, sinking heavily back onto the ground. He dropped his head into his hands and shuddered. Nathaniel frowned down at his friend and decided perhaps it was best to wait a moment or two before leaving. Silently, he reached into his pocket, producing the packet, one edge of which he unfolded to reveal the lock of hair within.

"Good gad, what color *is* that?" Rusty asked, scratching his cheek.

"A yellowy-browny sort of color," Jacob said, looking just as puzzled. "How do we call it?"

"I have always thought of Lady Anne as possessing a kind of brown hair. With golden highlights, yes, but definitely within the range of the brunette," Nathaniel stated.

"Truly? I should have said 'blond,' " came a deep voice from behind him.

All eyes lifted, and Nathaniel could not help the intake of

breath he took when he saw it was Kendrick Fitzhugh, Lord Crowell, standing there.

Their eyes locked, and a knowing smile began to creep over the other man's face.

Crowell nodded toward the packet of hair. "Given that I have knowledge of Lady Anne to be this morning missing a lock of hair of that very same color, and given that it is come from your very pocket, Lord Price, am I to understand I am now in the company of the Kissing Cavalier? Ah, I see by the faces of your friends, Lord Price, that I am quite correct in my assumptions." He stepped back, putting a hand to his chest, and stretched a leg as though at an introduction. Nathaniel felt the blood drain from his face. Of all the people to discover the secret of the Cavalier's identity! Lord Crowell—or Cruel Crowell, as others had called him—who had long since let it be known he had no liking for Nathaniel.

"Drat!" Rusty's concerned exclamation came low.

"Now only see what you have done," Francis said to Jacob, poking him with the end of his cane.

"I did?" Jacob squeaked, his voice loud in the open air.

"You insisted we see it. And lest we forget, the lock was brown, and you owe me a quid!"

"I still say—"

"Gentlemen, gentlemen!" Rusty stepped between them, interrupting the argument. "That is to no point at this moment." He looked up at the taller Lord Crowell, reaching up to drop a hand on Crowell's shoulder. "You will come with us to the nearest tavern, yes, and share a pint, will you not? After all, we have a little matter to discuss."

"A matter?" Lord Crowell asked with a tone that suggested he doubted Rusty had anything of import to say, ever. He then stared pointedly at the hand that touched the fabric of his form-fitted coat.

Rusty removed his hand, going a little pale under the high collar of his shirtpoints. "Er . . . yes. A matter of silence," he explained.

Nathaniel looked at Rusty with a mix of gratitude and surprise at this attempt to undo the damage already done, for it was usually Rusty who was the first to forswear any verbal negotiations for those that might be settled by a round of fisticuffs. That would hardly suit, however, for a quick glance revealed that Lord Crowell had brought none of his cronies with him, that he stood alone in this confrontation. So the meeting was as accidental as it seemed, for Crowell was never a one to jeer without an audience, not if he had a choice.

"Quite so. A matter for silence," came the mutters from the others as they all swept around Lord Crowell, making of him an island, shutting Nathaniel and Simon to the outside of their circle. Simon looked up briefly from his bleary-eyed seat on the ground.

"Rusty—" Nathaniel began, but was interrupted.

"Honor is at stake, you see," Rusty went on, his face still pale under the stiff silence in which Lord Crowell deigned to observe him.

"We ought not to have let the cat out of the bag; about our wagers. About Nathaniel being the Kissing Cavalier," Hugh rushed to explain.

"It is all our fault, you see," Rusty went on.

"My dear sirs," Crowell said, "I am sure you have some purpose in telling me this, but I can scarce imagine why you bother." He began to turn away.

Several sets of hands detained him, all withdrawn when his mouth turned hard and he gave their owners a speaking glance.

"The thing of it is this, my lord," Francis interjected, for once serious in look as well as tone, his words rapid and firm. "We all know that the *bon ton* tolerates these little episodes wherein their daughters are kissed only because the Cavalier remains an unknown. The minute a name is placed with the mask, their tolerance evaporates! We all know it is one thing to play a harmless and anonymous game, yet another to live with the consequences once it is no longer so anonymous."

"I daresay that is the risk the Cavalier—that Lord Price— has taken by playing his inane little game, is it not?" Crowell asked, managing to look bored and pleased all at once.

"But the result came about by no fault of his own. We have betrayed our friend by accident, it is true, but we intend to go forth and sin no more. That is to say, we have all sworn ourselves to silence regarding this little matter, and I am afraid you are likewise bound."

"Truly?" Crowell asked, his interest once again secured. His mouth now turned up into a smile—a cold thing nearly as hard as his scowl had been. "I declare I feel no such restrictions bind me."

Francis inclined his head. "It is true there is only one thing that works to bind your tongue, my lord.

"And that is?" Crowell reached into his fob pocket to pull forth his watch, flipping open the lid to studiously check the time.

"That all of us will remain silent, absolutely. If word spreads, we will all know its source: you, sir. You would be shown to be naught but a tattlemonger."

Crowell snapped his watch closed, looking up sharply as he placed it back in his fob pocket. Annoyance coursed over his face.

"Tattlemonger," came a hiss from the circle of men.

"No honor," came another.

Lord Crowell glared at each man surrounding him, his heated look causing soft-hearted Rusty to look down at his toes.

"I see," Crowell said at length. "You seek to impose silence on me by linking the telling of this little tale with my personal honor?"

"We do," Laffy said flatly.

Nathaniel stared at Crowell's face, amazed to see by the angry expression spreading there that the ruse had worked.

Of course, it was not really to be wondered at, for Crowell was a man who wished always to win the esteem of his fellow man, regardless of the worthiness of the task or event involved. That need was at the very root of the acrimony Crowell had ever displayed in his company, Nathaniel knew. Crowell's burning desire to be admired, and a resentment at seeing any such admiration or respect displayed toward anyone else, directed every one of the man's actions. It was his yearning to be thought ever the man of the hour that led Crowell to do such things as cheat in a race, never realizing the winning of the race was not the way to win his fellow man's regard, but rather that such regard could only be obtained through the manner in which the competition was executed.

Crowell's eyes narrowed, and his mouth worked to one side for a moment before he inclined his head. "Gentlemen," he growled, by way of agreement.

It was that same need, Nathaniel knew, that henceforth would prevent Crowell from speaking out, for he would do nothing so obvious, nothing that would clearly point the finger of blame his way.

A collective sigh of relief filled the air, although for himself, Nathaniel felt no such relief. There were some men who ought not be backed into a corner, and Crowell was such a man.

Francis clapped Nathaniel on the shoulder, saying in a low voice, "Well, we have righted that error, I believe."

"However," Crowell said not half a moment later, one eyebrow suddenly arching triumphantly, mirroring the arc his mouth formed as he showed his teeth in a smile. "Since I am in no way to profit from this game of yours, I demand a compensation for my silence."

"Poor time to wager against Cap'n Nate," Laffy drawled in a loud whisper to Francis. "There's but one more kiss to be had, and then the whole thing's over. I daresay everyone knows he's going to complete the thing."

"Not a wager, sir!" Crowell announced, pointing his chin toward Laffy. "A privilege."

Nathaniel frowned. Whatever it was to be, he knew he would not care for the words to follow. There was too much pleasure lurking around that severe mouth to be otherwise.

"A simple change, that is all I wish."

"Go on, Crowell, spit it out," Simon growled from his seat, his head still in his hands.

Crowell turned to glance down in Simon's direction, but then turned back to the circle around him. "Such looks, gentlemen! I daresay you misjudge me. All I demand is this: the right to name the lady whose final kiss must be obtained by our friend Lord Price here."

A stunned silence followed this pronouncement, as looks were exchanged and shoulders shrugged.

"Seems fair enough," Laffy agreed reluctantly.

"Exactly so," Crowell stated. He took a step forward so that the circle around him broke open, allowing him to stride before Nathaniel.

"And the lady?" Nathaniel asked, unable to comprehend what name could give the man such an air of smugness. Would he name some ancient dowager, or someone burdened with a feeble mind? Someone unfortunately scarred by the pox, or some lowly bumpkin? It was but a kiss, after all—so why that superior stare?

"Not a lady, Price," Crowell said, his grin growing.

"The Regent, perhaps? Or my horse?" Nathaniel suggested, striving to keep his face blankly arranged, so as not to give Crowell even a moment's satisfaction.

"You are not so much a high-flyer as to obtain the first, and it would be too simple for you to obtain the second," Crowell sniffed. "No, sir, I suggest a challenge to you, a true dare. I say you must obtain the kiss of not one young lady, but two: the Misses Alexander."

Nathaniel blinked, Rusty whistled, Simon grunted, and Crowell laughed.

"Yes, the most guarded pair of misses ever to set foot in London! The Daughters of The Keep, as their home has been deemed. You must have a kiss from both, as well as a lock from each of their fair golden heads."

"Gabrielle and Eleanor?" Simon demanded, scowling as he suddenly lurched to his feet. "My cousins? Do we speak of my cousins?"

"Simon, never mind," Nathaniel said, putting a hand on his arm to hold him back. "It was never part of the original wager. I need not agree to this change."

"You need respond to nothing this man says," Simon said darkly, his words still slurred.

"Indeed? Why, may I ask? Is it because we cannot agree your cousins are beautiful enough to be considered worthy of the Cavalier's kiss?" Crowell demanded in an arch voice. He spoke to Simon, but he looked to Nathaniel.

Nathaniel allowed his lips to stretch thinly over his teeth, forcing back words of response. There was no point in aggravating Crowell, and certainly no point in allowing Simon's upset to grow. It was inevitable what would happen if a fight should suddenly erupt and Simon's uncle learn that his nephew had been in yet another kick-up.

"They are beautiful indeed!" Simon went on, one hand waving in the air in over-sized gestures. Nathaniel wished he would not gesticulate so, but at least a fist had not yet been formed. Still, Crowell watched Simon's every move, undoubtedly ready to respond with his own fists if need be. "Every man here would have to agree m'cousins are Incomparables," Simon declared.

"Simon," Nathaniel tried to interrupt, "there is already a name on the list I was given—"

"Well," Jacob said, a little too loudly for it to be missed, "what is all the fuss about?" When everyone looked to him, Jacob colored under the attention. "You said you could kiss anyone in London, Nathaniel. Why not the twins? Just 'cause they are Simon's cousins don't mean they ain't beautiful, does it?"

Nathaniel shook his head. "Beautiful—yes, yes! But you must see how awkward a position this puts me in, with Simon my best friend and all—"

"So you will not accept the challenge, despite my granted right to put it to you?" Crowell asked in his haughtiest tone. "Well, what can this mean? Are you saying the twins are not beautiful, not deserving of the Cavalier's Kiss?"

Simon's fingers at last curled into a fist, and he lunged toward the other man. Crowell stepped back sprightly, leaving Simon's fist with no target to strike. The force of his swing took him off balance, and Simon sprawled to the ground at Crowell's feet.

Simon shook his head, his face darkening, and then tilted it back to look up at the man standing at the ready over him. "I will take no more of this, Crowell! You have bandied my cousins' names about, and that is unacceptable. I demand that—"

"He has, it is true, Simon," Nathaniel cut him off, before the fateful words could be said, before Simon could seal his fate by issuing a challenge for a duel. "He has bandied their names. And there is only one way to redeem their honor," he hurried on, thinking quickly. "I shall visit your cousins as the Cavalier, with your permission, of course, and that shall be all to the good, for then they shall be counted among London's beauties. Such an act could only serve to enhance their reputations rather than take anything away from them, surely."

Simon looked up, seeming to gather his wits of a sudden. The fogginess in his gaze receded, replaced by a grudging agreement that perhaps such a path might be the better one to take. Nathaniel saw the sudden flash of understanding there, the sudden acknowledgment that Nathaniel had just saved him from a duel—and consequently, for now, from the army.

Simon nodded once, stiffly, in the manner of a man accepting charity against his preference, then all fight left him, and he nodded again. "Of course you have my permission," he mumbled, stretching out a hand to his friend.

Nathaniel linked hands with him, pulling Simon to his unsteady feet, and they both turned back to Lord Crowell.

"Are you satisfied, Crowell?" Nathaniel asked coolly.

"Largely so. Of course, you do know Mr. Walford may not help you," Crowell said, nodding at Simon. "He may not grant you access to The Keep, or arrange to have his cousins meet with you in a dark corridor, or anything of that wise."

"Are you saying I may not even speak with Simon?" Nathaniel ground out.

"Oh, speak away! Make all the plans you like—only you must obtain the twins' lock by your own devices, just as you have all the others. Is that not fair?"

Nathaniel reluctantly nodded.

"Then it is agreed?"

"Agreed," Nathaniel said from between tight lips.

"Agreed," Simon echoed, the cloudiness of too much drink having returned to his eyes.

"And of course you further realize there must be a penalty to pay if you do not succeed."

"Penalty?" Nathaniel made a motion, attempting to dismiss the word.

"Of course! What challenge is there without a penalty to be paid! Do not tell me your fellows put no forfeiture on you?"

At the shaking heads around him, Crowell blew a puff of disbelief. "I thought you were gambling men. Well, I assure you I am. The forfeiture is this then, Captain Nathaniel," he said, putting a sneering emphasis on the title. "If you win, you take my coach-and-four, and if you fail, I take yours."

"No!" Simon cried out.

"Not the bays!" Francis hissed from between clenched teeth.

"Our racing coaches, of course, sirs!" Crowell insisted. "My matching greys against your bays, Price. What do you say, or are you less sure of your ability in the art of love than you are in the art of the whip?"

Nathaniel eyed the man before him. Perhaps, just perhaps, if Nathaniel took the man's pride and joy from him, perhaps if he won the gleaming maroon coach with its four perfectly matched greys, Crowell would call an end to this unspoken competition of theirs. Too, if Nathaniel took away the favorite toy of the leader of the Devil's Drivers, the streets would be a little safer, if nothing else. Yes, perhaps if he allowed the man a length of rope, the fool would hang his pride with it.

Of course, Nathaniel would have to win the wager to do so. And that was not as easy a task as it might seem to anyone who did not know how closely guarded the Alexander twins were. He knew better, knew of the footman hired to walk the halls at night, knew of the locks on all ground floor doors and windows, knew of Sir Newland's insistence that all commerce take place in the green parlor rather than in the kitchens, since that fellow would not venture into the latter and yet insisted on frequently being present whenever the household accounts were settled. Nathaniel knew the girls never spent a moment alone with any male, not even their cousin Simon. The Keep was aptly named, a stone fortress designed to keep out the unpleasantnesses of the world, and keep in the untouchable innocence of the twins.

Crowell gazed at him, a half-smile sitting on his lips.

"Done!" Nathaniel announced of a sudden. He inclined his head, his agreement met by the disbelieving sound of sucked-in breaths and murmured oaths from his fellows. To a man, they knew he did not lightly risk his specially crafted coach, with its unique light frame and its well-trained team, the lead vehicle of their driving club. "Are you now completely satisfied?" he demanded of Crowell.

"Oh, more than satisfied," came the answer. "Delighted, I assure you." Crowell reached for his hat, tipping it momentarily. "Since all is settled, gentlemen, I bid you a good evening."

He turned away, back to the nearby path, but not before Nathaniel had one last occasion to witness the man's smug smile.

"Well," Francis said, dusting his hands together as though to rid himself of any dirt that Crowell may have somehow left in his wake. "You simply must win this wager now, Nathaniel. It is not just a matter of my twenty quid anymore, you realize. Now it is a matter of letting Crowell know which of you is the better man."

"I only hope it may end this competition in which we have been locked."

Simon frowned, and shook his head. Nathaniel looked away, not wanting to interpret that gesture, not wanting to acknowledge that Crowell's appetite for mischief might never be satisfied.

"Ride with me to The Keep," Simon requested in a weary voice as he bent to scoop up a half-full bottle of wine. He tipped the bottle to his lips and took a deep draught before going on. "There might as well come some good from this evening, so you ought to have a look about and get a feel for how you are to vanquish over such a place. You know all London refers to Uncle Newt's home as The Keep for good reason."

Nathaniel took up his friend's arm once again to drape over his shoulders, the better to lead the man forth. "I know," he said with forced humor. "But I have yet to hear any nicknames for his carriages."

"Ah," said Simon, a grin spreading across his face.

And it all might be worth the bother and inconvenience and risk, Nathaniel thought with a sigh, if only there were the slightest chance he might discover Miss Gabrielle or Miss Eleanor Alexander was The Woman of two months ago. Unfortunately, he knew the girls well enough to be certain there was absolutely no hope of that. Neither of them would have the slightest idea how to kiss, and the woman at the masquerade had demonstrated she not only knew how, but enjoyed the task a great deal. There had been a depth to her words, too, a vibrant intelligence neither of the Alexander twins had ever demonstrated.

So, getting a kiss and a lock of hair from each of Simon's cousins was just one more of life's little twists to be endured until it was over. Please God end it soon! Then he could get back to leading his life as usual.

He studiously ignored a niggling doubt nipping at the corners of his mind, a tiny little voice that seemed to be saying life would never be what it once had been, that "usual" was gone forever.

Four

Joan looked out the upstairs window, knowing at once that the man who helped Simon up the steps was Lord Price. She had seen him bring Simon home enough times to know how he moved beneath the burden of Simon's weight. She knew how the merest sliver of moonlight could sneak around his hat brim to highlight his dark hair until it seemed to glisten like a deep pond just before dawn. She knew the patience he would display, either matching his steps to Simon's erratic ones, or else calmly pausing for the time it might take for Simon to be sick as a cat in the bushes beside the front steps.

She also knew she was top over tails in love with Lord Price, that she had been so for ages.

Lord Price had never realized she was the woman at the masquerade. That thought deflated her spirits each time she thought of it. In two months, he had never looked at her with any dawning awareness, any sudden thought to ask if she might have once worn a mask and kissed a man in the dark.

Now she was tempted to retreat, to hide in her room from the warm, friendly, and totally unlover-like gaze he would cast upon her.

Only she knew that Simon must not be caught out drunk—Joan had heard enough of Uncle Newland's loud lecture earlier this evening to know what one more proof of folly would mean for her cousin. She must go down and help Lord Price get Simon to his room as quietly and quickly as possible.

She did not know how to feel when Lord Price looked up

at her as she tiptoed down the stairs, for his look was one of gratification. If only it could be so just because she had come to meet him, not because she might serve to help save poor Simon from his own imprudence.

She dismissed the servant who kept watch all night—Uncle Newland hired a man just for that purpose, lest someone try to sneak in despite locked doors and windows, a ten foot garden wall in back, and his own frequent nighttime wanderings, which were ripe with suspicion that he had "heard a noise."

"Miss Galloway," Lord Price greeted her in a whisper. "You have come at a very opportune moment."

"I know," she said on a sigh, motioning that the two of them were to follow her.

"I am not drunk, you know, Joanie," Simon said, attempting to straighten his knees, only to tilt dangerously, causing Lord Price to grunt with effort at keeping him upright.

"Shhh! Simon, you must lower your voice," she told him, turning to lead the way up the stairs.

She did not need to tell Lord Price to keep to the left to avoid causing the steps to squeak, for this was hardly the first time he had brought Simon home surreptitiously. Neither did she tell him to wait a few steps down until she could be sure no one lingered in the hallway leading to Simon's room. She merely waved them up once she had seen the way was clear, not needing to speak the words.

It was a quick scramble then to Simon's chambers, a whispered, "Thank you!" from Lord Price, and the door was closed upon her, leaving her alone in the dark hall.

Joan turned back toward the stairs, kicking the hem of her skirt before her, for there was no point in kicking herself. It would just add to the pain she already knew this evening.

"Not that I blame him," she whispered to the nearest painting she passed. "For after all, I am only 'Simon's cousin.' Why should Lord Price ever cast his eyes my way? Simon has spoken to him for years upon years of his 'cousin Joanie,' and all the scrapes we got in when he came to visit—I dare-

say Lord Price thinks of me as something near to a sister."
She frowned at the next portrait. "If he thinks of me at all."

Suddenly a door opened before her, nearly striking her.
Joan gave a tiny yelp, and stepped around it.

"Joan!" her Uncle Newland, still dressed but with a nightcap warming his balding pate, bellowed from where he stood
in the open doorway. Then it was his turn to startle as he
caught sight of her. "Merciful heavens, Joan! What are you
doing gallivanting about without a candle?"

She did not bother to answer, knowing full well her uncle
would charge on, answer or no.

"What I want to know is this: where is Simon? You know
very well he was not at supper. Has he come in yet?"

"Yes, Uncle."

"Drunk, I suppose?"

"He spoke very clearly to me, Uncle," Joan replied straight-
faced. Not even for Simon would she tell a lie, but she was
not above telling only as much of the truth as seemed best.
"He has already retired for the evening."

"Indeed? Well then, I shall go and have a talk—"

"Mr. Alexander," interrupted a voice.

Joan and her uncle turned as one to see Lord Price coming
down the hall, a flickering candle held before him.

"How pleasant that I have this opportunity to wish you a
good evening." Uncle Newland pressed his lips together, apparently vexed at having his train of thought interrupted, but
good manners won out. "Lord Price. How do you do this
evening?"

"Very well, thank you. I am afraid, however, that I must
make a short evening of it, and so your nephew was good
enough to bid me *adieu* despite previous plans to play a hand
or two."

Uncle Newland frowned slightly—he did not approve of
playing at cards. "Gone to bed, has he?"

"Indeed, sir."

"And you are on your way out?"

Lord Price nodded. "Just so."

"Joan, girl, you will call a servant to show him out, will you not?" Uncle Newland demanded. He did not wait to hear her murmured agreement, but turned his gaze back to Lord Price, a speculative gleam apparent in his eyes even in the dim light. "She's a good girl," Uncle Newland pronounced, motioning toward Joan with a hitch of his head. "Needs a husband, though. Don't you, girl?"

Joan blessed the dimness of the corridor, hoping Lord Price's single candle could not show him how her face flamed with embarrassment.

"Every girl's wish, I should think," Lord Price said, not looking her way.

"Uncle—" Joan began, mortified to be once again the subject of her uncle's awkward attempts to find her a husband. It was not so much that he cared for her future, but rather that he preferred it not be spent with *him*. And of all the men in the world to be so blatant, so clumsy with!—anyone other than Lord Price would have been humiliating, but this was agonizing.

"Doesn't have two pennies to rub together, but she can work hard and her health is sound. She's m'sister's girl, you know. M'sister married a Galloway. That would be Lord Stanmore. Makes Joan here a viscount's daughter. Could be considered a bit of a prize, she could."

Unspoken words hung between them. Uncle might as well have said: *for a lower-status baron like you, Lord Price.*

Uncle Newland smiled, a rather grimly artificial gesture, and suggested, "Wouldn't know of anyone who's seeking a wife, would you, Price?"

Joan turned away from their visitor abruptly, knowing she was unable to keep the distress from her face. "Let us not detain Lord Price, Uncle. Come, sir, this way, and I shall find a servant to escort you out," she said brusquely, stepping away quickly, without looking back to offer her uncle a good night, or to see if Lord Price followed her.

She heard the two men murmur farewells. She was at the top of the stairs before Lord Price caught up to her, his candle flickering from the haste he had made to catch up to her.

"I daresay you have saved Simon from discovery," Joan murmured, her words rushed.

When he did not respond at once, she glanced at him long enough to see him incline his head in acknowledgment of that fact. He lifted the candle. "Do you retire for the evening? You have no candle—may I offer you mine?"

Her embarrassment melted, becoming a mere regret, the kind she was becoming used to in these past two months. *But how kind!* she thought as he passed the candlestick to her. It had certainly never occurred to Uncle Newland to offer her a candle, nor even to be concerned that she was left alone in the dark with a man. Such a thing would never happen were she one of his beloved twin daughters, but she was only the impoverished offspring of Uncle's less-than-beloved brother-in-law.

"Yes, please. That would be very kind," she answered him. And how good of him not to make allusions to her uncle's dreadful matchmaking efforts.

But she already knew he was the manner of man to attempt to put others at ease. Even given his usual casual inattention toward her, he was never unkind. He sometimes recommended books, having learned from Simon of her interest in tales of derring-do, of haunted castles and pirate ships and distressed heroines. That was one of the things that drew her to him, actually, that he was not afraid to admit to a fondness for such Minerva Press novels over the scholarly tomes she knew he read as well. That he did not sneer at her for preferring fancy over facts when it came to her reading list. That, unlike Aunt Hannah, he did not find her tastes to be too common.

She stopped at the foot of the stairs that led up, yet one more story, to her room. She turned to him, momentarily voiceless as she looked up into his eyes, those dark orbs now made darker yet by the gloom of the hallway. Even in day-

light, the deep rich brown of his gaze all but hid the pupil
from the casual glance, with long lashes framing them that
would have made his face too pretty if not for the sharpness
of bone under the skin of his cheeks and jaw. He possessed
a mouth with little curvature, but it had a balance of width
and length—a mouth so different from a woman's, a mouth
to draw the eye and hold it a moment too long.

She wished she might say something clever and charming,
and he would laugh, and then they would linger on the stairs,
and after a while they would move down to the front parlor
to play a hand or two of rummy, or talk of novels they had
read, or. . . .

"The Guardian is close behind us," he said, indicating with
a movement of his head the house's nocturnal footman, now
glimpsed walking slowly down the hallway toward them.

"Good evening then," she said, her voice tight with disappointment, but then that was what came of wishing.

"Good evening, Miss Galloway," he said, making her a
polite bow.

It flitted through her mind that when he had surrendered
the candle to her, their fingers had not so much as touched
for a brief moment during the transfer.

"Good evening, Lord Price," she repeated quietly, waiting
until he was down the stairs and too far away to hear before
she allowed herself to sigh.

The coins clinked as they dropped into the guardsman's
outstretched hand. That was one-tenth of the month's pin
money Uncle Newland provided Joan, gone in a blink. "Lord
Stanmore," she supplied the guard with the name of the man
she had come to see, even though by now he ought to know
whom she visited each week.

The guardsman gave Joan a grunt of acknowledgment, unlocked the iron gate with one of his many keys, and escorted
her into the close, rank air of Newgate Prison.

Joan avoided looking closely at the miserable prisoners they passed, tried not to hear their moans or sobs. Almost worse were those who made no sound, who did not stir, but lay immobile, defeated, hopeless. She could do nothing for them, or only very little in the form of the basket of food she brought, which she knew Papa would share as best he may.

Perhaps because he shared the little she brought, or perhaps because of his title, Papa had been granted a three-walled niche to himself. How low he had come, that a tiny pocket of privacy was to be considered a privilege! If only they had funds, then she could buy him a private cell, and furnish it even—but of course, their lack of funds was what brought him here to begin with. He would come away from this place in time, she knew. The rents on their country estate were still being gathered, and he assured her that five years' rent would erase his total debt—but even five days was a very long time in a place such as this.

He stood at the mouth of his niche as she approached, and once again she knew a kind of gratitude that at least he need not wear an ankle chain as some others did.

"Joan," he greeted her, his voice a heart-breaking mix of relief and regret to have her come to him here.

She rushed up to him, swinging her bundles aside so that she might lean into him, kissing him, doing her best to ignore the undeniable scents of incarceration surrounding him in this place. There were too many bodies gone too long without bathing, and spoiled straw and raw waste, and the inescapable choking reek of smoke from the ill-tended lamps and the open fires over which prisoners occasionally cooked.

As the guard turned and left them, she stepped back, looking her father over in the dim light. "How are you?" she asked.

"Fine, fine," Papa answered, as he always answered.

"I have brought some of yesterday's buns, and some ham and cheese. And a fresh bundle of clothing." She set her basket down, and pressed the bundle into his arms. Along with a few meager family mementos, Joan had managed to secure

Papa's clothing from her old home before it was locked up tight, the servants dismissed, and her access to the building denied.

"Thank you," Papa murmured, setting the bundle on the simple cot she had persuaded Uncle Newland to purchase for him. She had shamed her uncle into that much, even though he would not take Papa's debts onto himself.

"I should end in Debtor's Prison myself!" Uncle Newland had claimed, though his oft-repeated claim of being "only a third son" did not fool Joan for a moment as to the actual extent of his wealth. Uncle Newland had pockets of money— Joan knew, for she had heard his plans often enough to "buy" his daughters continental titles.

"You will marry the twins to fortune hunters?" Joan had questioned him in horror when first she had moved into his home and learned of his plans.

"Indeed! For what manner of man would care to share their titles but fortune hunters? They'll give me what I want— Gabrielle and Eleanor will be something more than just a mere third son's daughters, I can tell you—and I shall give the fellows what they want: plump pockets."

"But what if these men are unkind? Or spendthrifts?"

"It matters not. The girls can always move home again if they do not care for their marriages. Once they have the titles, I haven't a care what follows with the fellows themselves. They want to gamble away their settlements, or drink themselves mindless, 'tis no matter of mine."

Joan faulted him for his cavalier designs for his daughters, but she could not totally fault him for refusing to pay Papa's way to freedom. Had not Papa himself told her often enough to sleep in the bed she had made? She could hardly reprove Uncle Newland for taking the same attitude himself.

Papa coughed, the sound more labored than during her last visit, drawing her attention back to the moment.

"That sounds worse," she said, at once pulling off a glove to feel his forehead.

He took her hand away, patting it between his two. "I am fine," he assured her again.

A lie. She had touched him long enough to feel a warmth not generated by the clammy, cold stone walls around them.

"And how are you?" he asked, turning to remove the bundle from the cot, indicating she should sit down. "Are Newland and Hannah treating you better?"

"Oh, I am still a very convenient chaperone who need not be paid," Joan said, forcing a lightness into her tone as she sat on the cot. Papa required lightness as much as he required the extra food and clean clothes she brought. "And, although they remain as silly a pair as ever was, Gabrielle and Eleanor are dears in their own way."

"But they let you know you have come down in the world, do they not?"

"But of course they do," she said. "Have I not?" She had meant to be humorous, but a cloud passed over Papa's features.

"I am so sorry for my folly——" he began.

She would not let him apologize again. "Papa, do you know what I have learned?" she interrupted brightly. "Did you know that people have a nickname for Uncle Newland's home?"

Papa nodded. "The Keep."

"Exactly! It was Heloise Lewis who told me that. I can only wonder I did not think of it myself, what with those high stone walls, the way we must see the doors are locked every time we come in or out of an evening, and the way Uncle all but has a footman at every door, day and night. Sometimes I think I must be living with royalty, so closely is the house guarded!"

"Newland always did surround those girls with wool wrappings. Always had aspirations for them to rise above themselves."

"I daresay he may succeed."

"So, Heloise Lewis told you the name, eh?" Papa asked as he put some ham and cheese between two halves of a bun. Joan was aware of eager eyes shining from the shadows, eyes waiting for her to leave, for then Papa would share the basket's contents, but not until she was gone. She might have believed he ate all the food himself except for his progressive thinness, and because only last week one of the women prisoners had caught up Joan's hand long enough to bless her for bringing the food, and her father for sharing it. It was little more than scraps, but that was all that was left to her after the staff had their share from Uncle's table.

"That is well," Papa went on. "That means you are getting out and about. For a while, I thought Newland meant to keep you ever in the background."

"Two months of me seems to be enough to convince him otherwise," Joan said, feeling a blush creep up her cheeks at the memory of last night's encounter with Lord Price.

"A blush, Joanie? Why is that?" Papa asked after swallowing the bite he'd taken. "Good gad, he has not betrothed you to some oaf or—?"

"No, Papa," she said, shaking her head, but a sudden need for honesty led her to add, "Not that he hasn't made an attempt with every fellow who crosses over the threshold."

Papa lifted his eyebrows, encouraging her to go on.

"I daresay it has occurred to him that if I am to remain on the shelf, it would be his shelf. So he leads every stray male to my side, bids me open my mouth and show them my teeth, and then asks them if they'll have me," she said, giving a short laugh.

"Oh, Joanie," Papa moaned, sitting down beside her, the moan turning into a short cough. "How could I ever have led you to this?"

" 'Tis really not so bad as all that, Papa," she hurried to assure him, waving a hand as though to dash away his distress. "It is in some regards rather amusing, in fact."

"You are not a very good liar, Joan."

She slanted him a look, then sighed. "That is your fault. You raised me to be honest. But truly, at least Uncle Newland means well. I should not complain that he attempts to find me a husband, for that could possibly change all our circumstances, could it not?" She stopped, biting back the words that sprang to mind, the oft-considered question of where all her suitors had gone the moment Papa was arrested. Even Lord Crowell, whom she had rather thought might be on the verge of asking for her hand, had never come to call upon her at Uncle Newland's. He had not been one of the fellows led over the threshold to her side, even though she had made a point of letting him know at Lady Hall's dinner party a month ago that she had gone to live with her relatives.

Joan shook her head, to clear it of this nagging question, and smiled at her papa in reassurance. "The twins have not two thoughts between them, but they are usually quite pleasant. If I am an unpaid servant to them, well, I can think of much more difficult or unpleasant duties to perform. And Uncle Newland is providing me with pin money, which he need not. I have managed to save four pounds already. I know 'tis not much, but every little bit may help to pay our debts."

Papa frowned, coming to his feet to pace the small confines of his niche. "You should spend it, Joan! Lord knows you deserve a boiled treat or a ribbon or two, like any other young lady."

He did not say her ability to save two pounds a month would never come near paying their debts, but they both knew it. She could save the other two pounds a month if she did not come to see him, but that expense she would not give up, and it would make such little difference in the matter of his unpaid notes anyway.

"It is only a little over a month until my twenty-first birthday. I shall have Grandmama's money then."

Papa shook his head, not bothering to remind her that the sum she was to inherit was hardly princely. He had already assured her the amount would not even satisfy Kendall the pastry chef.

"Perhaps if I were to take employment—"

"No!" he shouted as he rounded on her, but then suffered

a paroxysm of coughing. She flew to her feet, coming to his side to pat his back. She bit her lip, not daring to let the specter of prison fever remain before her mind's eye.

After a moment, his coughing quieted, and he repeated, "No. I will not have you working just to get me out of prison. I forbid it! You are safe at your uncle's house, and you will remain there. It was not you who put me in here but myself. And I shall get myself out, in time."

Hc repeated his dictate several times before he would let her leave. As she followed the guardsman out, Joan reflected on Papa's words, that he would get himself out, given time.

Time. The one thing she was terribly worried Papa might not have, not if he were left in his prison world of permanent chill, poor food, bad air, and no doctor's care.

No matter what Papa said, she had to do something to get him out of there, and soon.

Such thoughts circulated through her mind as she returned from the prison. She was so absorbed in her worries, it was a moment before she realized the name being called from the street was her own.

She looked up to see Simon, and riding in the gig at his side, Lord Price. Simon waved to her, and she watched as Lord Price said something, perhaps—to judge from his expression—advising Simon not to treat his cousin so vulgarly. That would be his way, ever thoughtful.

Simon guided the gig around to her side of the street, calling a greeting of, "Joanie! Wool-gathering, were you?"

"I was indeed."

"Miss Galloway," Lord Price greeted her, leaping down from the vehicle and removing his hat in one smooth motion.

"Lord Price."

"But where is your maid? Surely you are not walking alone?" Simon asked with a frown. He did not come down, needing to control the horse.

"She asked to return to the house," Joan explained, afraid her cheeks pinkened to be caught out in this impropriety before Lord Price. "Sometimes I stay rather long at the . . . at visiting my papa, and if Margie stays and waits for me, she cannot complete all her other duties. I cannot bear for her to get in a difficulty because of me."

Simon growled. "As she would, if I know Uncle Newt. He'd dock her wages if he found a fire unlaid or a linen unpressed."

"You are very thoughtful," Lord Price said to Joan, and then she was sure her face reddened at the sincerity in his voice.

"Come along then, Joanie. We shall take you back to the house," Simon announced before she could murmur a reply.

Lord Price at once extended his hand, and Joan slipped hers into his. His other hand came around to lightly touch her waist to assist her as she stepped up into the gig. She took a shaky breath, for her lungs did not seem to work quite as they ought now that Lord Price had touched her.

He stepped back, breaking contact. "Simon, I shall see you later then, at the driver's meeting?"

Joan looked to Simon as he answered "yes," hoping her cousin would offer to surrender his seat to the other man. Of course, it would have been entirely improper for her to ride alone without a chaperone with a man unrelated to her, but such a slight indiscretion—in an open gig, in broad daylight—would be little enough fodder for those who would later gather over cups of the day's scandal broth. To her chagrin, Simon made no such offer.

"Good! You must attend the meeting tonight, for Francis claims there is a better way to hold six ribbons at once, and means to make a demonstration for us," Lord Price said.

"I could not possibly miss that. I am rather fond of watching Francis miss the mark."

Lord Price shook his head and laughed. He lifted his hand in a farewell salute, then turned away, Simon's farewell setting him on his way.

Joan sat back in her seat, sighing with regret that it was not Lord Price she sat beside, even while part of her reveled in the fact he had been willing to give up his seat to her. Of course, that was no more than one might expect from a gentleman, but there had been too many occasions of late when she had been treated as something less than a gentlewoman. Lord Price, and Simon, of course, treated her as the viscount's daughter she was—even be it an impoverished one.

Lord Price clapped his hat back on his head as he made his way down the street, Joan's gaze following his progress as he made his way past a series of shop windows. He had such a confident air about him that, when added to the grace of motion that was his, made it a pleasure merely to watch him walk. Joan was aware how her side tingled just where his fingers had brushed, and she could not stop herself from wrapping her arms around her middle, as though to hold the feeling to her just a little longer.

She ought to tell him she was the woman at the masquerade. She ought to put aside her goosish fears that he might be disappointed to find the mystery woman was no one other than her. Yes, next time they met she would ask if she might have her mask back.

She sighed with contentment at this decision, then looked up to see Lord Price greeting Althea Perriman with a tip of his hat. Althea took his arm, smiled up at him, and chimed with a distinctive cry, "Lord Price! My dear fellow, how famous it is to see you again. Are you quite recovered from Lady Shannenley's ball? I declare I never laughed so gaily, and all because you were such a tease, you rogue!"

Lord Price leaned down to say something close to Althea's ear. The girl giggled, and Lord Price laughed aloud. Althea's maid looked on with a benevolent smile, as if she had witnessed shared whispers between these two before.

As Simon urged the gig forward, Joan's last glimpse at Lord Price saw him resume his stroll, Althea on his arm, the two strolling down the walk before the shop windows, animated conversation flowing easily between them.

Joan sighed again, putting away the bright daydream she'd

had, but not quite quickly enough to avoid the bitter taste of tarnish it left in her mouth.

Simon went directly home, setting Joan down before the house after casting her a third curious glance. She had not responded to his first two silent inquiries, and she did not respond to this last one either. If Simon had noted she had fallen into a sullen silence, she certainly was of no mind to explain its origin to him. She turned to the house, gratefully leaving Simon to drive the gig around to the mews.

Pulling off her gloves—not one finger at a time to be careful of the stitches but all at once in a pet—she proceeded to Uncle Newland's library. The thought of reading a romantic work left her cold, but perhaps there was some manner of adventurous tale in one of her usually beloved Minerva Press novels to divert her from the heaviness that wound around her heart.

She had just settled before the fire with an unopened book in hand when Uncle Newland's butler, Seymour, came into the front parlor to inform Joan she had a gentleman caller.

"A caller? For me?" she repeated. Oh, surely not Lord Price? But no, why would he call for her? He never had, coming to the Alexander home only because of Simon. "Are you certain the gentleman did not propose to see Miss Gabrielle or Miss Eleanor?"

"Yes, Miss, he did not, Miss. The gentleman asked to see you."

"Gentleman?" she repeated, trying to imagine who it might be.

Her astonishment was complete when Seymour supplied the man's name: "Lord Crowell to see you, Miss."

Five

"Miss Galloway," Lord Crowell greeted her, offering a smile and his hand to her as she entered the front parlor.

She accepted the gesture, allowing herself to be led to Aunt Hannah's elaborate Egyptian lounging sofa. "Lord Crowell."

"How well you appear," he said, sitting down next to her.

Joan made an effort to keep her brows from coming together, forced her mouth not to thin into a line that might reflect the perplexed wariness his presence brought her. What had kept him away from her side for two months, only to now suddenly reappear? Certainly he had not been traveling, for this past month she had seen him at any number of gatherings. In fact, he had danced with Gabrielle a fortnight ago at Lord Amhart's ball, never acknowledging—or perhaps never seeing—the plain and recently penniless Joan ensconced among the matrons and chaperones.

"What . . . ?" She started to ask what he was doing there, but manners came to the fore, so instead she asked, "What would you care to have sent in for refreshments?"

"Anything, dear lady."

Joan turned to ask the butler if he would inform the kitchen that a tray was needed, only to discover he had left the room, leaving her unchaperoned. She frowned quickly, taking care to erase the reaction before turning back to Lord Crowell. She did not wish him to note her annoyance at how the servant's attitude of benign neglect so clearly reflected her uncle's. At least Seymour had left the door open, so there was some hint of propriety in this visitation.

"I shall ring," she informed him, starting to stand.

Lord Crowell shook his head, so that she sank back to her seat. "But you need not. I am content just to be with you, Miss Galloway. I need nothing more than your company."

Joan looked into his face—a little too near her own, she felt—but could not say what emotion lay hidden in his eyes. Once she had thought he had cared for her, and certainly he had courted her. Had he come to renew that connection?

"I believe I have some happy news for you, my dear lady," Lord Crowell said, taking up one of her hands.

"Happy news?" she repeated, wishing she had kept her gloves on, even if he might have noted the careful stitching she had done to hide the fact the gloves were slightly tattered cast-me-downs from Eleanor.

"I have come to tell you that I very much want to aid in your papa's release from prison."

Joan's lips parted in surprise, and she felt her eyes grow wide. "Truly?"

"Truly."

"And how may this be accomplished?" she asked breathlessly, not quite daring to believe in the possibility.

"I would pay his debts for him, of course. Oh, not all of them, but enough for the immediate charge to be dropped against him, and for him to be set free, you see. He would need to retire to the country at once, of course, or else back in he goes as soon as another creditor pays the fee to have him arrested, but I have no doubt your papa would make good use of such an opportunity to flee London were it but given him."

"Lord Crowell!" she cried, her free hand flying to press against her throat, where she could feel her heart beginning to pound with elation at the thought of Papa coming away from prison. Then the steady thump skipped a beat as she could not help but wonder why Lord Crowell made such a proposition? What had brought him here today with this fine offer?

There was only one reason Joan could think of: marriage. With her. To her! Had she then, after all, not been mistaken in his intention those months past?

"How wondrous an offer, my lord! But why ever would you care to do such a thing?"

"Ah. As to that, my dear," he said, releasing her hand as he stood. He crossed to the double doors that led into the front parlor and shut them without hurry.

Joan stared at the closed doors, well aware of the impropriety even while a touch of confusion caused her to frown again. Why did he close the doors? Had he come directly to see her, or had he first called upon Uncle Newland? Uncle was, after all, her guardian of sorts, and it would be rather unusual for a gentleman to ask a lady for her hand before obtaining her relative's approval. She ought to have asked Seymour how long Lord Crowell had been here—for as pleased as Uncle Newland would be to learn of any offer that might make her someone else's burden, he would also desire that proper decorum be followed. She had thought Lord Crowell had arrived but moments before Seymour announced his presence, but perhaps Lord Crowell called on Uncle at another, earlier time? Or perhaps Lord Crowell—Kendrick, she tested his Christian name in her mind—wished to be certain of her feelings before he spoke to her uncle at all?

He came back to her side, and Joan felt a prickle of uncertainty, but perhaps this was caused by the sudden realization that she was content Lord Crowell made no effort to once again take up her hand. How odd. In all the novels, the hero always took up the heroine's hand as he made his proposal—though this was not a novel, of course.

Perhaps she desired to remain separate from his touch because of two months' worth of neglect, which could not be dismissed in a moment's time and not without explanation. Or perhaps it was what her eyes told her: there was something about the way Lord Crowell held his shoulders, something in the set of his mouth that did not seem loverlike, that made her vision of an impassioned proposal tilt askew like a poorly hung portrait. And yet, he smiled, gazing directly into her eyes, and she thought perhaps she was making too much of things.

"Why would I care to see to it that your papa is released from gaol?" he restated her question, leaning toward her.

"Yes indeed, why?" she murmured, feeling the hairs on the back of her neck stand up. Was that because she thought he intended to kiss her, or was this shiver of uncertainty caused by something less sweet, less welcome?

"I wish to please you, of course."

"And I must please you in return?" she returned at once, a sense of unease growing despite her efforts to tamp it down, to ignore it at least until he had said his piece. She retreated from him, leaning back against the sofa support to allow a few more inches between them. "In what way would that be?"

"You appear alarmed, my dear Miss Galloway. There is no need. I am not proposing any low course. Not at all! I wish a simple favor from you, that is all." He moved, closing the new-made space between them.

Disappointment warred with the dim hope still inside her breast. *A favor?* That she would marry him? She did not think he meant so flattering a thing, but it was still, despite his strange ways, a possibility. Not that she was entirely sure she would agree to such a thing anyway, not with this odd vacillation of feeling on her part.

"What I ask of you is no more than you already do, Miss Galloway. All I want is an assurance that you will keep your cousins safe from the effects of rumormongering."

"What?" Joan stared at him, utterly perplexed. Was he, then, in love with one of her cousins?

"You have heard of the Kissing Cavalier?"

She nodded, making a gesture with her hand to indicate her bewilderment at the change in topic.

"I happen to know that he means to take a kiss and a lock of hair from both your cousins. All I want you to do is make sure he never succeeds. You are now forewarned, which is to say forearmed against him, and therefore in a position to defy him. Now, that is a simple enough thing to ask, is it not, to obtain your papa's release?"

"I do not see how one fits with the other," she murmured, looking to the pattern on the carpet as if clarification might be found there. It was certainly not to be found in Lord Crowell's expression, which revealed nothing greater than a mere mild amusement. So! He was not here to propose at all! How like a goose she had behaved, the reflection giving a sting to her next words. "Unless," she said, lifting her head to stare once again into his face, "Unless you know who the Kissing Cavalier is. And unless, for some particular reason, you wish him to fail at kissing my cousins."

"That is all quite true," he said, smiling brightly at her. It was a handsome smile—one of the things about him that had caught her eye when first they had met.

Joan pressed her tongue against her teeth, thinking rapidly. Lord Crowell looked on with apparent patience, still with a hint of a smile about his mouth.

"But what is it you ask me?" she asked at length. "It is true I play chaperone to my cousins, and that I spend more time these days watching them dance than dancing myself, but I cannot see how I may forward your interest in this matter . . . ?"

"You must become their guardian, of course. They must never be outside your presence. Never! The Kissing Cavalier obtains his kisses by sneaking into gardens and onto balconies, and by stopping carriages at night. So, it is a simple thing for you to foil him; if you must go out of a night, insist your outings be attended by outriders, even in the better districts, and instruct them to challenge anyone who approaches the carriage. Lord . . . that is to say, the Kissing Cavalier, would not venture near a coach manned by armed guards. You must never allow the girls to walk anywhere alone, and most especially not as a twosome, for he must kiss both girls. You must also bar their windows and lock the doors at night. All those manner of things. Do you see how simple a thing it would be?" His smile widened, inviting her to agree.

"But for how long?" she asked, her hands folding tightly together in her lap.

He appeared startled. "Ah . . . yes! It could not go on so forever, could it? But no limit was set . . . hmmm. Well, not to worry. I shall see that a time limit is established." Lord Crowell frowned, and murmured, "I should have insisted upon a week, but I know the fellow's mates . . . they are like as not to insist otherwise." He shook his head, then laughed. "I have it! Our Cavalier advertised, and so shall I. I shall give him two weeks from the date of the advertisement's posting, and not a moment more. None could call a fortnight unfair."

"But would this fellow have a mind to follow the dictates of your advertisement?"

Lord Crowell's eyes sparkled, becoming darker with some manner of emotion. "Oh, yes, he will follow it." He smiled down at her, seemingly well-pleased. "Only say yes, and I shall away, to begin the process of soliciting your papa's release."

Joan leapt to her feet, crossing her arms before her. "I cannot like this," she voiced the very thought that tumbled a warning through her brain. "There is something . . . it makes me uneasy, this entire business. It seems oddly like a betrayal of some sort."

"A betrayal? Of whom? Certainly not of your cousins, as you would only be protecting them from the very manner of scandal of which your uncle would hardly approve. He would be grateful, in point of fact, should you attend to your cousins so well."

"Then why not merely tell him of your suspicions about the Cavalier?" Joan demanded.

"Because he cannot arrange to be at Miss Gabrielle and Miss Eleanor's side at all times, as you can. He would merely order you to see to their protection, and then where would you be? Performing your duty to them, yes, but without the added benefit of seeing your father's debts relieved long enough for him to flee to the safety of the country."

Joan turned away from him abruptly, not wanting him to see how forcefully the truth of his words struck her. But he was only too right; she would still do her best to see Gabrielle and Eleanor came to no harm—the very idea of being subjected to a publicized kiss would be considered by Uncle Newland as a blight on his daughters' heretofore indisputably spotless reputations—and Papa would be in none the better a situation for it. And there was even something more than that, for as much as her two cousins often affected a witless air, they were pleasant girls who largely meant no harm to others. Joan would not see them hurt—and she could only imagine, given past experience, that at least one of them was bound to be heart-sore following any attention from the Kissing Cavalier.

Unknown to Uncle, but quite well-known to Joan, was the fact that both girls were not as utterly innocent as their father and their public reputations would have them be. Both had known the touch of lips, for they had paid the young stable lad, Jimmy, a tuppence for each kiss he gave them—at least until Joan had discovered their game and put an end to it, persuading her unknowing uncle to send the lad to "help out at the home farm" in Kent.

Joan had learned that the twins were romantic in nature, the very kind to take such silly things as kisses far too seriously—for each had declared her undying love for the stable lad for nearly full two weeks. How they had moped and sat about with handkerchiefs pressed to their eyes when he was sent away . . . ! Until, of course, they had both fallen madly in love with Lord Byron following their reading of *The Giaour* aloud to one another. And Heaven only knew how many other lads had been persuaded to provide instruction in the art of dalliance! When she questioned them, the girls would admit to no other escapades, then collapse into each others' arms in a fit of giggles.

Yes, the girls were silly creatures to take such fancies as holding a simple kiss so closely to one's heart, and yet, Joan sighed silently, perhaps not so silly. Anyway, not at being moved by a kiss—for had she not herself enjoyed a kiss that had branded her memory, that made her pine to spend time with the man who had shared that extraordinary kiss with her?

No, it was one thing to "fall in love" with a stable lad or a poet, another altogether to dally with a man who was determined to be light with his affections. The Kissing Cavalier was most obviously of that sort.

The twins must never know the sting of kissing an unobtainable ideal.

Behind her, Joan heard Lord Crowell give a small cough. She gritted her teeth. She could not be sure, but it seemed an affected sound, and she could not help but wonder if he meant to turn her thoughts toward the condition of prison fever so rampant in gaol these days. But, no, she thought as she allowed her jaw to relax, that was unkind of her. She need only look to today to see how recent events had bowed her usual good judgment!—she was becoming suspicious in nature, not only of her cousins but now of Lord Crowell.

Joan turned suddenly to face him. "I shall do it, but only under two conditions. One, we must repay you, as soon as Papa is in a position to do so."

"Naturally." Lord Crowell inclined his head.

Joan kept the corners of her mouth from turning down yet again. It was only reasonable that Lord Crowell expect to be repaid, but she could not help the feeling of disapproval she felt at the knowledge he had never intended to be altruistic, that he had some active stake in this curious sport of thwarting the Kissing Cavalier.

"What is the second?" he asked.

"That you tell me why you wish so much for the Cavalier to fail."

"Ah. The reason is simple." He crossed one leg over the other. "I am a friend of the family, and naturally I do not wish to see any harm come to Mr. Alexander or his daughters. I know, indeed as does all of London, that Mr. Alexander has proved a stringent parent in hopes that his daughters may wed where they wish. When I learned of Lord . . . of the Cavalier's plans, it behooved me as a friend to see what I might do to counter the villain's schemes."

Joan sat down again by way of comment, for she had no response she could voice. She could not say she was convinced by his testimonial, but there was just enough conviction in his demeanor and choice of words to keep her from challenging his claims aloud. True, he was known to the Alexanders, even if Joan had failed to note any particular attachment prior to this day. She took a breath, to steady herself, then looked up. "How soon before Papa can be released from Newgate?"

"A few days at most, my dear. I understand it was the chef, Kendall, who called upon the law to intervene in this matter?"

She nodded.

"I will see it is all settled as soon as may be. And, do not fear, I will assure your papa that he need not begin repaying me right away."

Joan took a step back. "He would not be able to," she declared. Dare she ask the question in her mind? She lifted her chin. "But pray tell, Lord Crowell, what if Papa can never repay you? I have learned his debts are severe, and it may be years before he has a penny to spare. There are expenses that come, you must know, even with living in the country, and I am told he has numerous lenders waiting for repayment."

Lord Crowell's smile did not falter, but something dark passed through his eyes. "Would I not, too, be one of the lenders he owed?" he asked, his voice even, perhaps even cool. Then he nodded once, ever so slightly, and the coolness was washed away by a warmth—was it a true warmth?— that came to his features.

"But, my dear, we need not worry about such things. I'm sure your father will find a way to repay me."

Joan felt a shiver run up her spine, not sure if it boded a sense of unease at something in his tone, or rather a tremor of familial pride. Papa would repay Lord Crowell, she would see to that, and the sooner the better.

"There is always the inheritance I am to have at my next birthday," she stated. There, that would tell him that one way or another, the Galloways would not end in debt to him, not for very long anyway.

"Inheritance?"

She almost smiled, knowing her assertion had indeed made her point for her, for he gave her an attentive, level look. "I am to inherit a sum from my grandmama. On my birthday, which is but one month away."

"Your grandmama had personal funds, did she? Quite apart from what your father inherited?"

"Indeed," Joan replied.

She was both pleased and piqued to see she had commanded his interest. "She always felt a woman ought to have access to her own funds." Funds! A fancy word for a mere two hundred pounds, and that the entire sum.

"I see. Well, that is always a possibility. We never know what the future will hold," he said, following his words with a smile and a thoughtful look.

It was the kind of smile, the sort of considering look, to make a woman's heartbeat pulse just a little faster, for it was not an idle look. It seemed to hint at some joining of their "futures." There was something in his voice that implied that this debt of her father's might be forgiven were she Lord Crowell's wife. How simple life would become if only that were true! She would no longer be a financial burden to Papa, and this new debt to Lord Crowell would surely be excused should Papa become Lord Crowell's father-in-law.

The only problem was, she thought with a sudden deep flutter in her stomach, that her heart raced with a sharp aversion, rather than anticipation, at the thought of marrying Lord Crowell.

Surely he could not be thinking of marriage, not after all he had said to her! But there was time to think all of that through later. Right now it was enough to know Papa would soon be freed from prison. Lord Crowell had, after all, made at least that much of her hopes possible, and she could only be grateful for that.

Lord Crowell took up her hand and executed a kiss over it, a gesture that was perfectly proper and not to be disdained, even though she had to fight an impulse to snatch her hand away. He then leaned close to her, to speak near her ear as though they were not already quite alone and unwitnessed behind closed doors. His tall frame leaning into hers created an intimacy, and his breath was warm on her ear. "Just keep the twins from The Cavalier," he said in a very low voice.

She pulled back, more nonplused by the instruction than she would have been by murmured endearments. "I know how to best tend to my cousins' well-being," she snapped.

He touched the point of her chin with one fingertip. It could have been an admirer's touch, Joan thought at once, if it were not for the flicker of apprehension it sent coursing through her. "How fortunate for your papa," he said.

She felt her eyes widen, and saw his answering smile, a brief smile that would never have warmed her even if it had lasted. He stepped back and bowed, and Joan curtsied in return out of pure habit, at a loss for how else to respond. Lord

Crowell turned, crossing to the doors, and left without a further word or glance in her direction.

Joan slowly became aware of the clenched hands pressed
too firmly to her stomach, and with some effort forced her
arms to relax and her fingers to uncurl. She could not say
for certain, but had Lord Crowell just threatened her papa's
well-being should she fail to keep the Kissing Cavalier from
the twins?

At that moment, she knew without doubt that she could
never love the man.

But, a small, bitter-edged internal voice pointed out, could
she dare to relinquish him as a possible suitor all the same?

Six

Nathaniel stood among the dense shrubs in the Alexander garden, observing the rear wall of The Keep through the night's gloom. He waited to see the glowing red end of a cheroot, and was rewarded several moments later for his patience by the sight. He heard the scuff of the footman's shoes against the stones of the rear walk, and watched as the dark shape of the man moved away, toward the front of the house.

Nathaniel waited for the particular clink of the front gate returning on its hinges before he moved out of the shadows, knowing the footman would spend at least ten minutes flirting with the neighbor's chambermaid before returning from his nightly walk.

Nathaniel moved to the base of the house, gazing up the grey, flush stones of The Keep. He shook his head in consternation. "Which set of windows belongs to the twins?" he murmured to himself. There were no bedchambers on the ground level, he knew from his own time spent here, but he was not so familiar with the first story, and certainly not at all with the second story. There was even a partial third story, a set of dormers presumably used by the servants or for storage.

Nathaniel twitched his mouth from side to side, as if the motion could somehow serve to realign his mask, which had slipped a bit to the left. All he knew was that the other night Miss Galloway had begun to climb yet another set of stairs, so obviously the women were housed high in The Keep. Not surprising, that, for if Mr. Alexander had a tendency to watch over every valuable with a sharp eye, it was to be expected he would put his beloved daughters high above harm's way. All that being said, it was mildly amusing that Mr. Alexander had no care for the amount of window tax he would have to pay—for the town house was designed without a care toward limiting the number of windows. Mr. Alexander liked to watch his pennies, but he also liked to display his wealth, for there were six windows across each level of his home's façade. Six windows per level—so which of them belonged to the twins?

If only he could have had Simon let him into the house! That simple endeavor appealed far more than the scheme now before Nathaniel—but such collusion on Simon's part would be only too obvious, and Simon would suffer for it. What if something went wrong? What if the "Cavalier's" escape route (the backstairs) were barred to him? What if Nathaniel were captured at the task? No, Simon could play no part in Nathaniel's arrival within the home.

Hearing a girl's laugh carried by the night wind, Nathaniel hoisted the coiled rope from his shoulder, sure the footman was otherwise engaged.

Simon's chambers were farmost to the left, so it was sensible to assume the girls' rooms were just above his, a good twenty feet above the sunken stone garden path below. Nathaniel inspected the cruel-looking tip of the grappling hook tied to the end of his rope, worrying for a moment that he might chip one or more of Mr. Alexander's roof tiles or pull down a chimney by mistake. There was nothing for it, however, for he must have access to the twins if he were to have a kiss from them. Simon could not leave a window unlocked for him—that would have violated the agreement with Lord Crowell—but he and Nathaniel had felt it was no violation to have Simon confirm that usually the windows of the higher stories indeed seldom went unlocked, for Uncle Newland placed a great deal of confidence in the impregnability of his home with its attendant guards. Climbing

the sheer walls—the point of least concern for the master of
the house—was the best way to assure an approach to Miss
Gabrielle and Miss Eleanor. Certainly it was the least likely
approach that Mr. Alexander would expect did he but know
of his daughters' part to play in this final business of the
Kissing Cavalier.

Nathaniel hefted the metal hook, getting a feel for the
weight of it, and stepped back, swinging it to and fro. A few
wide arcs, and then he released the hook, sending it flying
upward. It sailed at an angle, carrying the length of rope with
it, until suddenly he could see it had nowhere near enough
thrust to reach the roofline. Instead the heavy weight clanked
against the stone side of the house, the rope slithering down
the stonework like a frenzied snake, as the metal hook gave
a long ringing tone. It rang out—loudly, Nathaniel thought
with a silent curse—until it made a dull thud as it struck the
ground in the flower patch below. Nathaniel winced and held
his breath, but no guardsman came running. Perhaps there
was some small advantage to the thickness of the stone walls,
for the sound did not seem to have carried inside at all.

He dug through the daisies and buttercups there until he
found the hook, at once coiling its rope and binding it; he
would not be using that again. It made far too much noise,
was wickedly dangerous with that sharp hook it sported, and
was as likely as not to get him noticed as he attempted to
go about his business, so it must be put aside.

He tossed the rope away, his gaze rising up the sheer, cold
stone wall before him. There was only a little frieze of stonework decoration, not even wide enough to support a toehold,
halfway up the building. So, if not the grappling hook, then
how was Nathaniel to scale the outside of the building?

He almost turned away, almost gave up the idea of besieg-
ing the twins in their Keep, but then his gaze fell on the
flowers before him. The daisies and buttercups twined around
the base of a wisteria-draped trellis—a trellis that climbed all
the way to the roof!

Nathaniel sighed and shook his head, annoyed at himself for even considering the hackneyed approach of climbing a flower trellis, but the only other choice was to turn away and give up for the night. "And bear this wager even a day longer?" he murmured to himself, and that was enough to convince him to give climbing the trellis a try.

He found fingerholds despite the thick covering of spring leaves and fragrant wisteria blossoms, and after one false start managed to find toeholds as well. Perhaps he ought to have removed his shoes—he wore dancing pumps because of the added padding at his calves that gave him that much more of a disguised appearance, and his hessians would never fit over the padding—but the latticing was widely spaced, giving the toe of his shoe working space, so he decided to continue upward as he was.

The wooden latticing groaned under his weight, so that he paused five feet above the ground, bouncing to test and see if the wood might give way. It did not; in fact it seemed sturdier than one might think, but perhaps that was because the tangle of old growth helped to reinforce the framework.

He continued upward cautiously, judging the trellis's construction as best he could in the dim moonlight and amidst the flower's tendrils, quickly releasing any support that seemed loose or weak. As he moved up to where he had just released a handhold, a sprig of the wisteria sprang up to slap him in the face, the faint scent of the plant reminding him for a moment of Miss Galloway. He had not been aware he carried such a memory, and for a moment the thought gave him pause before he resumed his climb, only to get another sprig in the face for his trouble.

"Pray God this wager is over tonight," he muttered to himself.

The thought of passing time reminded him of the advertisement he had read just this afternoon in the *Gazette*. It had been accredited to one "Lord C.," but Nathaniel had known it was Crowell's notice even without that proof.

The notice had read: "Kissing Cavalier, Be Aware That a Time Limit is Forthwith Established. You Have Two Weeks From the Date of This Sheet to Complete Your Task, Else All is Forfeited. Lord C."

The cheek of the man! A time limit had never been discussed, never agreed upon, yet Crowell had managed to place one on Nathaniel nonetheless. Of course, he could always take out a notice of his own, denying any time limit, but that would look petty. He had but one—well, two—kisses left to collect and then he was done. Two weeks was more than enough time, or at least ought to be.

That thought made Nathaniel frown and nearly miss a toehold. Why had Crowell allowed so long a time? Did he think it sporting—or did he know something Nathaniel did not, something that would keep the twins ever out of Nathaniel's reach? "Curse it!" he said, freezing in place. Could it be the Alexanders were leaving town? "Then I shall simply have to follow them," he assured himself. Mollified at that thought, he resumed his climb, ignoring the itch of the mask where it stretched over his nose.

He came level with the topmost window—which he saw at once was a good twelve inches away from the trellis. Making his way to the far right, Nathaniel made the mistake of looking down. He swallowed, casting his glance once again to the window, which now seemed to be twice as far away. He reached out a tentative hand, finding the distance was easily spanned, but that the window did not budge upward at his light touch. There was nothing to grasp, no outer handle by which to pull the window up—if it was even unlocked, as Simon had indicated it ought to be.

Nathaniel leaned out a little farther. The trellis groaned, and there was a popping sound.

His fingers pressed firmly against the glass, upward in motion, alarm giving him strength. The window made a sound somewhere between a snap and a moan, and slipped upward, now opening easily.

Nathaniel moved a little farther up the trellis, so that he could slip his leg through the open window. With a twist, a breathless prayer, a suspension by one hand, and a thrust of his lower limbs, he found himself halfway through the opening. Then it was just a matter of kicking free of the entangling drapery as he released his death's grip on the trellis, and a mere matter of pulling his head and shoulders inside.

He took a deep breath, but before he could let it out he recalled where he was and his need for silent caution. He turned from the window, half-crouched, ready for a footman's fist clipping him on the ear or to hear the click of a pistol being cocked, only to find no one near at hand. He had, indeed, made his way unnoted into someone's sleeping chamber.

Breathing out a sigh of relief, Nathaniel stood up straight. He reached to the curtain behind him, moving the fabric back so that moonlight could invade the room. Ah yes, there was the bed, and, yes, there was someone asleep upon it. A single person. Curious. He had envisioned the twins sharing a bed-chamber, but then again they were indulged by their parents, so might very well have their own separate rooms.

There was no point in hesitancy. He crossed the room as swiftly as he might while still taking care not to be so noisy as to absolutely terrify the girl should she wake and see his approach.

She lay burrowed in her pillows, her sleeping cap in place, her back turned to him. She breathed evenly, peacefully. Nathaniel hesitated, not sure if he ought to take her shoulders and turn her to face him, or lean upon the bed, bury his head in the tangle of linens, and swoop a kiss from her all at once. He decided the latter would be preferable, and braced himself with one quick breath in and out. He slipped the scissors from his waistcoat pocket, holding the small pair cradled in his hand so as to avoid accidentally harming anyone. Then he leaned over her, pushed down the ticking, and somehow managed to find her lips with his own, all in less than two seconds.

The girl awoke with a start, her hands coming to his shoulders and shoving him away almost before his lips had finished touching hers. She sat up, gasping, a shocked stare upon her face and made a strangled sound that was surely a precursor to a scream.

"Shhh!" Nathaniel urged, keeping the scissors hidden yet, for that would surely alarm the girl. "It is only the Kissing Cavalier," he explained, speaking hurriedly, remembering to deepen his voice to disguise it. "I required a kiss of you, and now, if you will but let me take a little snippet of hair, I will leave you in a trice."

The girl pulled in her breath, but the scream she had been about to utter did not materialize. "Cavalier?" she said, her voice thin and squeaky. She stared at him with rounded eyes, the covers now pulled up under her chin where she sat upon the bed.

"I mean no harm, truly," he told her, making a gesture with the hand not holding the scissors, to indicate a kind of apology or at least a lack of threat. "I shall be out the window before you can say—" His voice faltered, for only now did he see the girl did not possess the distinctive burnished-gold locks of one of the Alexander twins. This girl's hair was decidedly brown. This girl . . . this girl was Joan Galloway, Simon's other cousin-in-residence!

"Oh," he said, taking a step back. "Oh, well. Er. It seems I have quite found the wrong room."

"Lord Crowell was right. You *did* come," Miss Galloway declared. "The Kissing Cavalier. I do not think I truly believed him."

She shook her head, her eyes still too wide, although even in the dim light Nathaniel could see a large measure of her fear had evaporated at hearing his sobriquet. That sudden lack of dread had been the same with the last three females he had kissed while in the guise of the Cavalier—the only good he had ever seen come of society's penchant for tattlemongering. Because of that tattlemongering, it was well known the Cavalier never hurt anyone, that it was but a game he played. Now, yet again, that knowledge worked to his advantage.

Miss Galloway and he stared at one another in silence. He could only guess at her thoughts . . . but, for himself, Nathaniel was suddenly struck dumb as he realized the portent of her words: Lord Crowell had been here before him! Crowell had warned the household of the "Cavalier's" most recent wager. The cad! Had Crowell no honor? The man had refused any advantage to Nathaniel, but had made and taken one for himself. The bounder!

"That mask makes you appear rather witless," Miss Galloway informed him, a tentative finger rising to indicate the fabric covering his face. "If you cut off the bottom half, it would not be quite so foolish-looking as it is now, with only your eyes and mouth showing as they do."

She had certainly lost a good deal of her fear of him, he thought, faintly stung by her unsolicited comment, but her loss of fear was all to the good. Thankfully, no one had responded to the sound of voices in her room, though that was not to say someone might not soon, or for some other reason come to her chamber. There was no time to waste. Surely a maid slept nearby . . . ? Nathaniel frowned, belatedly realizing what a tiny room this was, how it had but one door leading out of it, presumably to a hallway. Where did her maid sleep?

"So you really have come to kiss Gabrielle and Eleanor," Miss Galloway said softly, giving him a considering look.

He slipped the scissors into his pocket, and sketched her a quick bow. "I beg your pardon—"

He got no further, for his words were lost as a pillow struck him across the face.

"Get out! Get out, you rogue! You will not be kissing my cousins, not tonight, not any night," Miss Galloway, who had come of a sudden from the bed, cried as she repeated the blow a second and a third time.

Nathaniel stumbled back, giving a disbelieving grunt as the pillow struck him again, and then a half-laugh from sheer surprise. "Stop! Ouch! That pillow has quills in it. You are— ouch! You are hurting me," he said in hushed tones, raising his hands to try and deflect the blows.

"I mean to hurt you, nodcock! And I shall go on hurting you until you leave!"

"Shh! Madam, please. Your voice—ouch!" he cried, his tone rising to match hers, for what was the point of being quiet when her cries must have surely already awakened the entire household? "I am leaving!" he declared, taking a leap back, out of harm's reach, toward the door.

The attack came again, redoubled in effort.

"Not that way!" she informed him, her words choppy from her efforts. "Back out the window, you fiend."

"I shall fall and be killed!" he said sternly, only to contradict the firmness of his statement by grinning at the sight of Miss Galloway with her cap askew, a determined glint that even the dim moonlight picked out sparkling in her eyes, and her flailing pillow. He sobered immediately when yet another blow hit him full in the face.

He stood up straight, and thankfully the gesture served to call a halt to the blows for a moment. "If you will but leave off and give me a moment to make my escape, madam, please!" he huffed.

The pillow struck him again, this time upside the left ear.

"That is not amusing," he said, pointing a finger at her.

"No mercy, sir! I have none, and you should know it! For the final time: get out!" she cried, swinging the pillow yet again.

"My pleasure," he announced, the final word obscured by another buffet from the wielded pillow.

Nathaniel drew back sharply, admitting defeat. It was a quick scramble to the window, a lunge, and he was of a sudden hanging tenuously by his hands from the trellis, his feet kicking out at the window frame as he worked to free his lower body of the room.

He had just swung one leg free—thankfully finding purchase on the trellis with his foot—when the pillow struck him yet again, this time on the back of his head.

"Stop that, you vixen!" he cried around the edge of his mask. Her blow had knocked his face covering askew, so that the edge stretched over his lip rather painfully and his vision was almost entirely blocked. In the back of his mind he noted that somewhere a dog barked, the sound quickly joined by the howls of yet other dogs. Why were the dogs' howlings not joined by the sound of hurried feet, of servants' hands reaching out to apprehend him?

And, stranger yet, Miss Galloway had not struck him again with the pillow.

"You truly might have killed me, you know!" he groused aloud, hoping to divert any further attack even as he dared to release his hold with one hand just long enough to tug the mask back down into place.

"I am gratified," he stated as he settled the eyeholes so that he could finally see again, "that you have seen reason, madam. I promise you I will bother you no more." He nodded in her direction and began his descent, moving far more rapidly than he had during his ascent.

At her continued silence, he looked up to see Miss Galloway—rather charming now in her nighttime plaits and now that she had righted her cap—staring down at him wide-eyed, the pillow still in her hands, now tightly clutched before her.

"And my cousins?" she spoke belatedly, the words seeming to burst from her lips. "Will you leave them be as well?"

"Of course not," he replied, leaping the last few feet to the ground. He straightened and looked up, allowing himself to grin at her, now the danger of being caught inside the house was past. "I am sworn to have their kisses, I am afraid. I cannot leave it undone."

"You will not succeed," she told him.

"Why not?" he asked, his grin widening.

"Because there are too many people dedicated to seeing that you will not."

"Including you, Fair Dragon?"

She was silent a moment, and when she spoke her voice was soft, "Including me, Cavalier."

"We shall have to see then, shall we not, who proves correct in this matter," he replied, offering her a bow. He stood, blew her a kiss—cocky of him, but she deserved it after that assault with the pillow—and retreated to the shadows of the yard.

Nathaniel whistled a merry tune as he moved to retrieve his rope and hook, and as he made his way toward the garden wall, knowing any footmen who came were now too late to stop his retreat. He scaled the wall easily, vaguely satisfied to know that his mistaking the room had been turned from disaster into something that left him chuckling in light-hearted amusement.

Joan stared down into the darkness of the street long after the man was gone. "The man," indeed! It had been no one other than Lord Price. As soon as his mask had slipped, as soon as she had seen his mouth revealed, heard his voice when he forgot to artificially lower it, she had known it was he.

Lord Price was the Kissing Cavalier!

Joan planted her elbows on the windowsill, lowering her chin to the pillow she still held scrunched in her hands. Lord Price, of all men! Lord Price, who had declared his intention to take a kiss from Gabrielle and Eleanor, had vowed to not give up that quest. He would try again, and again. There was some manner of honor at stake here, some manly competition between him and Lord Crowell, of that she was certain.

That was, she saw now, why Lord Crowell had come to call on her, of course: somehow he also knew who played the role of Cavalier. Lord Crowell had entered into some manner of wager—or whatever it was that drove two men into such folly—with Lord Price, forearmed with a prior acquaintance with Joan, well aware whose cousin Joan was. He had not come today to call upon *her,* not with thoughts of marriage in his head, not with thoughts of her as a person for that matter, and not even truly to help her father. No, he had come merely to manipulate and extract a promise from her, a promise that served him in this other matter. That was as transparent as glass now, making all his former words clear to her.

And, annoyingly, she knew she *would* thwart Lord Price. She had sworn she would. She had agreed to do as Lord Crowell asked so that Papa could be freed from the dangers of imprisonment, and that need was still as real as it had ever been.

Joan scowled into the night, resenting the fact she had been dealt into a game she had never wished to play.

Oh, but what harm would there be if Lord Price won, if the twins surrendered a kiss? A tiny scandal might attach itself to their names, but even Uncle Newland, given time, would have to see how inconsequential such a thing was. And who knew, perhaps it would even establish the girls' standing all the more, to have been "victims" of the Cavalier, the kisser of "great beauties."

But . . . there was a little matter of Joan's pledge, even if it had been given in innocence. She had promised a service in exchange for the funds that would secure Papa's release, that would free him from that place of smoke and coughs and prison fever. A bargain, however deceptively begun, had been struck. Could she turn away from it now? Even if she could throw over her promise to Lord Crowell, could risk his reprisal against her father, could she be sure it would serve Eleanor and Gabrielle's best interest?

Lord Price had declared he could not leave his task undone—and neither could she.

How ludicrous! The one man Joan longed most in this world to kiss again herself was the same man she must prevent from kissing her cousins. How wretchedly ironic!

Her thoughts skittered away from the disparity of the situation, pausing at the recollection that not more than five minutes ago, she had awakened to Lord Price's kiss. True, it had been the barest of kisses, not meant for her, and too brief a thing to reignite the magic of two months ago. Yet all the same, her fingers rose to touch her lips, as if to hold the sensation of his mouth on hers there a moment longer.

Disappointment washed over her as she lowered her hand to once again mangle the pillow. He had meant to kiss someone else, not her. How careless Lord Price was with his kisses! They obviously meant little to him, that he could so lightly take on this pledge to acquire kisses from numerous pretty girls. Did he even remember the kiss he and she had shared at the masquerade? Or did he kiss everyone that way? Was he as cavalier as his name implied?

Joan squeezed the pillow even tighter, staring out into the darkness of the late night. Obviously, Lord Price was just like a hundred other men. He was the sort who was unwilling to take an offered, true heart, content with only the inane game of borrowing kisses instead.

"The problem with that assessment," she whispered to herself, "is that I cannot quite believe it."

The Lord Price she knew was ever kind, ever thoughtful. And no matter how she approached the memory of their shared kiss of so many weeks ago, there was no denying something special had happened, that he had felt it, too.

Still, she had to remember Lord Price had in some way agreed to play this kissing game. The question came from wondering why he played it? What deviltry had provoked him into a role so unlike his usual ways?

The answer was easily reached: Lord Crowell, of course. Lord Crowell had, somehow, ordered the events Lord Price must now play out, just as he had with Joan.

She sighed, having no doubt that Lord Price had been as manipulated in his bid to kiss the twins as she was in her vow to keep him from it. After all, she had seen the advertisement placed by "Lord C.," and without doubt Lord Price had seen it as well. "Two weeks" the notice had read. Two weeks until this charade was over.

All at once, Joan shivered, possessed of a chill, causing her to toss aside the pillow and reach to close the window. The chill was not caused by the night air however, she realized as she set the latch in place with suddenly trembling hands, but rather by the abrupt understanding that came to her. When she had said she knew her duty to her cousins, Lord Crowell had replied, "How fortunate for your papa."

She had wondered then if those words were some manner of threat, and now she knew they were, oh yes, most assuredly. If, before the two weeks were up, the Cavalier—Lord Price—succeeded in kissing the twins, Joan feared she knew what would happen, what price would be exacted for her failure: Lord Crowell would demand he be repaid his money at once.

Papa would be unable to pay, of course, and it would be straight back to Newgate for him.

Either Joan or Lord Price must lose at this game of kisses. And she dare not let it be her.

Seven

Perhaps I ought not have cut off the bottom half of this mask, Nathaniel thought again as he touched his bared chin. Surely the moonlight reflected off the lower half of his face even though he lingered in the shadows?

He shook his head, lowering his hand to where he held the reins of his hired nag. What did it matter that Miss Galloway had said the full-face version made him appear witless? After all, this was a witless business to begin with, and he might as well look the part as he waited here. Still, even in the midst of folly, a man did not care to look more want-witted than necessary, and so now he sat and wondered if his face reflected the faint moonlight.

The rumbling of wheels over cobblestones wrenched his attention back to the dark road before him. The moonlight was just bright enough for Nathaniel to make out the coachman, whose grey-shaded livery he knew would have proved in daylight to be colored blue and silver, perched atop the approaching carriage. Just as he had predicted, the Alexander carriage was returning home from the theatre by way of a small side street. The traffic here tonight had been near to nonexistent, just as he had hoped it would be.

He kicked his heels, urging the nag forward. He pulled her to a skidding stop before the startled coachman, who just barely managed to halt his team. The road was narrow, and there would be no maneuvering around Nathaniel's mount.

" 'Tis I!" Nathaniel announced in his deepened voice, "The Kissing Cavalier."

"Gor!" said the coachman as he reached under the box on which he sat. He pulled forth a long-barreled pistol, cocking the weapon and aiming it at Nathaniel's chest. "Miss said as you might try'n stop us tonight," the man announced, peering cautiously through the dimness.

"Devil take it!" Nathaniel cried in surprise, pulling back on the reins so that the horse backed away a few steps, tossing its head in protest. "Friend, I mean no harm."

"That's as may be—" the coachman began.

"Hiram!" came a voice from the carriage. Nathaniel glanced away from the coachman just long enough to see Miss Galloway's head sticking out the coach window.

"Hiram!" she called again, her voice alarmed. "Pray do not shoot him!"

"I'll have to, Miss, if'n he moves toward the coach."

"Well then, move away, Mr. Cavalier," she called, her voice ringing with a thread of dismay that seemed to indicate she was more worried about seeing his blood spilled than she was by his intent in stopping them. She put a hand out the window to wave Nathaniel away, rather like shooing a goose from one's path.

"All I want is a kiss from the Misses Alexander," Nathaniel called back, still eyeing the unwavering firearm aimed his way.

"And a lock of their hair, sir! But you will have neither. Now, go away!" Miss Galloway withdrew inside the coach.

It was on the tip of Nathaniel's tongue to respond that her conversation last night had also included instructions for him to "go away" and that his intentions still did not include plans to comply, but it would have been unchivalrous to reveal he had been in her room.

"You do know," he called back, "that we could all be done with this, if you would but allow me a moment's time and a moment's indulgence?"

There was silence from the carriage, followed by a distinct blend of two girlish giggles. A brusque, though indecipherable word brought a halt to the giggles, and then Miss Galloway leaned out the window once more.

"I am starting to think Hiram should shoot you after all," she said, scowling at Nathaniel. It was not a very fierce scowl however—indeed, she appeared to be fighting to keep more than a thread of amusement from entering her voice.

"What a blood-thirsty creature you are, madam! Ought I be more alarmed than I am?"

"I care not, sir, whether you are alarmed or not. I only wish you to allow us unmolested passage. In fact, we go now, and you may either move out of harm's way, or else answer for the consequences. Hiram, take us home."

Nathaniel had to put heel to horse abruptly, for the coachman did not put down his pistol before giving a loud "hah!" to the horses, who lunged forward at the sudden slack in the ribbons. Hiram kept his eyes trained on Nathaniel all the while, pistol ever at the ready, as Nathaniel moved out of the way and the carriage rolled forward.

"Bravo, coachman!" Nathaniel called at the man's deft handling of four horses with but one hand. He gave the man a salute of respect.

"Gor!" came Hiram's response, followed by a shake of the head, presumably at the ways of the gentility.

The edge of a bonnet showed at the still open window and was abruptly thrust forward with a short, muffled cry of protest, fully revealing Miss Galloway's face to him again, as two golden heads pressed close behind, twin pairs of light-colored eyes peering back at him. There were flashes of white teeth, accompanied by trills of feminine laughter.

"Until we meet again!" he called after the ladies, bowing to them as best he could while still astride his horse.

"Until we meet again," came the reply—from Miss Gabrielle, he thought, although it was often difficult to tell one twin from the other even in a well-lit room. Miss Galloway sat back abruptly, pulling the twins away from the window with her.

Nathaniel turned his horse, shaking his head at the incompletion of his task—again.

Miss Galloway, it seemed, was entirely sincere in her intention to keep her cousins free of kisses. Of course, it was only right of her to see her uncle's wishes in the matter were carried through, but surely it was not too great a transgression against the man's plans to allow one little buss each? It was true that the continental fellows Nathaniel had known were often shocked at what they perceived as too much freedom of movement among the English female, too little attention to strict chaperonage, but a tiny lapse or two from absolute propriety would surely never keep an interested *parti* from offering for a young lady with an otherwise blameless history?

It could be supposed the twins themselves did not object overmuch to the idea of an innocent kiss or two, at least to judge by their evident amusement tonight, but perhaps that was why their cousin sought to serve as guardian to them? She must protect them from their own inclinations—and that was never the easiest of tasks. Nathaniel knew that fact well enough himself, for he had wished to save Simon from his own proclivity for mischief a hundred times, most often failing miserably.

So, Miss Galloway had just proved that the contemptible Lord Crowell had stacked the deck well. He had cleverly selected a devoted, female sentry, one who for reasons of her own seemed utterly determined to keep Nathaniel from his task, and—worse luck, at least for tonight—capable of acting upon her determination. With an ironic grin, Nathaniel found he was not quite sure if he ought to detest Crowell for so shrewdly skewing the odds, or else admire the man's resourcefulness.

Shaking his head ruefully, Nathaniel reflected that as a gentleman, he ought to relinquish the field to Miss Galloway.

Indeed he would, were it not for one thing: Simon. It did not matter that Nathaniel stood to lose his favorite coach and team to Lord Crowell, nor that his driving fellows would be bitterly disappointed at the loss. But Simon mattered. And Simon would, undeniably and inevitably, come to the point of ruination should Crowell win this wager. It was as certain as sun in summer, for Simon would never be able to stand for Crowell's smug exultation upon winning. And Crowell would be smug, there was no doubt of that. Smug, and crowing, and taunting, until Simon lost his temper. Simon had once already been on the verge of calling the man out. If a duel ever took place, there were only three possible endings to come from it: one was that Simon would kill Crowell, and then have to flee the country for breaking the law against dueling; the second was that he would merely wound Crowell, or be wounded himself—but then there would be no keeping the truth from Newland Alexander, and thus would Simon find himself posthaste in the army. The third was that Simon would be killed—and that was too heinous a thought to be contemplated.

No, Nathaniel could not retreat from the field of battle. If Miss Galloway had determined to wage war against him for such a little thing as two kisses and two locks of hair, then war it must be.

Perhaps, after all this dementia was behind them, Nathaniel could persuade Simon's uncle to allow the two of them to do a Grand Tour of sorts. The lengthy war with France had prevented any true Grand Tour for years, but there were ports that could be visited yet—perhaps Mr. Alexander would finally concede to the old suggestion. Now, with two daughters coming out who needed seeing to, he might not be so dismissive of Nathaniel's offer to finance such a venture. Perhaps.

Time for such plans later. For now, Nathaniel must first get this quest for kisses behind him. He was not sure what to make of the unease that filled him at the thought of staging a campaign against Miss Galloway. It rather made his stomach sour.

He decided to attribute the sensation to the distasteful business of having to appear less than the gentleman before a lady. However, he gave himself the cold comfort of thinking, there was nothing for it. Simon's life and happiness must be held paramount over the social pretensions of two young ladies. Eventually Miss Galloway would relax her guard, or not think far enough ahead, or not allow for her opponent's determination, and the wager would be won, the deed done, the event behind them all.

Nathaniel tilted back his head to gaze up at the stars. "Sooner would be better than later," he told the heavens.

No star winked and no cloud chased before the moon, the heavens refusing him any manner of reply. Nathaniel shook his head and laughed at himself as he reached to remove his hat and the half-mask. He laughed again at the memory of Miss Galloway's tart tongue and her frivolous young charges. He looked down at the mask, wondering briefly if Miss Galloway had noted the change he'd made to it? No matter. He stuffed it in his pocket with a sigh as he urged the horse forward with a kick of his heels.

"Take me home, old bones," he told the horse. "Then you may go back to your warm stable, and I to my supper."

Supper. There was to be a late-night supper tonight, one he had promised to Simon. He recalled the night's invitation to join Simon at the Alexander home. That presumably meant supper would be spent with Miss Galloway and the Misses Alexander as well.

Another smile spread over his face as Nathaniel began to plan how to turn the midnight meal to his advantage.

Joan ignored Lord Price's smile, looking to the table cloth, thoroughly annoyed with him. How dare he come to this house, eat this food, all the while plotting to assail the daughters of the house? It quite smacked of poor taste! *True, 'tis but a kiss he wants,* Joan thought with an internal frown, but his apparent ease with making a duplicitous incursion—under a longstanding and thorough disguise as "friend"—piqued.

Eleanor was not so willing to look away from his attentive visage however. Joan watched from under her lashes as her cousin chattered and tittered, asking Lord Price what he thought of Lord So-and-So's new curricle and Lady Thus-and-This's French lace pelisse. Was not the weather yet too cool? Did he think picnicking weather would come upon them soon? Did he care for picnics? How delightful! They would have to enjoy one together, would they not? Oh yes, Gabrielle adored picnics! What a splendid outing they could make of it, the three of them.

"Four of you, you mean," Uncle Newland put in, pointing his fork at Joan to indicate her inclusion in any plans.

"Of course," Eleanor said, not even bothering to glance her father's way. "But we need not belabor that point. Joan goes everywhere with us."

Like the family pet, Joan thought to herself, schooling her face so as not to reflect the thought. Really! the evening had put her in a dreadful mood.

"But as to outings," Lord Price said, "does anyone dare to be out and about with this Cavalier fellow haunting the streets?"

Joan looked up in surprise, to try and see some hint of deeper meaning on Lord Price's face at this seemingly innocent question, only to find a blandly innocent countenance there. What purpose did it serve him to mention his own secret persona?

"The man is a menace!" Uncle Newland pronounced.

"A menace," Aunt Hannah echoed, her bonnet bobbing as she nodded agreement with her husband.

"You heard our tale of him already," Gabrielle said to Lord Price, leaning forward in a manner that blocked Eleanor's view down the table to where he sat. Eleanor sat up as straight as she could, scowling momentarily at her sister before she tilted flush against her chairback, her head at a peculiar angle, to maintain a view of their guest from that awkward position.

"But you never said: Were you frightened of him? Did he truly seem a menace?" Lord Price asked Gabrielle.

"Oh, never so! He is a Gentleman Brigand."

"That is a total improbability, Gabrielle. There cannot be such a creature as a Gentleman Brigand," Joan said, taking pains not to give Lord Price the speaking look she longed to send his way. He obviously did not feel a barb had been sent flying, however, for a quick glance in his direction revealed an upward pull to his mouth.

"You know what I mean," Gabrielle pouted at Joan. "A Gentleman of the Road. A Courtly Criminal. A Refined Felon—"

"Gabby, have done!" Simon growled, making a show of rolling his eyes.

"And you may stop rolling your eyes, Simon," Gabrielle replied. She dismissed him without another look or word, turning to Joan. "Dear cousin, what do you mean?"

"I simply meant some words cannot go together, such as 'Gentleman Brigade.' They form what is called an oxymoron."

"Oxy—?" Gabrielle blinked. "Are you saying I am some manner of moron?"

Joan might have laughed, but instead she explained, "No, dear girl. 'Oxymoron' is from the Greek, meaning one has made a combination of contradictory words. Such as 'a simple complexity.' "

"Oh pooh, Joan! Whoever knows such a thing?" Gabrielle announced with a graceful little shrug. "You really must try not to spout such things, or else you will end by looking like a bluestocking, Joanie."

Simon put down his fork with a clatter. "Must you be a bluestocking to know how to use your own language?" he challenged.

Uncle Newland frowned at Simon's tone, but Gabrielle answered, "Yes, you must."

No one corrected the girl, perhaps because she looked so pleased with her own logic. Nathaniel smiled pleasantly, although that might be a devil of humor dancing in his glittering eyes. As for Joan, she put her tongue against her teeth, not because she felt her cousin's reasoning had won the point, but to keep back the comments she herself so longed to make. She itched to cry forth the fact she knew who the Cavalier was.

There was nothing to stop her from denouncing him, of course. That would put an end to this charade. She ought to do it. She was, in some respects, obliged to do it. She ought to just speak right up and say Lord Price was the Cavalier, for he would not lie about it, she felt sure, not once she made the pronouncement. He was a scapegrace for playing the part—even be it under some pressure from Lord Crowell—but he was not a liar. He would own to the truth if he were challenged.

Then do it, she told herself, *speak up!* But her tongue stayed firmly planted behind her teeth.

There was the matter of Lord Crowell to keep her silent. But surely he would not be so mean-spirited as to say voiding their agreement was the same as allowing Lord Price to win? Surely he would not see to it that Papa's imprisonment continued? He was not that mean-spirited, no, of course not. But she knew with a sinking feeling she would only be unwise to trust in his kindness. No, never again, not after she had comprehended his threat against Papa! But surely there was a limit to the man's lack of charity in pursuit of his goal?

Joan did not know, not with any certainty.

But that was not foremost in her mind. That was not what kept her from stating the truth right here and now: she wanted to beat Lord Price at his own game. That kept her silent as much as anything.

Joan did not want to win by "default." She wanted Lord

Price to see she could be clever, and persistent, and gracious in her triumph. She wanted him to see kisses were not always a casual thing, that harm could come to those who misused the sensitivities of others. And once he saw all those things, there was a tiny, slim chance he might see past all the kisses, all the games, and note the woman who had dared to challenge him. See her worth was something more than the depth of her father's pockets or his title, see past the lack of esteem afforded her by her cousins.

Oh yes, part of her wanted Lord Price to fail: that he might come to see her for who she was, that she might repay him for never seeing her in truth, never realizing the depth of feeling they had once shared in a darkened hallway, however fleetingly.

Yet another part of her wished he would succeed, that Uncle Newland's decrees would be, for once, overridden, that Lord Price would best Lord Crowell despite the man's machinations. There was even a part of her that wanted Lord Price to triumph for no reason she could put a name to, but whatever caused that urge also caused a tightness in her chest.

"Joan?" a voice brought her back to the conversation at the table. She looked up, seeing it was Gabrielle who had spoken to her.

"I am sorry. My mind was in the clouds," Joan explained, blushing at the admission.

"I asked what we are doing tomorrow," Gabrielle explained, then turned to nod in Lord Price's direction.

Joan understood at once that the question had surely originated from him. So, he wished to know their plans for the morrow, did he? That he might plan another "encounter with the Cavalier?"

"We are off to Covent Garden," Eleanor supplied before Joan could open her mouth to speak. "Do you not recall that I wished to find a new fan to replace the one Mr. Quoddy sat upon, Gabby?"

"You will have two footmen in attendance, should you put

so little as a toe outside the door," Uncle Newland declared, rapping his knuckles against the tabletop. Aunt Hannah startled at the sound, then nodded in agreement.

"Oh, Papa!" Gabrielle scoffed with a laugh. "Who would be so foolish as to attempt to steal a kiss in the middle of Covent Garden? Why, we could venture there alone," Gabrielle slid a sideways glance at Lord Price, invitation in her voice and look, "and be as safe as babes in their cradles."

Joan looked closely at Gabrielle, wondering if the girl somehow knew it was the Cavalier she gave such an obvious enticement to? But, no, she saw from the clear-eyed expression in her cousin's eyes that Gabrielle was thinking more of kisses than of characters. Could Gabrielle be thinking of herself and Lord Price as a couple? Surely not for marriage— Gabrielle's fate was as good as set, for Uncle Newland would agree to no less than a continental marriage—but perhaps for dalliance?

Joan sat back in her chair, experiencing a sudden sense of botheration at the very idea of her cousin being wooed by Lord Price.

"I will have you know, Gabrielle, that this Cavalier fellow slipped into a crowded garden party at Sir Garrett's home and still managed to come away with a snippet of the eldest daughter's hair! You will have two footmen, or you will not go!" Uncle Newland ordered.

Gabrielle wrinkled her small nose in a gesture of reluctant acceptance as Aunt Hannah murmured, "Of course they will have, my dear."

"And the rest of your day's plans? Do you go to the Vicomte de Lisle's musicale tomorrow evening?" Lord Price asked the table at large.

"Indeed!" Eleanor answered eagerly, now leaning far forward in her chair to speak to him. The edge of the fichu she had tucked into her décolletage—a rather deep one, which even the fichu only nominally served to cover—dipping into the gravy on her dish for her trouble. "I so look forward to an evening of music. Do you not, Lord Price?"

Lord Price inclined his head. "Most decidedly."

"Eleanor! Only see what you have done to your dress," Aunt Hannah cried, causing her daughter to look down her front and give a mew of displeased surprise.

"Oh dear, you will have to change at once," Gabrielle pronounced with a cat's smile, turning at once back to Lord Price.

"And you will have to come with me!" Eleanor stated firmly.

"Do not be silly. Joan, you will help her, will you not?"

Joan bit back the reply that came to mind—that the twins had two lady's maids to serve their needs—and stood.

Gabrielle beamed, pleased with her little triumph over her twin, her self-satisfaction serving to goad Joan into stating the obvious. "Do you gentlemen retire to your port now?"

Gabrielle's smile slipped at the nods all around. Joan gave the girl credit, however, for she stood with a show of grace, and due to the late hour bid the gentlemen good night without making any fuss about meeting again after their port.

"Good evening, Ladies," Lord Price said, and for a moment his gaze met Joan's. There was laughing humor there in his dark eyes, and it was with a physical and quite pleasant shock that Joan realized the humor was shared particularly with her. A moment later he had hooded his eyes, removing from her any further glimpse into his thoughts—rather wisely, she judged, if he did not intend to confess from where this sudden, new awareness of one another had sprung. And it *was* a new awareness, the result of experiences shared. Both knew what had happened in her bedchamber just last night, but neither could admit it to the other.

She had two advantages over him, two reasons she turned away to avoid the possibility of him returning his gaze to hers and perhaps reading more than he ought there. The first was that she knew he was the Cavalier, where he did not know she knew it, and the second was that she knew of one other occurrence they had shared: that midnight kiss two months ago.

Temptation nibbled at her, tweaking her, telling her to lift her eyes to his once more, to let him see in her gaze what she could not bring her lips to say. *I was that woman—*

"Joan, whatever are you doing standing there gaping at the carpet?" Aunt Hannah interrupted her thoughts.

"It needs cleaning," she mumbled, turning at once to flee Aunt Hannah's gaze and any other possibilities rife within the room.

Once outside the doors to the dining room, however, she was stopped by the serious countenance of Gabrielle, who pouted out, "You needn't have mentioned port quite so soon. I vow you have a positive knack for spoiling sport, Cousin Joan."

"Do I?" Joan asked, hiding a tremulous smile even while she thought to herself: *only see how tomorrow goes!* For she had no doubt the Cavalier meant to put in an appearance at tomorrow night's entertainment, and Joan meant to spoil that sport as well.

Eight

Joan did not approach the waiting carriage until she saw the last section of trellis come down. The gardener looked to her for her approval, got it by way of a nod and a smile, and began to instruct his underlings how to set the bed of buttercups and daisies to rights.

Joan turned to where Gabrielle and Eleanor sat impatiently waiting for her, the footman handing her up into the landau.

"The windows are all locked, even the servants', and the trellis cut away from beneath the wisteria. Are you content now?" Gabrielle huffed.

"Quite so."

"I still say no one would ever be so foolhardy as to climb a flower trellis," Eleanor sniffed.

Joan made no reply, never having confessed to the Cavalier's invasion of her room. If Uncle ever knew the Cavalier had already been in his home, he might very well sweep his daughters off to the safety of the country, Season or no Season. In the wilds of Kent, Joan would not be present when Papa was released from gaol, and she would lose near any hope of attaching a husband for herself, so such a case was to be avoided. How could she ever help Papa with his financial woes if she never married?

She put the thought of marriage aside, for after her experience with Lord Crowell, the subject made her ill-tempered. Instead, she concentrated on the beauty of this bright May morning, glad the driver had chosen to open the calash tops of the landau even though the breeze was yet a bit brisk this morning.

Their driver put them down at the piazza, promising to bring the carriage around to the same place in two hours. The groom rode off with the carriage and driver, while the two footmen who had been ordered to accompany them fell in step behind the ladies. Gabrielle and Eleanor, hand-in-hand, led the way through the market stalls, pointing out items of interest. Gabrielle leaned over a pretty fan of shell-colored lace, only to sigh and turn away, a clear sign the item was priced even beyond her generous allotment of pin money.

Oh dear, thought Joan. That would be the only fan Gabrielle would see all day that would please her now. Therefore, before Gabrielle would consent to return home to attempt to persuade her papa to gift her with the money to pay the difference she would first require them to look at every other fan in the market.

That was exactly how it went, of course. Gabrielle looked at every stall, then proceeded on to the shops surrounding the piazza, Eleanor a willing accomplice.

A half an hour later, Joan wandered the edges of the third mantua-maker's shop they had entered, idly taking in the displays of fans, combs, pins, and fabrics. She sighed once over a new pair of gloves that only served as a reminder new things were beyond her until such time as Papa turned his finances to the better, or until she married. There was that word again: marriage.

She had been not unlike Eleanor and Gabrielle at one time, not so long ago, a few months only. Oh heavens, could it really have only been two months? She had been, like them, concerned with being seen in the latest vogue, taken up with the thought of a new bonnet or gewgaw. Life had been easy, pleasant, settled in its course. She had borrowed books from the lending library whenever she pleased, never giving a thought to the cost. She had burned oil lamps well past dark, smiling indulgently at Mrs. Lyle's comments about the expensive luxury of reading at night and how poor it surely was for the eyes. She had given away the very kind of gloves she now mended. Yes, life had been easy and predictable, and in truth Joan could not really fault her cousins for enjoying the leisure and assets that life afforded them. It was no more their fault they were well-to-do than it was hers for having tumbled from that very same exalted station.

Joan sighed again, raising her gaze to glance in one of the shop's many mirrors. The bonnet she wore was well enough, for now, but in two more months it would certainly be dated and showing wear. Ah well, it was always possible one of the twins would see that she received one of their cast-offs.

Joan looked beyond the bonnet to the look of faintly amused chagrin on her face, and then her gaze focused on a bit of movement in the reflected alley just outside the window. The mirror was pocked and wavy, but not so distorted as to prevent her from seeing a man with a large, flamboyant hat slipping up the alley between this building and the next.

Joan spun from the mirror to look out the window directly, catching clear sight of a masked face as the man neared.

The Cavalier! Lord Price. The cheek of the man, to charge them in broad daylight!

"Gabrielle! Eleanor!" Joan cried, hurrying toward them.

"Whatever is the matter?" Eleanor demanded, looking alarmed.

Joan opened her mouth to explain, but the eager light that came into Gabrielle's eyes made her think twice, especially when Gabrielle looked around with an anticipatory smile settling on her lips.

"I can only think of one thing to make our cousin grow so suddenly pale," Gabrielle told Eleanor.

"You cannot mean . . . ?" Eleanor cried, her eyes going round and a smile crossing her mouth as well, as she turned to Joan.

Joan was saved from making an answer, for the shopkeeper, one Mrs. Richman, came forward with a box she had brought from her back room. "Here are the Italian fans I was telling you about—"

"Do you have a private showing room?" Joan interrupted, already putting one hand on each of the twins' elbows and propelling them toward the rear of the shop, ignoring their noises of protest.

"Indeed, madam. Does madam want—?"

"Madam most certainly does," Joan replied. "Take these ladies there, at once! Keep them there until I say otherwise."

The shopkeeper started to protest this strange request, but just then the shop door opened and Lord Price stepped in, his mask—now halved, exposing his fine mouth—and fancy hat in place. The shopkeeper took one look and whimpered, and at once shooed the twins in front of her through a curtain at the back of the shop.

The lower half of Lord Price's face flushed scarlet, and Joan could swear he grit his teeth in embarrassment. Good! He ought to be embarrassed by all this foolishness.

Joan backed up, until the curtain to the showing room brushed the back of her bonnet. She put out an arm on either side as thought to prevent him from passing her by. Behind her she could feel a flurry at the cloth curtain, as though hands tugged at the fabric, seeking to part it open.

Lord Price gazed at her, not moving, until she began to feel a little silly in her dramatic pose.

"How long do you intend to stand there like that?" he asked dryly.

"As long as it takes for you to go away."

"That could be a long time."

"I do not think so. You dare not stay long, not with our footmen near at hand, and not dressed so in the middle of the day."

A sigh and a delighted gasp behind Joan convinced her that twin pairs of blue eyes were without doubt now peeping past the edges of the fabric curtain.

"Your footmen are across the street helping a pieman with

an overturned cart. But do not look so distressed, madam—I assure you I did not tip the fellows wares for him. It was happenstance that gave me this opportunity, one I plan to take full advantage of. I am only grateful your footmen do not think much can happen to three ladies inside a shop. Now, either step aside, or else I shall have to consider pushing past you that we all may be done with this in a trice," he informed her.

"Oh, do move aside, Joan!" one of the twins whispered loudly.

Joan stared up at Lord Price, not sure if he meant to do as he threatened or not. "You changed your mask," she countered.

A tinge of red returned to his jawline. "At your suggestion, madam. You see, not all your words fall on deaf ears."

"Then hear these: leave us be."

"I cannot."

Joan blew out a frustrated breath. "I thought you were supposed to *receive* your kisses, not *steal* them from unwilling young ladies."

"Steal?" He drew himself up, as though affronted. "Would it necessarily be so? Let me speak to the Misses Alexander there, and I shall ask them—"

"I should not mind, Joanie, if it were but a kiss!" a voice chimed from behind the curtain.

"Eleanor! Be silent!" Joan admonished.

Lord Price spread his hands, his gesture clearly suggesting there was no theft involved.

Joan felt her face coloring, finding both her position—poised as she was like some manner of enraged she-bear—and the conversation preposterous.

"Truly, madam, your guardianship does you credit, but now we have it from Miss Eleanor that she would not mind, it behooves you to step aside," Lord Price said logically.

Joan floundered for a reply, unable to deny what they all had heard. "Do kisses have so little meaning for you then?"

she blurted out, at once horrified to hear her foremost thought expressed aloud.

"Meaning?" Lord Price frowned, his dark eyes taking on a serious cast.

Joan took a deep breath. "Why do you do it, unless it has some meaning?"

Lord Price blinked once, and shifted his weight to his rear foot. "To win a wager," he explained.

"Ah," Joan said, aware her mouth turned down at the corners. "Of course. Just as I thought."

"How disapproving you sound."

"I *am* disapproving!"

" 'Tis a harmless enough game," he said in a quiet voice.

He met her gaze for a long moment, then looked to the floor, away from her steady regard, either moved by her disapproval or some other sensibility of his own.

"But let me ask you this, madam," he added, at length raising his gaze back to hers, his voice grown firm again. "How is it that you disapprove so much? What is a kiss to you?"

She could have explained about Uncle Newland's wishes for his daughters. She could have explained about familial duty and all of that. But instead, knowing it was Lord Price to whom she spoke, she could only think of the real reason she did not want her cousins kissed by this man. "It is just that—"

Now it was her turn to look away, lowering her arms to her sides as she pulled her lower lip between her teeth. Ah well, it was better said, for he seemed to be truly listening to her, truly attempting to understand her objection.

"I rather suppose you will think me foolish, but I think a kiss can be a special thing. A way to show affection or regard. A promise to come to know someone better, to desire more of their company, of their consideration." Joan remembered such a kiss, and had to close her eyes for a moment to banish a tremble from entering her speech. "It is that I think hearts can be broken when kisses are lightly given and received."

She opened her eyes again to find Lord Price staring at her, his hand to his chin, a considering look apparent around his exposed mouth, in his dark eyes.

How could anyone not see it was him? She saw the familiar mouth; the long, straight ridge of his nose beneath the mask; the rise of cheekbones there; the fringe of dark brown hair escaping from beneath the stretch of fabric near his temple. His clothes were unfamiliar, and thick-soled shoes perhaps served to disguise his height by an added inch or so. She was fairly certain some padding had been added to accentuate his lower legs and shoulders, bringing them to rather imposing dimensions. The hat served to draw the eye away from gazing too long at the half-hidden face—yet she could no longer be deceived. Even if she had not heard him use his true voice, there was no mistaking the way he held himself, the way he moved.

"There *can* be . . . magic in a kiss," he admitted slowly, still staring at her from his mask's eye slits.

She felt her own eyes begin to widen, her jaw slackened just a little, as it dawned on her that the consideration with which he regarded her meant he was remembering a kiss as well. Oh, sweet Heaven!, he was wondering if it had been her, was pondering whether her mouth could have shaped so intimately to his . . . !

Panic seized her, for in his gaze, too, she saw him struggle with the thought, with the possibility: *Simon's cousin?* He might as well have shouted it. *Miss Joan Galloway? The penniless Viscount Stanmore's daughter?* his eyes asked. Oh, why, oh why had she mentioned kisses in regards to herself? And why must he look at her with such discomfiture at the thought it might be her he had kissed?

"Not that I have ever been kissed," she lied, her hands knotting into fists where she pressed them into her skirts. A lie! she had told a lie, something she had not done in years, not since leaving the schoolroom. Where were her scruples? Gone, gone, for another lie bubbled easily to her lips. "But if I had, I am sure I would only wish a kiss from someone who had pledged his troth to me."

"Never been kissed?" he asked very softly. His expression cleared, then darkened, and cleared again. "Never even in sport?"

"Why, of course not. Never!" she cried out, the relief on his face striking such a blow near her heart that the lie came easily, a way of relieving the terrible ache that centered there.

"Never?" she heard Gabrielle ask Eleanor.

"Then perhaps, madam, and I beg your pardon for saying it, but perhaps you are not the best one to judge whether my kiss is right or not for your cousins," Lord Price said.

"I wish you would go," she said in utter misery, looking to his shoes, not his masked face, blinking rapidly to keep back tears.

Silence fell, broken only by the ticking of a mantel clock above the shop's hearth.

A flash of movement caused Joan to look up, taking half a step back with a small sound of alarm, pressing her skirts against the curtain at her back. But, although the Cavalier moved, it was only to make her a bow.

"Madam is upset," he said in his disguised voice. "We will wait on this for another day, I think." He stood, giving her a level look, then turned and crossed the distance to the door, exiting without another word.

"Gabby, who do you think that is?" Eleanor broke the silence, her voice pitched high with excitement as she flung the curtain aside. The cousins crowded around Joan, speaking around Joan almost as if she were not there.

"Lord Warner, I was thinking. Or perhaps Frederick Pennyman."

"Oh never! Freddy is a foot too short to be this fellow. I think the Kissing Cavalier is Sir Daniel, or Mr. Cartwright."

"Mr. Cartwright less two stones, perhaps," Gabrielle mused.

"Of course, Freddy has been gone from society for three months now, so I suppose he might have lost the weight . . . ."

"Let us return home," Joan suggested quietly.

The girls did not object to this suggestion, resettling their shawls about their shoulders as Joan thanked the shopkeeper for her assistance. The twins followed Joan from the shop, their banter continuing.

"If I did not know better, I might guess the Cavalier is Simon," Eleanor laughed.

Gabrielle waved a dismissive hand. "He is never so gallant. No, not Simon, but it is one of his friends, mark my word."

"What of Lord Price?" Eleanor cried, clapping her hands together. "Oh, would that not be famous?"

"Widgeon! Lord Price never stoops to such antics," Gabrielle reproved.

Eleanor sighed. "Too true," she agreed.

All joy in the bright day gone, Joan leaned back in the landau and only wished Gabrielle's words really were true.

Nathaniel rode to a deserted street, divesting himself of his costume's hat, mask, coat, and waistcoat as he rode. He pulled up the reins long enough to dismount, stowing his disguise in a cloth bag behind the saddle. He hoped Sir Francis's hat would be sadly crushed by its ill-treatment, and grinned with a rather wicked satisfaction at the thought. He pulled free his own coat—much the worse for having been rolled and placed in the sack—and remounted. He kicked his horse into a trot, his mood well-suited to the jarring pace.

This business with the Alexander twins was going on too long, becoming far more difficult than it ought to be, and all because of Miss Galloway. He should have ignored his finer instincts today, should have hardened his heart to the upset in her voice, should have barged past her, kissed the twins, taken the tokens, and been done with it. But no! The sight of a miserable Miss Galloway had turned away his steps, had caused him to halt the contest for yet another day.

And where did that misery come from? What had made her unable to meet his eye? What had caused her voice to lower, had made him feel less like a vanquisher and more like a despoiler?

Of course, it was entirely possible Miss Galloway had put on a cloak of anguish, that she had *meant* him to feel uneasy. Certainly she had shown a touch of dramatic aptitude when she had thrown wide her arms to block his path, and when she had accused him of stealing kisses. She had intended for him to feel like a thief, and dash it if she had not succeeded to a certain degree!

Do kisses have so little meaning? she had asked him, and for one wild moment he had thought she looked right through his mask, saw not the Cavalier, but *him,* spoke to *him.* And for an even wilder moment he had thought she might be, could be the woman from the masquerade. Joan Galloway, Simon's cousin!

However, she had negated the thought once she claimed never to have been kissed. That could be a lie, of course. In fact, there was a kind of fire in her dark eyes when she spoke this that made her words suspect—but that could be caused by embarrassment. Easy enough to believe in her embarrassment, for it could be no pleasure for a woman of her age—she must be, what, twenty?—to admit to a lack of kisses, especially a woman who seemed aware of her rather conventional appearance. Bringing her to the point of such a confession had made him feel unwittingly unkind and terribly maladroit.

The truth was, he would have been stomping on her exposed feelings—real or unreal, as they might be—by demanding she step aside and give up her post of sentinel to the twins. As much as he longed to have all this behind him, as much as it would have made all their lives simpler, he had been unable to so deliberately play the churl.

His eyes narrowed. *Something* was amiss here, but he could

not put his finger on it. Either she experienced some real distress, or else she played some deep game. Too, there was the oddity of her room last night. Why had no one come flying at the cries and scuffling they had made? Why did she have such a small, humble room, so far up in the house, rather more like a servant's than one intended for a member of the family? Why had she not had a maid near at hand to tend to her needs of a night? It was not as if the house were not large enough to provide adequate chambers. It was almost as if she were being treated as something less than any other member of the house, including the disfavored Simon. Peculiar. Nathaniel must make a point of asking Simon about the situation.

"Humph!" he growled aloud, alarming his horse into a momentary skitter.

But there was the trick of the thing, of course: to not be lulled away from his task by other thoughts. Howsoever she was situated, the fact was Miss Galloway had sworn to keep him from kissing her cousins, but kiss them he would.

Lord Crowell had done his meddling well, bringing two reluctant players into his game and fixing them in place. Nathaniel could not know why Miss Galloway was compelled to her course, but it could not be ignored that she had agreed to become part of this, had allowed herself to be put in the middle of a high stakes competition. She could hardly blame anyone but herself if the stakes became too steep. She should not blame Nathaniel when he played the hand dealt to him.

He only hoped she understood that.

Nine

The soft light cascading down from the Vicomte de Lisle's music room chandelier made Eleanor's coiled hair gleam like polished brass as she leaned over in her chair. In a low voice near Joan's ear, she asked, "That was a lie this afternoon, was it not, Cousin Joan? About never having been kissed?"

Gabrielle leaned around her sister from her farther seat, blue eyes glinting with eagerness to hear the response.

Joan was saved from having to answer by a sudden bluster from Uncle Newland on her other side. "Lord Price!" he called, standing and motioning.

Uncle Newland's greeting overrode the hum of thirty-odd voices in the room, and even the discordant sounds from the six-member troupe of musicians tuning their instruments. Joan blushed at her uncle's over-hearty greeting, afraid to even think what it might mean for her. Uncle Newland had little enough interest in Lord Price's company, and certainly no wish to bring the man to the attention of the twins. Simon had declined an invitation to the Vicomte's musicale tonight, so that left only one thought as to why Uncle Newland sought Lord Price's company tonight.

She was not mistaken. Uncle Newland promptly led Lord Price to their row of chairs, bidding him take the free one at Joan's right. He then promptly suggested the twins go with him to fetch a glass of wine, and without another word abandoned Joan and the very man he had waylaid.

It took a great deal of effort, but Joan brought her chin

up and met Lord Price's gaze. "Good evening, Lord Price," she said, hoping her mortification at being made to look like an unwanted item at a cut rate sale did not show on her face.

"Good evening, Miss Galloway."

An awkward silence fell between them. Joan cast about in her mind for something to say, some words that would set him free from having to politely remain at her side. However, the phrases that sprang to mind would surely sound rude, as if she were dismissing him rather than releasing him.

"Your uncle is quite the eccentric," Lord Price broke the silence.

How considerate of him to offer her an excuse upon which to hang her uncle's behavior! But she was unwilling to accept something so sadly near to pity. "Now that," she said, "is one word for Uncle Newland. It is not the one I would apply."

He nodded once, briefly, and a ghost of a smile touched his mouth. "I see Simon is more than right when he tells me you wish to return to your own home," he said, and she was glad to see it was not pity after all, but something more like understanding that shone from his eyes.

"I do," she said, and then had to blink to keep moisture from obscuring her vision.

"Home is a far friendlier place than anywhere else."

How perceptive of him; it was clear he knew or suspected her life had changed for the worse in Uncle Newland's keeping.

She nodded a response, not quite trusting her voice to remain even should she dare to speak. No wonder she adored Lord Price, for he had this way about him, an unfailing thoughtfulness that commiserated without belittling. Some men were deemed gallants, some were gentled by a meekness or mildness of nature, but Lord Price's genuine graciousness came from the fundamental fact that he possessed a good heart.

Even now it was clear he saw she suffered some manner of distress and responded in a way to ease her through it. He allowed the solicitude to recede from his gaze, pulled back from the edge of personal confidences upon which they had teetered, and smiled a smile meant to invite her into a jest. "It is fascinating," he said, slanting one side of his mouth to show he did not mean the word in a praiseworthy sense.

She was grateful he had changed both the topic and the mood, although she could not imagine what his comment meant. "Fascinating?"

"The hair," Lord Price explained. He nodded toward a corner of the room. Her gaze followed to where a young woman stood. At the woman's temple a lock of hair was missing, and no effort had been made to disguise its loss. "There must be ten females in this room strangely shorn of a lock of hair tonight."

"Ah yes! The fashion some ladies have adopted. *A la Cavalier,* they call it."

He sat back, pretending to be shocked. "Adopted? Why, do you say you believe the locks were taken by someone other than the Kissing Cavalier?"

"I should be surprised if their locks were lost to anyone other than their lady's maids."

His smile widened. He leaned close to her to agree in a conspiratorial undertone, "I more than suspect you are right, Miss Joan."

Miss Joan. It was the first time he had ever called her anything other than "Miss Galloway." Joan felt the bones in her body soften, becoming just a trifle more malleable than they had been a moment before. She rather doubted her legs could support her should she choose to stand at this moment, and was grateful for the hard chair beneath her. The use of her Christian name—a privilege taken, not requested, although she certainly would have granted him the permission to use it—implied some social intimacy that their association until now had lacked.

His name, *Nathaniel,* formed on her lips, but that would be too much familiarity for one day. She could not call him by it, not without a request from him that she should, and never would she ask if she might. Perhaps soon it would be asked, and then it would flow easily from her tongue, seeming natural, seeming right and fitting. Or would the sound jolt him as the sound of her own name had jolted her, coming as it did from that finely-shaped mouth of his?

"I understand there was an attempt by the Cavalier against the twins this afternoon," he said, bringing her back to the moment.

Now, why does he insist on pursuing the topic of the Cavalier? she asked herself. It was almost as if he wished to be caught out as the scoundrel! Joan nodded a response, watching his face.

"Simon told me this afternoon—"

Late this afternoon, she silently amended, knowing full well where he had been earlier in the day. How clever of him to weave himself an alibi without having to tell a single mistruth.

"—that your Uncle was most certainly overset at the news of the Cavalier's approach to your cousins."

Ah, so *that* was what Lord Price wanted: to know how Uncle Newland meant to counter the Cavalier's offensive. Well, he would learn precious little from her! Just when he had said something that made her feel all light and floaty, he had to bring her back to earth by attempting to use her as nothing more than a source for information. It was true he was a good-hearted man, but he was also a man who wanted to win a wager. Wanted it enough to come to the very person who meant to stand between him and success.

She smiled, and he did not seem to notice it was a slightly cooler smile than it would have been a minute earlier. "Uncle certainly was overset," she admitted.

"I daresay he will bring in more footmen, day and night, at The Keep, eh?"

"Mmmm."

An $18.49
value.
FREE!
No obligation
to buy
anything, ever.

"And more armed outriders with the carriages as well, I suppose?"

"Mmmm."

"And curtail the girls' outings?"

"Ah," she said, proud of the noncommittal sound.

Lord Price considered her, his head slightly to one side, his expression becoming strangely muted. He shook his head and crossed his arms over his chest, and she had to think he had given up trying to extract any helpful information from her.

Another silence fell, but this time it was not awkward. Perhaps that was caused by something to do with a brand new easiness of manner between them.

It was with a physical shock that Joan realized a momentous event had just passed, unnoted and until now unhailed: she and Lord Price had somehow, almost magically, changed their connection from a mere occasional exchange of limited words—that of the name of a book or the fineness of the weather—and had somehow, almost magically, slipped into a version of companionship. They had shared a moment of mutual understanding, had looked into each others' faces, had seen each other as people rather than as someone else's friend or cousin, and had taken that first tottering step that sometimes leads to friendship.

The realization was both exhilarating and startling, and the newness of the revelation left her without the ability to pull quite enough oxygen from the air she breathed, making her a little dizzy.

"I should not care to be the Cavalier, I know that," Lord Price said quietly at her side, in a musing manner that suggested the words meant exactly what they said.

Joan mentally pushed aside her own astonishment to listen to the tenor underlying his words. For the second time she wondered how Simon's friend, the one friend she would never have envisioned taking on such a silly prank, had come to play the part of the Kissing Cavalier. It was quite simply so unlike him. What forces had Lord Crowell brought to bear to drive this man to take on this obligation? An obligation he presumably—even evidently—did not relish? What would cause a man to act so out of character?

"Why do you think someone would pose as the Kissing Cavalier?" she asked, watching his face, his eyes. "To be fashionable in some manner? To escape *ennui?* Or because he is not a handsome man and so feels he could not take so many kisses except from behind a mask?"

"Must his reasons be so ignoble as those?" he asked, a fire flaring in the back of his eyes. "Could he not be forced to the situation? Perhaps to save a friend?" He spoke casually, but a minute downward twitch to the right corner of his mouth betrayed it was done so with an effort.

And then she knew, as surely as if he had said it plainly: the wager must be won to save Simon from some dire fate.

Of course.

She herself had overheard Uncle Newland's warning to Simon, knew how perilously close her cousin was to disaster. Lord Price was surely saving Simon from just such a disaster.

Joan felt a frown begin to form, not wanting to grant Lord Price's performance as the Cavalier any leniency, not wanting to forgive him for his role-playing. But it was too late; he was instantly forgiven once she comprehended it was not just a game, not just for sport, but for Simon. How could she possibly think poorly of Lord Price, suspecting as she did now that he only acted as a friend ought? And she knew, oh yes she had learned, that Lord Crowell was not only capable of coercing one's behavior, but of using any tool, any threat, to do so. It was no difficulty to believe Lord Price had been put in a place where he must act to save another, for was she not doing just the same?

Joan raised a hand to her forehead, as if to push away the headache that all these turbulent thoughts threatened to bring with them. She longed to ask Lord Price what it was that motivated him, what it was he was saving Simon from, but of course she could not.

She almost laughed wryly, realizing that they both danced to the tune of the same piper. A piper whom she had pledged to follow, to support with her deeds.

She had already done Lord Crowell a disservice. The other night, in her bedchamber, when she had blurted out to Lord Price that it was Lord Crowell who had told her the Cavalier was going to call on the twins, she had worked against Lord Crowell, without ever knowing she was doing so.

And as much as it galled, she had to remember it was Lord Crowell who was helping her family, arranging Papa's release from gaol. It was Lord Crowell who had offered her a way out of her troubles, albeit with a price. It was to Lord Crowell she owed any kind of loyalty in this matter of the Cavalier, whether she liked it or not.

Unless . . . unless someone else provided the funds for Papa's release? What if the very man who was supposed to kiss her cousins was also the man who assisted Papa . . . ?

But what of Eleanor and Gabrielle? What was Joan's responsibility to them? Even if Lord Crowell had no part in all this, was not Joan still bound to her familial duty of watching over the twins? Would she owe Lord Price the kisses he sought from Gabrielle and Eleanor if it were he who loaned Papa the necessary funds? Would he reveal his secret identity so that he might press such an advantage? Could she flout her uncle's wishes so openly? Would she be ruining the twins' lives to save her Papa's?

She glanced up at Lord Price, but he had turned his face away, lost to his own thoughts. Yet another realization spun into the confusion in Joan's mind: What kept Lord Price from walking into the Alexander home as himself, kissing the girls, and taking his tokens of golden hair, for that matter? Why had he not ended all this folly days ago by so simple a solution?

Joan had already decided only an urgent need to protect Simon would compel Lord Price to take part in this wager in the first place, so how could she think anything less than that a matter of equal or greater urgency prevented him from taking such an easy path in completing his task? Yet, why must he do so in the guise of Cavalier?

Again the answer was simple and clear: Lord Crowell. Lord Crowell did not only play the tune, but told them all how to dance to it.

Devil take the man! she thought vehemently, using the most offensive curse she knew. How easily he had led her, had duped her! And she had no doubt Lord Price had been made to shuffle to one of Crowell's tunes as well, and all undoubtedly to save Simon from himself.

So then, if Joan asked Lord Price if he might be the one to lend her the necessary funds, would she be upsetting more than one apple cart? What repercussions would result? Dare she ask?

Dare she not, and thereby remain beholden to Lord Crowell?

She wet her lips, more than half-convinced she would ask, but the words never came forth. Just at that moment Lord Crowell sat down in the vacant chair before Joan. Lord Price, at her side, made a small sound rather like a growl.

Lord Crowell turned to face them, a smile in place. It was, yes, a handsome smile she observed as though from a distance, her mind still reeling from the questions that ran through it. But even in the midst of her distraction, a part of her confirmed it was not a truly kind smile.

"Miss Galloway," Lord Crowell greeted her. "I come with happy tidings! Your papa is released and has repaired to your uncle's home."

Her hands formed into fists, too much emotion coursing through her for them to lie still in her lap. Joy flooded her, instantly followed by gratitude that he had not said aloud where her papa was released from, then by the need to go to her father, to see his release for herself. Just as rapidly, there descended upon her a great disappointment.

It was done. There was no going back. Lord Crowell had

delivered on his end of their agreement. Even if there were no familial loyalties in question here, even if Lord Price would have said "yes" to the coarse question of lending Papa the needed funds, now Joan was committed to upholding her end of the bargain she had made with Lord Crowell.

"Happy news," Lord Price said, his tone even. He looked to Joan, then to Lord Crowell, his expression becoming unreadable.

"Indeed it is!" Lord Crowell looked steadily at Joan, as if he could force her to read a message from his eyes.

"Of course I have not forgot our arrangement," she said to that silent statement.

"Arrangement?" Lord Price questioned.

"A minor matter, Price," Crowell replied coolly, though his smile stayed in place. "Nothing that could be considered your concern." He put one arm on the back of the chair in a way that looked anything but nonchalant, fixing his gaze on Lord Price. "In point of fact, I believe you have your own affairs to see to, do you not? It seems to me there is a little matter left yet undone, and with the time ticking away, too." He clicked his tongue disapprovingly, the cadence even and steady, like a clock's.

Lord Price exhibited no overtly noticeable response, but Joan saw the muscles of his jawline tighten. He did not slide his gaze toward her, did not threaten the man with a look to say Lord Crowell should take care with such baiting lest he reveal the Cavalier's identity. She could only admire his coolness, unable to match it herself with anything more quickwitted than a blank stare.

If she had doubted even slightly that it was Lord Crowell who caused Lord Price to play the Cavalier, she doubted it no longer.

"I must go," Joan announced, coming abruptly to her feet. "I wish to see Papa." She teetered just a little, dizzied yet by the overwhelming developments of this night.

"But the musicale has not even yet begun," Lord Crowell

said with a smoothness that made her think of oil on water. "And you really ought to allow your papa to wash away the stench—the aroma of his recent residence before you call upon him, my dear."

She could almost believe from his tone that consideration motivated his words. Almost, except such naivete was now behind her. Lord Crowell was so much more than he appeared, and so much less than the man he ought to be.

He patted the seat beside him. "Move here, my dear. Sit and abide with me a while. I shall entertain you through the evening."

"I must go to Papa," she insisted, beginning to feel slightly ill.

A hand touched her sleeve, anchoring her, making her swirling thoughts settle even as it urged her back into her chair. It was Nathaniel's hand, warm and strong.

"You have gone pale. Allow me to call for your carriage and to find Mr. Alexander for you," he offered.

"Thank you," she said, her voice near a whisper. Then, unable to help herself, she put her hand on his where it lay on her arm, tightening her fingers just enough to let him know it was no idle gesture on her part.

His other hand came to rest atop hers, squeezing acknowledgment in return. For a moment their eyes met, locked, and then he smiled a quick, reassuring smile. There was a nod, as if to say he understood the violence of her emotions, but of course he would think it was only in connection to her father's release.

He turned to Lord Crowell. "Do be of some use, fellow, and fetch the lady a glass of wine."

Crowell gave Lord Price a hooded look, but then a thin smile creased his lips. "Of course," he said, rising and offering them both a half-bow, accepting the momentary dismissal.

If Lord Price had done nothing else for her all night, that alone would have won him Joan's esteem.

Unfortunately, the respite from Lord Crowell's presence

was short-lived. He returned almost at once with two glasses
of wine, one of which he pressed into her nerveless fingers.
Joan avoided the man's steady gaze, instead looking to catch
sight of a returning Lord Price, or Uncle Newland, or even
the twins. Anyone to give her a reason to rise, murmur an
excuse, and flee this man's company.

Lord Crowell sat down beside her, leaning into her.

"I think you have the wrong impression of me," he said,
his breath stirring the curls at her nape. Joan shuddered, and
leaned away, prepared to leap to her feet if he moved so little
as an inch nearer.

"Do I?" she said, and even to her own ears the question
was biting.

"Indeed, my dear. But how can this be? Did I not seek
you out to help you? Did I not see that your father's immediate debt was paid, the bankruptcy dismissed for now? Did
I not do as I said I would by gaining your papa's release?
And all I have asked in return is that which a lady devoted
to her family would wish to do anyway. Tell me, my dear,
where have I offended? When have I done aught to put the
censure in your eyes?"

It was on the tip of her tongue to inform him she knew
of his wager with Lord Price, but a vision of Simon's face
flashed before her mind's eye. She hesitated, wondering what
threat had been made against her cousin. Another quandary!
How could she speak, not knowing what consequences it
would serve in that direction?

Thoroughly annoyed at the past two days—full as they
were of unexplained situations and tongue-binding twists—
Joan turned to him with a kind of smile. It might drip acid
inside her mouth, but the words that came forth were carefully
polite. "Why, Lord Crowell, have I been cross with you? I
daresay it was the shock of learning the happy news. But, oh
look, there is Lord Price with Uncle Newland, and he has
our cloaks. I must be leaving now, but before I do—" she
hesitated again, and now, reluctantly, the words nearly as sin-

cere on the inside as she made them on the outside, even though it was a reluctant admission, "—I do thank you for helping Papa to come away from that awful place."

"My pleasure, my dear. Do you know one of the ways you may repay me?"

One of the ways! she repeated to herself, scarcely suppressing a sneer of repulsion at his avarice, knowing every penny of the money for Papa's release must be repaid before her life could ever be free of Lord Crowell's unpleasant presence. And now he dared to demand even something more of her?

"Repay?" Uncle Newland asked as he approached, Lord Price following more slowly in his wake. The younger man gave Joan a considering look, but then she could not see his face for he moved to put her evening cape over her shoulders.

Joan flushed scarlet, perhaps from not seeing any way to avoid telling her uncle how Papa had come to be released from gaol, or perhaps from the light and momentary brush of warm fingers where her shoulder was bared by the line of her gown. "Uncle Newland, Lord Crowell has loaned Papa some funds," she said, hoping her voice did not sound as shaky as it felt. "Papa has been released, and awaits us even now at your home."

"Loaned him the funds, in fact?" Uncle Newland looked startled, the very picture of a man who could not fathom a reason why a stranger might act upon a charitable impulse. He stared at Lord Crowell, then looked to Joan, and then his features smoothed and cleared. "Oh, eh!" he said, and gave Lord Crowell a showy wink. "I see the way the wind blows!" He chuckled, gave another wink, and said to Joan, "Thought it blew toward Lord Price here, but you have fooled me, have you not, you little minx?" He turned back to Lord Crowell. "I'll not stand in the way, and so you should know. Be seeing you in my study soon, eh, my lord? Or, rather, my brother-in-law will, eh?"

Lord Crowell smiled—a beautiful, cold smile, she saw now—and spoke in an undertone, "We shall see."

Joan's heart chilled, the icy edges cutting off any words of denial that might have risen to her lips. All she could do was stare, not looking to Uncle Newland, who beamed with un-adulterated delight at the idea of marrying off his niece, and not to the twins, who stared in something like shock at the inference that their cousin might actually be considered for marriage before them. Certainly not to Lord Price, for she did not want to see what he might make of such an implied alliance.

Lord Crowell gave her a warm look, warm as the fur of seals but just as desolate as the frozen place called Russian America from whence they were imported, and Joan found the word "grasping" creeping across her tongue. She read it in his eyes. Oh yes, he was attracted to her, the kind of at-traction that sees how best to use another. She was the in-strument by which he would win his wager against Lord Price. She and her papa were financially beholden to him, and now she began to fear that he would use her in other ways until that monetary debt was once and for all settled. Too, there was even another kind of greed in his eyes, the greed that allowed him to think the viscount's daughter would be coming into a tidy sum once she was able to claim her grandmama's money. Joan wished to heaven she had never mentioned the bequest to him, had never allowed pride to make the sum seem ever so much more than it would be in truth. She wished she could look at him and say that he was not truly considering asking for her hand in marriage, but the appraising look he gave her made her fear otherwise.

However, there was one good thing to come of this day: at least now she absolutely knew what manner of man Lord Crowell was. When she thought of how she had once admired him, had encouraged his suit, had attempted to forgive his transgressions, a real and active nausea caused her to give a bubble of hysterical laughter.

Uncle Newland gave her a curious look, almost frowning. "See here, we've made the girl blush and giggle," he excused the high-pitched and emotional sound. He turned to Lord Crowell once more. "But you were speaking of repayment?"

"Indeed. I was hoping to repay this lady's kindness in allowing me to sit at her side tonight, by inviting her to drive with me tomorrow in the park."

"Of course—" Uncle Newland began.

"I intend to spend the day with my father," Joan interrupted. At her uncle's frown, she softened the abrupt statement a trifle by adding, "I know you understand my wish to be with him."

She turned, not awaiting a reply, gripping her cape with either hand as she stepped away as quickly as she could, that an alternative time not be proposed to her. Someone followed her, and she hoped it was not Uncle Newland as she willed her tongue to turn to stone, for that was the only way she could keep from crying out a denunciation of Lord Crowell—the man who could call in his debt at a moment's notice, the man who still held sway over Papa's fate.

The someone caught up with her in a few strides, and from the corner of her eye she saw it was Lord Price. That was almost worse than if it had been a blustering Uncle Newland demanding she go back and apologize for her curt behavior, for Lord Price was the last man she had wished to be a witness to her humiliation and distress.

To her surprise, and not some little relief, he said nothing, simply escorting her as she made her way to the waiting carriage. It was only when he was handing her in that he spoke. "I think you are wise to avoid Lord Crowell's company."

There it was again, that spark of rapport, that marking of the fact she had become visible to him, had become something other than merely "Simon's cousin." Not a friend, no she could not dare to say such a word, and not quite a woman to him either, not in the sense of male and female circling one another in the ancient dance of courtship, but rather something as basic and elementary as acknowledging her as a person in her own right. She had feelings and troubles, and his steady gaze claimed the increased intimacy of knowing her well enough to recognize the existence of her difficulties. Perhaps, just perhaps his regard and his words were meant to tell her that he even cared just a little that Lord Crowell and her uncle had humiliated her, that he would not add to her burdens and wished that somehow he might remove a portion of them.

"Thank you," she whispered. It was little enough reward, but anything else would have caused her to erupt into noisy sobs.

He nodded his head, then stepped back, making way for the twins and Uncle Newland to enter the carriage.

"We will have a talk about your behavior toward Lord Crowell," Uncle Newland said with a scowl as he settled in his seat.

Joan gave one last glance out the carriage, startled to find a disturbed look on Lord Price's face as he closed the carriage door. What caused him to frown so, however fleetingly? Or had the short-lived grimace merely been a reflection of her own heaving emotions? She could not say, but the memory of it cheered her somehow, just a little, as Uncle Newland proceeded to lecture her about propriety and expectations all the way home.

Ten

Less than half an hour later, Simon looked up from his seat in the tavern as Nathaniel, a steaming coffee mug in hand, took a seat beside him. "What, no locks of hair?" Simon asked with a false cheeriness that bode ill.

Nathaniel made no reply. Instead, he glanced around the room to see that Sir Francis, ensconced between two pretty serving maids who giggled at his witticisms, completed at three the total number of Price's Princes present this evening. Otherwise Simon and Nathaniel had a corner in the public room to themselves.

Nathaniel sipped his hot coffee, pleased to see Simon drinking nothing stronger than the hot, black liquid. Even so, Simon was in a dangerous mood.

Nathaniel did not answer his friend's question, fully aware Simon would already be in possession of the news that the Cavalier's attempt to waylay the Misses Alexander at a shop in Covent Garden earlier this afternoon had failed. "Come on then, out with it? What has happened now?" he asked instead, quietly.

Simon did not pretend to misunderstand the question, silently slipping a missive from his coat pocket and handing it to Nathaniel. It was a folded, sealed, and addressed note in Mr. Alexander's script, one obviously ready to be posted.

"Stealing your uncle's communications now, I see," Nathaniel told him, lifting the edge of the note with an already broken wax seal.

"For all the good it will do me. When Uncle Newt learns my father has not received this missive, he'll just send another, and another. Eventually, one must slip past my guard."

Nathaniel read the note:

Roger,

It has come to my attention that Simon is spending too much of his time at corruptive diversions, in addition to those already noted by you in prior communications. I speak here specifically of gambling and accruing debts thereof. It is my belief that it would be wise to limit the amount of funds available to your son, and do herein suggest his next quarterly payment be halved, that he might learn how better to allow for his expenses and not be wasteful with any surplus. In proof, I submit that only the other night he was playing at cards in his room, and cannot help but think this indicative of his immersion in morally unhealthy pursuits, that he would bring card games into my home, especially without first seeking my permission for same.

I humbly await your decision, which I will present to the boy in your stead.

Ever yours,
Newland

Nathaniel folded the note, handing it back to Simon, who proceeded to tear it in two.

"You can live on half your allowance," Nathaniel pointed out, watching as Simon tore both halves in half again.

"Can, but why should I?"

"I am sorry. It is my fault. That night we brought you home drunk, I told your uncle you and I were playing cards in your room. I did not consider he would disapprove of an idle game between friends."

"He does not! Not when he hosts a party," Simon said, laughing hollowly. "But it is fashionable, is it not, to have tables readied for your guests? He would not care to appear unfashionable, regardless of his personal convictions. No, Nathaniel, you are wrong to apologize. It is not your fault my uncle is a hypocrite! You could have told him we were sitting entirely still, breathing only, and he would have found something to object to in that."

Nathaniel could not argue the point, and so instead, changed the subject. "Your cousin, Miss Galloway- -her father is out of gaol. He is even now at your uncle's home, and Miss Galloway on her way to join him," Nathaniel said.

"Uncle Eugene? A free man again then? Ah, but you mean to divert me into remembering that others have it worse than I! Although, I wonder sometimes, for at least Joan's father knew what to expect from one day to the next while he was in gaol. At least he knew his fate," he said bitterly, tapping the table top twice with a sharp rap of the knuckles.

The fever of hurt and outrage fanned in Simon's sober eyes, giving him a wild, desperate look, only to sputter and settle back as he met Nathaniel's steady gaze. His rage died in the face of his friend's unspoken compassion. "I am sorry," he said, putting a hand to his forehead. "Sorry. I know my anger goes out of all bounds, all reason . . . ."

"You need to be your own man," Nathaniel said, knowing it was less possible than it sounded. Simon had tried before, had suggested ways for both he and his father to be content, but Mr. Walford had ever balked at his son's request. No, Simon could not travel abroad. No, he could not seek service in the government. "No son of mine shall toil for Whigs," he'd claim, and refuse to debate when Simon pointed out he would be toiling for Whigs were he consigned to the army as his father always threatened. No, Simon could not lower himself to become a Master of Hounds. No, he could not stay on the farm, for what polish could he learn from the bumpkins of Kent with whom he spent all his idle time? He would stop taking his father's money, would he? Then Simon could take the crown's instead, as a soldier in the army. He'd buy the boy a commission and see to that!

It seemed any matter of interest to Simon was unacceptable to Mr. Walford. Simon must be a man of wealth and leisure—yet not be tempted by all its attendant idleness and dissipation.

"But you say Uncle Eugene is free?" Simon questioned now, lowering his hand to focus on Nathaniel with a faint show of interest. "Never say Uncle Newt paid his way out of Newgate?"

Nathaniel shook his head. "Lord Crowell."

Simon stared, then gave a shake of his head and a weak laugh. "Pardon me, I thought you said 'Lord Crowell.' "

"I do not know why he did it. Not entirely," Nathaniel hedged, the last two words very faint even to his own ears.

Thankfully, Simon either did not hear or chose not to comment. Nathaniel, in a strange moment of divided loyalties, did not wish to speak of Miss Joan behind her back, especially as he was not completely sure what hold Lord Crowell had over her. He found himself hoping that hold was light and fleeting, that Cruel Crowell's apparent interest in Miss Joan was only some trifling thing that induced her to act the dragon guardian to her cousins at his bidding.

"Then we must go!" Simon declared, springing to his feet. "We cannot miss the reunion of father and daughter. This day needs some happy moment to it."

"I am not sure you should go there, not while you run yet so heated in your sentiments."

"Why not? I am not drunk," Simon declared in defiance.

"But you are angry. Your Uncle Newland will say just the wrong thing, you will remember his letter to your father, and Miss Galloway's reunion will be spoilt."

Simon put a hand on his friend's shoulder, saying with a quiet earnestness, "I would not do that to Joan. Never to Joan."

Nathaniel looked to the floor for a moment before he stood,

keeping his gaze away from Simon's. "Of course you would not."

They called a farewell to Sir Francis, and moved outside to where each had paid a boy to watch their horse. They mounted, heading without further word in the direction of Newland Alexander's home.

As they approached The Keep, Nathaniel gave its sheer walls a glance, not too surprised and some little amused to see that the wisteria remained, but now it looked fragile and abandoned, for the main part of the trellis upon which it had risen was stripped away where it had not been wed to the building by the vine and age. There would be no more climbing to Miss Joan's bedchamber that way. The windows were all closed, despite the fineness of the May evening, and he suspected they were locked. That would be under Miss Joan's order, he presumed, wryly smiling to himself.

"Simon," he said, looking away from the window that had once given him entree to the house's third-story. "How is it the girls sleep on the third floor?"

"They don't," came the reply. "Well, except for Joan."

"Joan? Why is Joan the only one on the third-story?"

Simon flushed and looked away. "Uncle Newt claims there is not adequate room for Joan on the second story. It is not true, of course. They could make a room, and a right comfortable one of it, too, from the storage chamber above the front parlor."

"I do not understand."

Simon's mouth worked. " 'Tis fairly simple, Nate. Uncle Newt wants Joan to know he believes she is not nearly as important as his beautiful girls, even if she is a viscount's daughter, and what clearer way to let her know than by giving her a tiny, cramped room nearly at the top of the house? I should be ashamed myself to give that room to a governess or a housekeeper, let alone my niece. But there you have it. That is my uncle all over again, of course."

"Does she have a maid?" Nathaniel asked, glancing again at the house before them.

Simon gave him a curious look. "Whoa-ho, my friend. Did I look so thunderous when I was angry just ten minutes ago? You quite frighten me with that wrathful glare! But, no," he said, as if he sensed Nathaniel was in little mood for humor or teasing. "No, she does not have a maid of her own. She is allowed to share one of the maids employed for the twins, when they have a moment to spare."

Nathaniel felt his frown deepen. "Small wonder Miss Joan wishes she could return to her papa's home."

"Miss *Joan,* is it?" Simon said, his eyebrows raising, but before Nathaniel could respond, Simon went on, "And the humor of the situation comes from knowing Gabrielle and Eleanor. Pampered and fêted, they are treated like little princesses, when in truth they are simple girls, ill-suited to the role Uncle Newland has declared they will play. Joan, for all that she is no beauty, has the grace and wit to be a *grande dame,* but Elly and Gabby will ever only be country girls with the barest town polish. I feel sorry for the flighty creatures, for they will not be happy in their marriages, not if Uncle Newt has his way in choosing the grooms."

"They do not seem . . . complex beings," Nathaniel agreed, something at a loss for the right phrase.

"Well said." Simon laughed, a clear, honest sound, as they stopped before the house. "How long ago did the Alexanders return?" he asked the groom who ran out to secure the horses.

"Five minutes, sir, no more."

"Good! We have missed the hugging and the kissing, but not the tales and hints of reproach. Come, Nathaniel—no, do not quail now! *Miss Joan* will not mind another witness to her happiness at her father's return. And I have need myself of a staunch supporter in case Uncle Newland's displeasure at having his 'wastrel brother-in-law' at hand spills over onto me."

Simon hurried ahead, and Nathaniel followed more slowly.

He nodded at the butler who held the door open for him, and came into the entry hall just in time to hear a dour Uncle Newland suggest they all retire to the front parlor. Mrs. Alexander nodded her agreement, her hands aflutter in an ineffectual motion that Nathaniel could only guess had been taking place since her brother-in-law had stepped into her home. There were nods and assenting murmurs all about at the thought of removing to the parlor, and one quick glance from Joan acknowledged Nathaniel's presence. She looked faintly surprised to see him there, but there was no refusal of his presence. That acknowledgment in some way made his steps less reluctant.

The group moved to the parlor, refreshments were rang for and seats taken. Joan sat at her father's side. Nathaniel saw that the hand which did not clasp a cloth occasionally to Lord Stanmore's mouth while he coughed was gathered up in Joan's delicate one, her eyes glistening with evident relief at his release each time she looked at him. The man had done his best to be in form, his freshly pressed clothing presumably newly donned, his longish white hair clean and brushed back, and there were freshly polished shoes on his feet. Aside from the occasional deep cough that had surely been bred by his stay in Newgate, all trace of gaol had been left behind. Nathaniel experienced a sense of satisfaction that the man had put himself to some bother to appear well before his daughter and her unsympathetic uncle.

"I have had a bit of time to think about the announcement I wish to make now," Lord Stanmore interrupted the general conversation, looking to his brother-in-law and then to his daughter.

Newland frowned, his expression frankly suspicious of a new announcement.

"I am going to retire to the country," Lord Stanmore went on. At his side, Joan nodded as though she had expected the news. Newland almost smiled and visibly relaxed. "My financial . . . er . . . embarrassments are still too plentiful for me to stay in London, else another claimant will surely soon pay the shilling for the . . . ahem! . . . arrest warrant. I know how awkward all this talk is for you, my dear," Lord Stanmore interrupted himself to say, squeezing his daughter's hand. He coughed into his cloth, shook his head at the seizure, and when it was under control went on. "But these things must be said. Once the sheriff is paid again the fee to exercise my arrest, I should be made to return to *that place,* and consequently in time be declared a bankrupt.

"Now, in the country, I am more than likely to avoid re-arrest, at least for quite some while. I have every hope that by living simply there, giving up for now the expenses of living in London, I shall be able to recover my losses all the more quickly, to pay my debts. Not to be gone forever, mind you! I foresee a time wherein I shall be able to return to London, to our former way of life."

Joan looked down to where her hand clenched her father's, and Nathaniel could not help but wonder if she averted her face from her papa's gaze to avoid allowing him to see the flicker of pained skepticism that crossed there.

"Until such a time, Joan," Lord Stanmore said, his voice lowering although he did not indulge his obvious embarrassment by looking away from where Joan raised her face in inquiry. "The truth, my dear, is that while I go to recoup my income in the country, you must remain here in London with your uncle and aunt."

Joan gave a small involuntary gasp, not quite able to hide her distress at the news.

"I shall be living very humbly, my dearest girl. You would have nothing! No new dresses, no entertainments, no society. You need to remain a part of the Season. I cannot give you that, not now, and not until much later. And later would not be soon enough, not to secure your future as it ought to be secured, while you are young and of an age for marriage. Here you can have suitors. Here are your Aunt Hannah's connections. You see how it is?"

Joan began to shake her head, but stopped herself, perhaps reading some urgency in her father's gaze. She worried her bottom lip, unwilling or unable to speak for a moment, her eyes searching his for some other answer she wished to see there.

When she did speak, the words were accompanied by a stiffening of the spine, by a regal lift of the head, by the flash of an almost steady smile. "Of course I see how it is," she told her papa, and the man was just deliberately blind enough or just desperate enough to take the words at face value. He crushed both her hands between his, nodding, and if the quiver of Joan's chin, or the false brightness of her tremulous smile gave him a sense of the sacrifice she had just made for him, he did not show it outwardly.

For himself, Nathaniel looked down at the fingers he had laced together in his lap, to grant her a few moment's privacy. Lord Stanmore asked that Joan not come with him, that she not burden her father with her care, with the worry of seeing she somehow found a marriage partner or other way of facing her future. He asked that she stay in this house where she knew only second-class status, that his new-bought freedom not include an equal freedom for her. It was not, strictly speaking, cruel of him—it could even be said he was only doing what was best for her in numerous ways, but it was also a death knell to the hopes she had cherished of returning to some form of the life she had once known.

And she had said "yes." Had given away all that was precious to her, that her father might know peace, might have a chance to rebuild his life without the restrictions and hesitations that come with tending to another's needs.

In the room's silence Nathaniel kept his head down, but from under his lashes he looked up at Joan, at that bravely held head. A tight band restricted his breathing for a moment, fading only slowly, and he realized the sensation was a kind of aching admiration for the smile she maintained, the lightness she kept in her voice, even if she could not keep the grief from darkening her brown eyes. How odd that she was not the kind of woman one thought of as beautiful, and yet at this moment, he could swear he'd never seen a finer, more noble profile.

A hand touched Nathaniel's shoulder as though in warning, pulling his attention up to where Simon stood at his side. A nod of Simon's head directed Nathaniel's attention to where Newland was speaking with a broad smile. "—going to pay that fellow back, eh? Well, I daresay there would be a simple enough way to reward Lord Crowell for his generosity, Eugene."

"Oh?" Lord Stanmore asked, hiding a dubious glance behind a coughing fit.

When he breathed freely again, Newland explained. "Crowell's all but said he wishes Joan for his bride."

Lord Stanmore turned to Joan, his expression questioning.

She shook her head vehemently, the brown pin curls at her temples trembling from the force of her denial. "I would not have him, Papa."

"What?" Newland cried. He thumped his fist against the arm of his chair, looking accusingly at his brother-in-law. "Whyever did you raise the girl to be so particular, Eugene?" He turned to Joan. "Tell me, whatever is wrong with Lord Crowell that you reject him so roundly?"

"I do not care for his company," Joan said stiffly.

Newland sat back, blowing his lips and waving away her reply. "The girl is utterly particular, and in no position to be so, I tell you!"

"It does not matter, Joan," her father assured her, patting her hand. "There are other suitors. I would not barter you away in exchange for the repayment of a debt to Lord Crowell."

Something in the set of her shoulders relaxed, and a glimmer of her former happiness returned. "I know you would not."

"Of course not," Lord Stanmore said.

Fortuitously, at that moment a light repast of tea and biscuits arrived, over which desultory conversation turned from the latest court gossip to road improvements, with everyone, even a disgruntled Newland, carefully avoiding any mention of prisons or debts or nieces who stay on beyond their welcome.

When Lord Stanmore could not stifle a yawn of exhaustion despite the fact dinner had yet to be served, Nathaniel rose at the cue and bid his hosts good evening. Mrs. Alexander called to Simon and insisted he escort Lord Stanmore to the proper room for the night, while she saw to having a warming pan and camphor wraps brought up to "Dear Eugene's" room. The twins offered in a chorus to escort their exiting guest to the door.

"Call Seymour," Newland muttered loud enough to be heard by all, " 'tis what I pay my butler to do." He did not say it loud enough however, to persuade the twins to act as though they had heard it, and they each took one of Lord Price's arms. At this Newland gave Joan a speaking glance, and the girl rose to her feet.

"I shall see our guest out as well," she announced, and if she resented the silent instruction, that resentment was hidden behind a calm and ordered face.

Joan led the way to the front entry. With the leisure to merely follow her and observe her as the twins nattered at him about the "Cavalier's attempt at Covent Garden today," it was with a start of surprise that Nathaniel realized he recognized the evening dress Joan wore. It was palest green gauze over a rich apricot, its hem stitched and ruched at regular intervals by a distinctive golden leaf pattern. Somewhere in the house there would be another dress much like it, only in lightest yellow and autumnal orange, for the twins had made a bit of a sensation when they had appeared together thusly clothed for Mrs. Alexander's pre-hunt dinner party at the tail end of last year's Season. They had made their brief, bright bow to society arrayed in the hues of autumn, rather daringly attired in colors bolder than most soon-to-be-presented young ladies would hazard. But since their quasi-debut had been kept brief, and the girls had been so fetching, the bolder colors had served the trick, making them the center of all attention for the fifteen minutes they remained at their mother's affair.

And now here was the dress, an obvious cast-down to Miss Joan Galloway. It suited her coloring in a different way than it had whichever Miss Alexander had worn it, although it was sadly two inches shorter than it ought be on the taller Joan, which would explain the plain white and rather incongruous lace that had been stitched to the hem. Too, her bosom filled the confines of her bodice more than either twin would have done, but Joan had cleverly managed to contrive the tightness to lift her bust upward to form attractively rounded prominences above the fabric rather than a mere strain at the seams.

Joan had done as well as she might with the highly recognizable gown, but still its blatant existence as a cast-off brought an unvoiced growl to the back of Nathaniel's throat. Newland Alexander could easily afford a few new dresses for the girl, that she need not be seen in her cousins' old gowns, but it was clear the man's basic parsimony left him willing to enact such an affront against his niece.

They halted before the door. Nathaniel turned, but neither twin released his arms, turning with him, smiling up at him.

"Tush, girls, you cannot keep Lord Price here all night," Joan chided.

"I only wish we could," Eleanor said, batting her lashes. "I vow I would sleep the better for knowing Lord Price would stand between me and any attack by the Cavalier."

"Surely not an attack," Nathaniel corrected. "An approach. But Simon assures me you ladies need not fear an encounter with the Cavalier, for the fellow would not dare strike here at your home, that it is too well guarded these days."

Was that a flicker of response from Joan? Simon had assured Nathaniel that Joan had never said one word to anyone about having a stranger in her room, but she would be remembering that event now.

"It is true that Papa and Joan have been making our home into a veritable fortress! Do you know she even had the wisteria trellis pulled down, just on the odd chance someone would be so foolhardy as to attempt to climb it!"

Nathaniel chose not to reply to this comment by anything more than a brief smile as he took a rapid step back, pulling free of the twins' hands. He immediately caught up a hand for each of the twins, making an airy kiss over each as he bowed to them, an act that made them titter with pleasure.

"I hear the Cavalier called on Lady Frederica in the folly her father added to their garden," Gabrielle said, keeping her hand resting in his.

"The one that looks like an old castle turret," Eleanor assured Joan and Nathaniel, her hand likewise still pressing against his own. "He chased her up the stairs, kissed her as she squealed—I have that from my maid who got it from Lady Frederica's maid—and snipped the lock of hair from her head before she had ceased to squeal. *I* would not squeal. *I* would ask for another kiss."

"Eleanor!" Joan cried, sliding Nathaniel an embarrassed glance. He only smiled at the girl's unfettered assertions, lowering his hands until the girls were forced to let go of his touch.

"I only wish I knew who the Cavalier is," Gabrielle pouted, "for I might be tempted to let him know how to prevail in the matter of sneaking into our home."

"Gabrielle!" Joan gasped.

Gabrielle ignored her. She leaned toward Lord Price and said in an audible whisper, "I would tell him about the sealed door at the back of the house that leads into the basement. It is all overgrown with ivy, but it is not really sealed, you see? It is Elly's and my secret door."

"Gabby!" Joan interrupted sternly, putting a hand on her cousin's arm and pulling her from Nathaniel's side.

Nathaniel stepped back, not quite able to keep from laughing just a little, unable to maintain a stoic face in light of the information he had just been granted. He struggled to tame a grin as he said, "Well then, a good evening to you all, Miss Gabrielle, Miss Eleanor." He gave them another quick bow, and turned to Joan. "Miss Joan," he said, catching up her hand, causing her to give a startled "oh!" as he sketched a kiss over it as he had for the twins.

"Good evening, Lord Price," she said, taking back her hand at once, and although the entry hall was dim, he thought a blush spread over her cheeks. It was too bad, really, that she had not expected to be included in the common-enough gallantry. That was what life with her aunt and uncle had schooled her to expect.

The twins returned to the front parlor, but not before casting Nathaniel lingering looks, calling out good-byes, and issuing little waves of farewell.

Nathaniel lowered his hand from returning those waves and sighed, aware that once again Joan's repute had been threatened by her careless cousins, for they had quite left Joan alone, albeit in the front entry, with a man. By the sudden stiffness in her person beside him, he strongly suspected Joan realized as much as well.

He hesitated a moment longer, some impulse causing him to say, "I suspect the ivy-covered door will soon be secured?"

"But of course," she replied. "Tonight."

"Then the girls' apparent scheme of having me spread 'accidental' word of their 'secret entrance' to the Cavalier's ears was to no effect."

"They are sweet things, but not very clever."

"Not when they mention the secret door in front of their guardian-cousin, no."

He grinned, and Joan smiled back, the smile continuing even when she ducked her head and folded her hands together at her waist.

"Good night, Lord Price," she said, lifting her head at an

angle, glancing at him from the corners of her eyes, her hands once again relaxing at her sides.

He could not say why, perhaps it was because he felt vexed by the woes this evening had brought her, but some flight of fancy caused him to catch up her hand and press another kiss there, one this time that actually brought his lower lip into contact with her ungloved hand. "Good night, Miss Joan," he murmured against her skin.

He turned and left, in some ways not surprised when no more words passed between them, for their mutual silence was a strangely comfortable one, like that between long-standing friends. Well, perhaps not comfortable exactly, for there was some curiosity on his part, a feeling of wishing to stay, to talk with Miss Joan a while, to learn what that blush of hers could possibly mean.

"Joan!" came Uncle Newland's voice, interrupting the pleasant haze that had kept her standing in the entry hall. "Joan!" he bellowed a second time, demanding she go to him in his private parlor.

Joan stepped reluctantly down the hallway, half inclined to pretend she had not heard him, the other half reluctantly knowing if he planned a lecture it would come tomorrow if it did not come tonight, and so she might as well get it over with.

She poked her head around the doorjamb of the open door. "Uncle?"

"Come in," he said gruffly, waving her in.

She went before his desk, behind which he sat in his big wing chair.

He did not ask her to sit, nor did he wait a moment, saying at once, "You have been spoilt, you know."

She said nothing, finding the accusation a hypocritical one coming from the father of the twins.

"You have been indulged. *I* will not indulge you!"

"Am I now to have only bread and water for my supper?" Joan asked, biting her lip at the thread of angry defiance she heard in her voice, knowing it would only goad him.

"A splendid idea! But I am not so cruel, my girl. No, I am a pleasant, caring fellow, and that is why I am telling you, here and now, that if Lord Crowell asks for your hand, I will grant it to him, and you *will* marry him."

She shook her head, just once, but the emphasis was such that once was enough.

Uncle Newland looked both baffled and annoyed. He pressed the fingers of one hand to his forehead. "But why this obstinacy, missy? Is it that you have developed a *tendre* for some other fellow? But who . . . could it be Lord Price? Do you love him or some such ridiculousness? I admit I thought the fellow was thinking of throwing his handkerchief in your direction, but he has not done so, now has he? No, my girl, you cannot be counting eggs when you do not even own chickens! 'Tis Crowell who will come up to snuff, mark my word. He'd care to marry above his station, I say, and your being a viscount's daughter is your greatest—well, your *only* asset! So 'tis Crowell you'll have, and with no fuss, mind you! You could do worse, far worse, and 'tis no small thing to be able to fashion yourself as a baroness. You'll have the pleasure of being called 'Lady.' "

"I would rather remain Miss Galloway."

"Put your nose in the air, would you? And such temper! Perhaps some suppers of naught but bread and water are exactly what you require, my girl, to lose a bit of that temper! My sister was an excitable girl, I recall—you inherited your temper from her and your impractical nature from your father."

Joan bit the tip of her tongue, to gain some control over the very temper he spoke of, before she spoke. "Uncle Newland, *I Will Not Marry Lord Crowell,*" she stated, each word slow and succinct.

He stared at her. He shook his head, lowered his fingers

from his forehead, and looked away. "That, my girl, is not for you to decide!" He frowned. "Granted, you will be of an age in a brief while, and I will not be able to gainsay your choices then. But being of age and being independent are too different things, and so long as you are in my home you must understand some things are expected of you. One of those things is that you will leave this house to live with your father—no, do not shake your head at me, missy—!"

"I will not go to Papa," Joan declared, ashamed of the tremble in her voice.

"That you will live with your papa, or else you will marry as soon as may be. If not Lord Crowell, then someone else. There may have been a time when I should have cared to see you married to a worthy man, but now I assure you that I will accept any *parti* you present to me. Be he a wastrel, a libertine, a merchant, or a pirate, you will have my blessing and hang to your place in society!"

Her uncle glared at her. Joan experienced a quiver that was not quite satisfaction, for threat underrode that glare. "As you say. I will seek a man I can bear to be married to," she said, the words thick and awkward in her mouth. It seemed too bald, too shallow, too unworthy a thing to declare an intention to marry just anyone for conveniency's sake alone.

"But, understand this as well, once you choose your bridegroom," Uncle Newland went on, pointing his forefinger at her, "you will leave with him and never come across my threshold as a charity case again. Never! If you will not listen to my council now, I shall not offer you succor later. I hope you believe me when I say this."

"I believe you."

Uncle Newland stood, dropping his shoulders and lifting his chin. "Then it is settled. You have until your birthday to find yourself a groom."

Joan's lips parted soundlessly, and she had to remind herself how to breathe before she could speak. "But . . . a month? I cannot marry in a month! What happens when this proves impossible?"

"You go to your father. I will not have you in my house one day longer than that. I am being magnanimous as it is."

"And the twins? What of them?" A little steel returned to Joan's jawline. "I thought Aunt Hannah looked rather pleased at the idea of retaining an unpaid servant in her home, namely me, to look after the twins."

"I can afford the hire of a dozen companions, you silly chit!" Newland growled.

Joan stared, then suddenly turned, walking carefully, stiffly from the room.

A silent moan grew behind her lips, filling her middle with an ache that spread to her limbs, setting them to tingling in something close to physical pain. She had lost everything, everything. Soon, she would have to move from this house that was no home, either to a husband's residence or to Papa. No, not Papa! How much more difficult it would be for him should she be with him, costing him the price of keeping her fed and clothed, however minimally. A husband, then. She must attract an offer—with only a month to do it!

No, a month was too short. She would have to go to Papa, for a little while at least, and there in Kent she would find someone to marry. A clergyman, perhaps, or . . . or, yes, even a merchant. Anyone who seemed kind, who seemed disposed to take on a girl with no prospects.

Some of the stiffness slipped away from her, her movements becoming more fluid. Uncle Newland's demand was not so far from what she had planned for herself anyway, was it? She had never meant to remain here in The Keep all her days. The change in her circumstance would just occur sooner than she had anticipated.

Her head came up as she thought that, yes, Uncle's demands were just fine with her. It did not matter that her mind shied from the thought of plotting a marriage—such machinations took place every day. She had ever put too fine a point upon the matter of marriage.

Joan found a footman and instructed him to see to securing the ivy-covered door that led into the basement. She then stopped at the dining room long enough to announce she had no interest in dinner, and moved abovestairs to her room. As she closed her chamber door behind her, she came to the conclusion that her life had taken a leap forward. In point of fact, she should be grateful to her uncle for showing her the way to get on with things. She ought to thank him for keeping her on for a month longer, that she might utilize every connection of Aunt Hannah's to search for her future husband, her future life. It might be that she would have to move to Kent to search for her mate, but until such a pass, she would do her best to search for him here in London, where the possibilities were surely far better. Oh yes, it was good to have a plan, a decision made!

Which made the fact that Joan proceeded to pummel her pillow to a flurry of loosely flying feathers an asinine and utterly nonsensical act. It had very little to do, she told herself as she struck the pillow repeatedly, with the realization that any hopes she had ever harbored about attracting Lord Price's regard were now for naught.

Eleven

Two evenings later, Joan waited for the carriage that would return her from the rout she had attended at Lady Boudreau's. The twins, less than pleased to be leaving at what they considered to be the early hour of midnight, stood a little apart from their cousin, attempting to whisper to one another. Joan almost smiled to herself, thinking the twins had never mastered the ability to whisper without being heard. Too, there was the sight of Lord Price making a hasty back-door exit to bring the amusement filtering up to tug at her mouth.

"Whatever is that *flash* in her eyes?" Joan heard Eleanor say in an attempt at speaking *sotto voce* to Gabrielle.

"I should think she was angry if it were not for the way she laughed and flirted all night. *Joan,* flirting! She is ever the one vexing us about being too coquettish!" Gabrielle returned, her whispering talents even less than her sister's.

"I should fear she is nipping at the sherry, for she is as gay as Seymour when he has had a glass too many, although I do not perceive the scent of it about her person."

"Can you hide the scent in some manner?" Gabrielle mused.

Joan mentally shook her head, turning her attention to the goings-on just beyond the confines of the portico under which they stood. Yes, there went a lone horse and rider. Without doubt it was Lord Price riding away.

As Joan climbed up into the carriage, she moved to one of the windows, peering out into the night in the direction

Lord Price had ridden. The carriage rocked forward, bringing an "ooh!" of surprise from the opposite squab.

The night was dark, with the moon on the wane, so it was a trifle surprising Joan was able to spy a dark smudge of movement among the small copse of trees to the right of the moving carriage. She stared at the smudge as it became a shape, the shape a mounted man, and as the man neared their carriage, he was seen to wear a large, floppy hat. "The Cavalier," she said, expressing no surprise.

She was startled, however, when a thump announced that Lord Price had not chosen to try and stop the carriage, but had instead lunged at it bodily. This was confirmed by the sight of the man's horse, its saddle empty, turning away from the rolling carriage, although the animal then checked its pace, moving to match that of the other horses pulling the vehicle. A scrambling sound and a shout from the driver assured Joan that Lord Price had not only successfully launched himself onto the coach, but had also managed to scramble up to its top. She breathed a sigh of relief that he had not been hurt, and drew in yet another for the thought that, by her instruction, the driver was unarmed and therefore would not shoot the interloper.

She was just as grateful when the coach slowed to a stop, however, for there was no way the driver could be both clubbing Lord Price and controlling the horses at once. She would not care to see Lord Price hurt.

As soon as the carriage shuddered to a stop, Joan threw open the door and leapt out. "Hiram!" she shouted at the driver.

He turned his face to look at her, all the while clucking soothing noises toward the nervous horses, and indicated with a shrug of his head that she ought look behind him. There, sprawled on the roof of the coach, lay Lord Price in his Cavalier costume.

"Good heavens, Hiram, is he dead?" she cried.

"Stunned, more belike! I think the bloke took a mighty

thump to the lungs when he leapt off'n his horse in that fool's way he did."

Joan put her hands to her skirts with every intention of climbing up the coach to see Lord Price's state for herself, but was stopped when he moaned and sluggishly sat up.

"I . . . can . . . breathe again!" he gasped, a hand to his chest.

Joan stared, alarmed by the wheezing quality of his voice, and not a little amused to see his silly hat was still in place atop his head. "Is it tied on?" she asked.

"My . . . breath?" he asked.

She gave a quick giggle. "No, your hat."

"No. It is just . . . very tight . . . if you must know. I happen to detest . . . the thing."

"Are you very hurt?"

"Very. But I am . . . warmed by . . . your concern, madam."

Her amusement faded. "Hiram, he says he is very hurt," she told the driver, as if he could not have heard the breathless words for himself.

"Serves him right."

"Hiram!"

"Well'n, what would you have me do, Miss? Play nursemaid to him? More belike I'll set me fists to him!"

"No, no," Lord Price said, lifting a hand as though to wave away anyone's concern. "I shall do as I am—" The words cut off abruptly, as Lord Price sprang to sudden energetic life, both hands reaching out, snagging the coach ribbons in one hand while hitting Hiram square in the chest with the other, sending the driver tumbling backward off the coach box.

Lord Price secured the ribbons, then leapt from the box. Joan cautiously came around the rear of the coach, watching as Lord Price bent down on one knee next to where Hiram lay sprawled on the stones of the road. "Are you all right, old fellow?" Lord Price inquired.

"I am *not!*" Hiram roared, then wheezed in a manner not unlike Lord Price's pretended manner just a moment ago.

"You are all right enough," Lord Price grinned under his mask. With one fluid motion he brought a length of rope from his pocket, bound Hiram's wrists, and turned to spring back up to the coach top.

"Why, you—!" Hiram gasped in outrage.

"Get the other horse!" Lord Price called over his shoulder, ordering Joan where she stood staring at his antics.

She came back around the coach to find his horse had halted nearby its beastly brethren. She moved toward the horse, crooning softly until she managed to catch a rein.

"It will be a simple matter to untie your driver," Lord Price informed her. "You and Hiram can ride home together on the horse. I apologize, I never meant to put you out from the carriage, but in truth this suits my purpose as well."

"In the coach—"

"The girls will be well cared for, I promise you! I shall have them home almost before you can arrive there yourself." Lord Price turned to the horses, crying out "Hah!" as he gave the horses their heads.

The animals sprang forward, snorting in wide-eyed alarm, quickly pulling the carriage away from where Joan stood, staring, one hand pressed to her mouth to keep a laugh from bursting from her lips.

Nathaniel made sure he drove far enough, with enough unpredictable turns, before he pulled the coach to the side of the road. He secured the reins once again, and leapt down from the box. He pulled open the carriage door, making a point of taking a step back so that the light from the carriage lamps could illuminate his disguised person for their edification.

"My gracious me!" came a feminine cry from the interior.

"Ladies, I will have my kisses now, if you please," he

announced, stepping again toward the carriage to lower the step and move inside.

"Kisses, is it?" came a voice out of the opposite squab.

The dim light from the carriage lamps provided some illumination, but still it was a moment before Nathaniel saw anything but darkness. "Kisses indeed," he replied, only to narrow his eyes and add with sudden rising aggravation, "But there is only one of you! Where is your sister?"

"I presume she is in Heaven," came the reply, amused and rather tremulous. "You see, she passed on these ten years and more ago."

Lord Price sat back, aware the voice was all wrong. "Would you mind moving into the light?" he asked suspiciously.

He was already quite sure the vehicle's occupant was neither Miss Gabrielle nor Miss Eleanor, but when she obligingly scooted forward into the light, Nathaniel was more than a little startled to find he shared the space of the carriage with Lady Bostwicke-Martin, a matron of ninety years if not a hundred. "But . . . I thought—!"

"Thought you'd kiss those two girls with the buttercup hair, did you not, eh?" Lady Bostwicke-Martin said for him, giving a long, deep chortle. She reached out with the folded fan in her hand, stabbing him with surprising strength in his shirtfront. "Miss Galloway said as how she could make you think you were after the right carriage, and by Jove, she was right!"

"Miss Galloway," he said in a low growl.

"I haven't had this much sport in a decade! Although I shall confess to you I was a trifle concerned you'd try to run with me to the Scottish border! Might have made you marry me, too, for such presumption and botheration, but then again I suppose a man who thought he'd plucked two plums instead of one would not be heading for Gretna Green. Too difficult to choose between the two Alexander girls, I daresay. Unless you have a preference, one over the other, hm?"

"I assure you, my lady, it was never my intention to elope with either of the Alexander twins," he replied stiffly.

"And why should you have when you can have their kisses for free? But, come along then, lad, take my kiss and my token, and we'll have done with our sport for the evening."

Nathaniel stared at her, swallowing with an audible gulp. "Lady Bostwicke-Martin—"

"Ah, so you know my name, do you? We have met, have we?" She reached out, toward his face. "Let me see under that mask of yours—"

"My lady!" he cried in alarm, grasping her hand.

"Shy? Well, lad, I am not going away from this encounter without *something* for my trouble. It will either be a kiss or else I shall know your identity—"

Nathaniel did not let her finish her sentence, leaning forward and rapidly pressing his mouth to hers. "There!" he said, annoyed at her for insisting and reluctantly amused at the triumphant smile that spread across her face. "Now, I shall take you home," he announced firmly. "Your direction is Grosvenor Square, is it not?"

She went into a paroxysm of chortles, rapping her fan against his shoulder in time to her uttered "heh-hehs!" of amusement. After a full minute, she was able to speak again, "I shall not agree or disagree until you snip a lock of my hair, my Kissing Cavalier."

With a sigh, Nathaniel complied, stuffing both the scissors and lock of hair in his coat pocket, knowing he would never, ever show the lock to his fellows, not if he ever wanted a moment free of badgering from that lot.

"First white one you've collected, I would wager!" Lady Bostwicke-Martin laughed again, a briefer amusement, until she nodded and allowed, "You have the way of it, my lad. Grosvenor Square it is. Oh, I can scarce wait to tell that conceited Hester Van Buren about this! She will be entirely enraged that *I* was your only elderly victim, not her! Proves my point I was ever the beauty between us, does it not? Heh-heh!"

Nathaniel closed the carriage on Lady Bostwicke-Martin's renewed sniggers of glee, and climbed upon the box once more.

As he settled the ribbons in his hands, he thought to himself that the attributes of cleverness and pride of purpose he had recently noted in Miss Galloway had proved to be a double-edged sword. That which made her admirable also made her a bothersome foe.

Nathaniel gritted his teeth, having a vision of a deliciously satisfying future moment when he might rip up one Miss Galloway with a well-placed phrase or two—until he began to laugh, without having meant to, the sound blending with the "heh-heh!" chuckles that penetrated the coach panels below. He had been bested, *again,* and even the thoroughly annoyed Nathaniel was not so hard-hearted as to deny Miss Galloway had done so with a superior flourish.

Hiram left Joan at the front door, where only Seymour raised an eyebrow at her belated return to the house.

"If you care to join the party of young persons," Seymour informed her, assuring her she had arrived after the twins and the party of six with which Joan had sent the young ladies home, "they have removed to the music room."

"There are new pups at the mews," Joan explained away her late arrival, internally frowning at having to make a statement that was true, yet in its intention to mislead, a lie. She handed Seymour her light wool pelisse, avoiding meeting his eye. Certainly there were new pups at the mews, but she had not stopped to admire them. This whole business with the Cavalier was making a liar of her! How extremely vexing the entire situation with Lord Price was coming to be.

As she untied her bonnet, Joan glanced down the hallway from whence came sounds of group merriment. The sense of vexation was replaced by a reluctance to join that group, but that, too, was a short-lived thought, replaced as a slow smile turned up the corners of her mouth as she tried to imagine the scene that must have ensued once Lord Price realized it was not the twins inside the coach he had ambushed, but rather a saucy old dowager. Oh, without a doubt Lady Bostwicke-Martin had given him an earful for his trouble! Joan grinned fully, having no doubt the lady had never been alarmed to find herself alone with the Kissing Cavalier, but rather quite the reverse.

She reached to hand Seymour her bonnet, only to discover he had gone from the entry, leaving her to her own devices. Her amusement faded as she was reminded yet again of her lower status in this household. Sighing, she went to hang her bonnet on a peg near the front door.

Joan's sigh turned into a *moue* of distaste as she decided she must join the festivities in the music room. If she were going to comply with Uncle Newland's demand, then it behooved her to meet as many eligible young men as she could. The sooner the better. Even a hurried wedding—short of an expensive and difficult to obtain special license—must have three weeks of posted banns before it could take place. Obviously, there would be no getting around the fact that she would have to spend some time with Papa in Kent, but if she could secure an offer before she had to leave London, where her chances of meeting "marriagables" were a hundredfold superior, she could go to him happily and not as a long-term burden.

Of course, that was why she could not let the Cavalier triumph, and why she must keep news of his attempts from Uncle Newland's ears as well, if she could but manage it. Any threat to the girls was a threat to her own access to society. Uncle Newland would think nothing of reeling his girls in, making them virtual prisoners in The Keep, and therefore Joan almost as great a prisoner at their side. With the twins she had access to more invitations, more soirées, more dances—in short, more opportunities to be with men. It did not matter that it made her fidget to think of using her cousins so callously for her own aims.

She tried to soothe her conscience by assuring herself she was also protecting them—helping to ensure that they have the better, brighter future their father had promised them.

With such thoughts in mind, she joined the party in the music room.

"Oh, Joan!" Gabrielle called at her entrance. "You make number nine! We haven't a seat for you," her cousin explained, indicating the card tables already set for whist.

"Miss Galloway must have my seat," Mr. Strathy offered, starting to push back his chair.

Gabrielle trilled out a laugh. "Heavens, no! Joan will not mind if she does not have a seat at play, will you, Joan?"

Ah, the old conundrum of whether to insist it was not necessary—a genteel reply that might impress the attendant males—or to insist she must play, to look the equal of her cousins. Joan chose the former, for at least then she could circulate among the three attending gentlemen.

So, I am reduced to stalking men, Joan thought as she settled with a forced smile on a settee next to Lord Mavenbury's place. She pushed down the unflattering impression, knowing others never suffered from a conscience when it came to the important matter of finding a lifemate. Like them, she would smile the smiles, offer the words the gentlemen might like to hear, would play the role of hostess so that they might see her talents in the area of social interchange. Would Mr. Strathy like more tea? A glass of wine perhaps, Lord Mavenbury? Mr. Pennelton, what a clever play that was!

As the evening wore on, the act of fawning grew increasingly distasteful to Joan, although no one else seemed to take exception to her actions. Even her cousins seemed to find nothing awry with her manner. When Mr. Strathy spent more time talking with her than he did at playing his cards, no one chided him except his partner, Miss Teasdale.

Still, Mr. Strathy's lengthy tales of past fishing adventures could only pale after awhile. Joan found she could not feign one more minute of interest in trout. She excused herself from his side, at the same moment deciding to cease her attempts at enticing any male regard her way, instead merely moving to please or make comfortable the guests as she might. She loaned Miss Thornwell a shawl against a draft, and refilled Lord Mavenbury's wineglass only because it truly was empty, lapsing back to her normal quiet demeanor.

This change served Joan well enough, for the remainder of the evening was less tedious than the beginning, but she had no regrets when she saw the evening of cards had come to an end.

As the guests rose to leave, she offered her farewells and slipped from the room, abandoning her duty as chaperone. After all, Uncle Newland had wandered into the room—presumably to see if any bibelots or silver had been pinched during the course of the evening—and his hawk's eye would be sure to see the twins received no untoward male advances as the guests made their farewells.

Joan moved up the stairs, regretting any times she had ever called her cousins superficial or shallow. She silently begged their forgiveness for such thoughts, not a little ashamed of her own dissembling display this night, one that surely exceeded any demonstration Gabrielle and Eleanor had ever made, for hers had been a knowing and utterly false attempt, using flattery to entice.

"Ah well," she told the line of Alexander familial portraits hanging on the corridor wall, "At least I learned how *not* to go about securing a husband." She shuddered in distaste and vowed to leave such blatant falseness behind.

She was just about to move up the second set of stairs when the voices of the twins preceded them up the lower steps. Joan paused at the landing, openly listening to their exchanged comments about the visitors, wondering with a half-smile if her own evaluation of Lord Mavenbury and the

Misters Strathy and Pennelton as Winkin, Blinkin, and Nod was unduly unkind of her.

"Lord Mavenbury would do," Eleanor said.

"Oh, never! He is not nearly wealthy enough. And even if he were, not nearly handsome enough."

"Handsome, pooh! Papa will not be disposed to favor anyone just because they are handsome. No, I tell you, if we are to hope to have British husbands, they must be exceedingly wealthy and well-titled."

"And there are simply throngs of such suitors pounding a path to our door, are there not?" Gabrielle said scathingly, the cutting words quickly followed by a deep sigh. "But you are right! Papa will never settle for any British gentleman of a title less than a viscount, and no less than an earl if he is not blessed with a fortune. Where and how are we two to ever attract such a one as that?"

"Such *two* as that," Eleanor corrected.

"Impossible!"

"I fear so."

"But I do not *want* to leave London!" Gabrielle wailed. "I do not *want* to marry some stuffy old Prussian or Russian or Spaniard, or . . . or anyone but an Englishman! I do not even want to marry an Irishman. I want someone who loves England, loves London, loves the gay life we could lead here. If Papa marries us to some foreign fellows, they will likely be two that stand on opposite sides of some war or other. They will drag us apart and forbid us to travel to see each other!"

Eleanor gave a sound of concern. "Never! Apart, for months on end, if not years? It cannot be! And, do you know, I have no doubt we would live in frozen palaces on frozen countrysides that only have spring and summer for one week a year! Life would be unbearable!"

Gabrielle was silent, causing Joan to lean over the stair rail to catch sight of the two girls hugging each other tightly.

Gabrielle broke away first, exclaiming, "Eleanor, you know what we must do! *We* must find husbands for ourselves."

"And how are we to do that?"

"Elope."

Stunned silence filled the corridor, then Eleanor gasped, "Elope?"

"Yes. It is the only way. Once we are married to our grooms, Papa cannot but accept them."

"But . . . who? How?"

"We must help each other." Gabrielle gave a satisfied smile. "I have someone in mind for myself already."

A matching smile spread over Eleanor's face. "I can think of a fellow I should care to marry myself."

"Lord Price!" they declared together.

"Oh, Lud!" Joan groaned softly, quickly covering her mouth.

The twins must not have heard her involuntary exclamation, for they stared only at each other, mouths rounded with surprise, expressions flushing red.

"But, I thought of him first—"

"I have ever had an eye turned toward Lord Price—"

"I daresay he has ever paid special attention to me—"

"Even though he is but a baron, it is my opinion he would do very well, for he is wealthy enough—"

The twins stared again, silent, stepping back from the embrace they had just shared.

Joan straightened, prepared to go to their sides to prevent the flurry of slaps or hair-pulling that seemed imminent, only to be halted by Eleanor's giggle.

"I know!" she exclaimed, "We must have a competition. Only one of us may win him, but that will be the one he prefers, so it serves us both well, for then we would know whom he cares for most. You and I shall both do our best to charm him, and whoever wins his heart, wins the man!"

"And the other of us?" Gabrielle asked.

"Shall presume upon her sister's newly betrothed bridegroom to help her find an Englishman to marry!"

"Oh, Eleanor, you have the very way of it! 'Tis settled. And I tell you now that *I* shall have the swansdown shawl when next Lord Price comes to call."

Eleanor squeaked, "Beast!" then laughingly claimed, "And *I* shall have Grandmama's pearls to wear!"

Gabrielle drew in a sharp breath, a short-lived denial, for the two girls moved on to their chambers, giggling side by side.

Joan started to go to them, to direct the two to put such flummery thoughts from their heads, but for each step she took toward their rooms, a thought sprang into her mind: they would defy their father? Not only dismiss his plans for them, but do so by way of contriving something as shocking as an elopement? They schemed to pursue Lord Price—of all men!—did they?

And who was she to say they must not? Joan's steps slowed even more. For all that it was ineligible that the Kissing Cavalier should win his kisses from the twins, there was no reason why Lord Price, as himself, should not marry one of her cousins, was there? Why had the thought never occurred to her before? It was true he had not shown any preference for the twins' company . . . or had it been just her own dusty dream of catching his regard that ever kept such a thought from her before?

What kept her from going to them and demanding they put aside such foolish plans? Was there more to her reluctance than a quiet fear the girls would see it was not so much the change in their futures she objected to, but the choice of who that future would be spent with?

Joan moved back to the stairs, mounting them one by one, her hand unsteady on the rail. The twins—one of them—could do it, could attract his heart. With their beautiful faces, their burnished-gold hair, their determination to be won, one of them could persuade Lord Price to make his offer.

"Persuade indeed!" Joan said aloud, shaking her head at the thought. No! Lord Price, for all that he had taken on the unwanted part of Cavalier to help Simon, was not the manner of man who could be "persuaded" to marry anyone. Temporarily charmed, perhaps, but never persuaded. If he chose to marry, it would be because he *chose* to marry and for no other reason.

Or, she caught her breath, if he were trapped into making an offer. It was not beneath her cousins to arrange an entrapment!

She would have to tell him, warn him. It was the only decent thing to do. The problem was, how did one bring up such a subject?

She would just have to find the words somehow, next time she saw him, despite any awkwardness involved.

As for the twins—well, if they were so goosish as to attempt to challenge their papa's dictates about whom they might marry, then they had no one to blame but themselves for the outcome of any silly wager, even if (or when) Lord Price served them back their own sauce by avoiding any need to offer for either of them. Yes, just as soon as he and she met again, Joan would find a way to take Lord Price aside and warn him of the twins' schemes.

She chose to ignore the satisfied sensation this thought sent shimmering through her as she moved up the stairs to find her bed for the night.

Twelve

"Hah!" Nathaniel cried, his voice ringing out in the late morning air as he flicked the long driving whip over the ears of the team before him. "So then, your help, good man!" he shouted to Simon over the thunder of pounding hooves.

"Certainly!" came Simon's shout in return. "You say you need a new approach to the twins?"

"I do! Cannot climb The Keep. Cannot waylay their coach. What then? Only a little over a week left in which to succeed!"

Nathaniel waited for an answer, aware that Simon was occupied in shifting his weight, leaning far out to the right, holding on to the special rail before him with both hands lest his feet slip out from under him. After the coach-and-four made its corner, Simon resumed his seat next to Nathaniel, watching the path ahead for any sign of difficulty.

"Surprise them then!"

"Surprise?" Nathaniel echoed.

"Come to them where they would never expect it."

Nathaniel shifted his hands, using the ribbons to hold back the right leader for a moment, until its counterpart matched pace. "Ah!" he said, pleased with the suggestion. He fed the leaders more of the ribbons, letting them stretch their legs now that they were on the straight length of the oval course.

Sir Francis leaned in from his precarious post on the added step over the left front wheel. "Avonleigh coming up on your left!" he hollered at Nathaniel.

"He is too late! We have the win, lads!" Nathaniel cried, just as Simon, and Laffy on his right, gave a whoop of triumph that also marked their coming first across the designated finish line, a chalk line laid down this morning which allowed enough room yet on the course that the coaches might slow and turn once they had crossed over it.

Nathaniel pulled in the reins, signaling the horses to a slower pace, anticipating the turn at the end of the course. Suddenly a coach cut before him, its leaders stamping and snorting, the aft wheel coming perilously close to Nathaniel's favorite leader.

"Watch your wheels, sir!" he shouted at the driver. It was a man on Crowell's team, one Mr. Nielson. At Nielson's side sat Crowell, who did not deign to turn his head or otherwise acknowledge Nathaniel's call. Their carriage swept a wide berth at the end of the path, sending up a spray of dirt and stones, startling a nurse on the neighboring walking path into sweeping her young charge up into her arms with a cry. Nielson laughed unkindly as their coach rolled back past Nathaniel's in the opposite direction.

Avonleigh's coach was next to roll beside Nathaniel's, although this time coming to a halt beside where Nathaniel had stopped. "Good race, Price," Lord Avonleigh acknowledged, touching his driving whip to the brim of his hat.

"My thanks," Nathaniel nodded in return. "I thought you would have that inside corner on the first turn."

"I thought so, too. I would have won if I had," Avonleigh grinned and saluted again just before giving his horses the signal to pull ahead.

Nathaniel readied his ribbons, following the slow turn of the other man. There, on the opposite path, stood Miss Joan and her charges, flanked by two large footmen.

They had obviously stopped to watch the race. Miss Gabrielle twirled her parasol above her head in a way that could only mean she meant to catch their attention, and Miss Eleanor was so bold as to wave across the dividing expanse.

Minding his team, Nathaniel brought the coach around so that it ran parallel to where the ladies waited. Miss Joan seemed bothered by something, the sun perhaps, for she tended to look at the ground and to frown when she must look up.

"Simon, Lord Price," Gabrielle greeted them, still twirling her parasol in a languid circle. "We saw you win the race. What a fine whip you are, my lord!"

"Thank you."

"I did not care for the way Lord Crowell's driver frightened that poor nurse," Eleanor put in, "but you are far too fine a fellow to ever do such a thing."

Nathaniel looked to Simon, who appeared startled by his cousin's discourse, and who gave Nathaniel a strange look. Not to wonder, though, for Nathaniel was just as startled, for it was almost as if the girls were . . . well, flirting with him! Why? They never had in the past, despite ample opportunity. "Er . . . thank you, Miss Alexander," Nathaniel answered.

"Of course, my lord. Do you think you might give me a ride on your marvelous coach? On the seat beside you? I vow I shall not be frightened if you drive slowly."

"Oh . . . certainly. How pleasant. A turn for each of the ladies then?"

After an insistent footman was allowed to assume the little jumpseat at the coach's rear, Eleanor had her ride at his side. This was followed by a ride for Gabrielle, who laughed at every word he uttered, even when he merely ordered a young boy to call back his dog lest the beast be run over. And both ladies lingered on the path once he had put them down, chatting and sharing a series of *bon mots* until Simon cried for them to "have done!" Yet the girls fell silent only when Nathaniel turned to Miss Joan to offer her a turn about the row with him.

"Joan?" said Eleanor as though in utter disbelief.

"Certainly. I presumed that each of you would—"

"You do not care to ride with Lord Price, do you, Joan?" Gabrielle broke in.

Joan lifted one eyebrow and calmly answered, "I certainly should like that very well."

The curious part was that once Joan was seated beside him, she fell utterly silent, looking for all the world as if she would rather not be there.

"Troubles, Miss Joan?"

She looked at Nathaniel sharply. "I beg your pardon?"

"I know it is a presumption for me to ask a personal question, but I cannot help but wonder why you were eager to take a drive, only to now wish yourself elsewhere," he explained.

"I don't wish myself elsewhere."

"Really? My mistake."

She looked down at her folded hands, and when she lifted her face again it was with an apology written across her lips. "I have been uncivil. I will confess I did not so much want a drive along the row as I wanted to be—" She stopped abruptly, coloring.

"To be acknowledged as your cousins' equal," he finished for her.

"Oh dear. So clear as that, is it? I am afraid that is how I was thinking of your offer. Trifling of me, I know, but I sometimes weary of being . . . of being invisible," she said, a breathless quality to her voice.

"You could never be invisible," he assured her, then looked away, not having expected the look of raw pleasure his comment gave her. Why, it quite transformed her, bringing her the kind of glow in a woman that often was superior to mere physical beauty. His stomach did a curious little flip, and out of nowhere it occurred to him that it had been at least two days since he had thought of the woman he had kissed at the masquerade. Knowing on the one hand this could not be that woman, on the other there was something about Miss Joan that had the ability to summon forth and then displace that other being in his thoughts. Curious, and oddly pleasing.

He shook off the sensation and searched about for a topic

of conversation. "Simon tells me your father left for the country early this morning."

She nodded solemnly, her glow dimming at his words. *That* had been a poor choice of topic, he realized at once. Ahead of them he spied a bevy of older females, all happily engaged in active conversation around a bench upon which resided yet another lady. "What happens there, do you think?" he asked, for that was certainly a preferable subject than reminding her of her father's leaving.

"You have not heard?" the woman at his side asked, smiling ever so slightly again. "Why, I thought everyone who ventured to the park today was regaled with the tale! That is Lady Bostwicke-Martin there. She is regaling any passersby with the story of how she was 'kissed and cropped by the Cavalier,' as I believe she said it."

Nathaniel's gaze flew to the woman on the bench—yes, the woman had her head of white hair exposed, free of a bonnet, where she now pointed, chatting and laughing happily.

He closed his eyes, suppressing a shudder, and when he opened them he was pleased to find merry brown eyes watching him. "I vow I believe her tale," Joan said. "Is it not too amusing? Whoever would have thought the Cavalier would kiss Lady Bostwicke-Martin?"

"Only Lady Bostwicke-Martin," Nathaniel replied, trying not to sound sour.

"I daresay you are right," Joan replied, smiling at him.

For one breathless moment he thought *she knows I am the Cavalier!*

But no, she couldn't know any such thing. His disguise was good, and no one else had ventured to guess it was him, at least not within his hearing. Yet if she knew, why did she hesitate in denouncing him? She would do so, for only look at how well she had done her duty of guarding her cousins; she would not neglect such a vast advantage, surely not if she knew Nathaniel was the Cavalier.

"Lord Price," she began, her face pensive. She meant to

tell him something, share something with him, he could see that by the way her hands fidgeted together, by the way she avoided his gaze. "There is a little matter concerning my—"

"Nathaniel!" interrupted Simon's voice, just as that fellow leapt up from where he ran beside the carriage, snagging a ride by clinging to the highly polished brass top rail and finding the racing side step with his feet. "As to that . . . er, former question you asked me . . . ?" he said, looking at Joan just long enough to greet her with a nod of his head, "Joanie."

"Simon," she returned, looking annoyed by his presence.

"Yes, our former conversation," Nathaniel replied, having to shake his head to recall that conversation. Oh yes, right, the bit about how he was to approach the twins—but what had Joan been about to say? "A little matter concerning my . . ." my what?

"I have had me a thought about our, er, subject," Simon pressed.

Nathaniel looked to Joan, who made a motion with her shoulders that said she no longer felt free to speak. He gave her a small nod, speaking quietly just to her. "Can your statement wait until we meet again?"

"Oh, yes, I rather suppose so," she agreed, looking both aggravated and relieved.

Nathaniel gave a quick frown, shrugged mentally, and told Simon, "All right, fellow." He pulled the horses to a halt at the place where they had picked up Miss Joan. Simon handed her down, and then scurried up to take her place, even as the girls' attendant footman again took up his position near the ladies.

"You ladies are returning home now?" Simon asked his cousins.

At their nods of assurance, Simon smiled approvingly. "Good. *Adieu.* Nathaniel, do drive on."

Nathaniel also bid the ladies farewell, glancing over his shoulder as the carriage rolled forward. He saw that Gabrielle twirled her parasol, Eleanor threw smiles, and Joan stared off to one side as if she were either wishing she might be anywhere but in the company of her cousins or else was deeply lost to thought.

"You had a notion?" Nathaniel asked when they were free of the presence of the ladies.

"Yes, a plan. It is just as I told you: do the unexpected. And so we shall."

"We? You may not help me."

"Oh, only a little. Only by leaving out a ladder, my friend."

"A ladder," Nathaniel repeated, then sighed, suspecting he would not like what Simon had planned.

Gabrielle leaned out the window, giggling without restraint, while Eleanor, at her side, called encouragement down to Nathaniel where he stood rooted to a ladder's rungs. Simon grinned from a neighboring window, out which Joan also leaned as she ordered, "Cavalier! Desist at once! This is folly."

"I would gladly comply," Nathaniel shouted up at her, "if you would but call off your dogs!" He looked down at the snarling, yipping animals, amid which stood a footman brandishing an umbrella. "Both kinds!" Nathaniel amended.

Simon laughed, the umbrella made a solid whacking sound against the ladder, and Eleanor called out, "Come all the way up, Mr. Cavalier!"

"Eleanor, be silent! What would your father say?" Joan cried, leaning out the window to give Eleanor a hard look.

"Oh pooh, Papa is not here!" returned Eleanor.

"And I want you girls to unlock your door this very instance!" Joan ordered.

Eleanor's only reply to that dictate was to grip the ladder with one hand and call down to the Cavalier, "Look, I have steadied it for you. You are safe to climb up!"

Eight feet below where Nathaniel perched on the ladder—a

tall rickety contraption no doubt used by the servants when it was time to sweep the roof clean each fall—the footman began to climb up. "Here now, we've orders, guv'nor!" called the man, "You'll have to come down at once."

"To be pummeled by zealous guards and mauled by a pack of mongrels who ought to have been left in the country where they belong? I think not," Nathaniel replied, climbing a few feet higher. Really, he was reluctant to go too high, in case the footman should think to tip the ladder. He looked up at the eagerly waiting twins, aware their room was not so high as Miss Joan's but nonetheless a sizable distance from the ground.

"Here now, them hounds ain't mongrels," argued the footman. "And, might I add, I don't see as you've much choice, guv'nor. You gotta go up or down, one way or t'other."

Nathaniel glanced up again, giving Simon a dark look, for that fellow was convulsed with laughter where he leaned against the window frame for support. Joan had gone from his side. Simon pointed down at his friend, seeming to wish to speak but unable to form the words for all his laughing.

From inside came the sound of pounding on a door and the steady call of Joan's voice demanding, "Gabrielle! Eleanor! Open this door at once!"

The twins ignored the command, eyes shining as they watched Nathaniel where he perched on the ladder. "Come along," urged Gabrielle. "You may take your kisses and your tokens ere the footman can ever pull you from the ladder."

Nathaniel was not so sure, and the thought of falling into the shrubberies onto a pair of scissors—albeit tiny scissors—gave him pause.

His gaze traveled upward, to where the long ladder rested against the roofline. He sighed—really, it sounded more like a growl—and scurried up the ladder. Eleanor squealed with delight, and then Gabrielle called "What now!" as he hastened past their window, on up the ladder. In a moment he was on the roof.

He gave a cry of "Whoa-ho!" as his smooth-soled dancing pumps skittered momentarily over the tiles, but a moment later he achieved purchase. He spread his arms, walking as rapidly as he dared, moving across the slanted surface, holding his breath as though the act could keep him from sliding from the rooftop. Behind him came the sound of someone ascending the ladder, and a moment later the clatter of soles on tiles.

Simon's laughter came again, this time from in front of Nathaniel instead of behind him. Nathaniel came to the roof edge, dropping to his knees to peer over the edge, finding as he had anticipated that Simon had moved to a side window, where he now leaned out, looking upward. "Good gad, man!" Simon called as he spotted Nathaniel, "Do you propose to leap onto the tree there?" Simon stifled his amusement long enough to point to the large oak spreading its limbs near the house.

"How I ever let you talk me into this asinine daytime assault—!" Nathaniel hissed down to Simon, cutting off his own comment as he saw out of the corner of his eye that the footman, the fellow's eyes wide with a care for his own personal well-being, diffidently approached.

"You will never make it. You will break your neck!" Simon called up, the laughter dissipating. "Do not be a fool, man!"

"Too late for that!" Nathaniel replied.

The footman was only six feet away. Nathaniel rose slowly, allowing a friendly smile to grow below his mask. He spread his arms as if to say "you have me caught," and when he saw the footman nod as though agreeing with this sentiment, he sprang forward, all but leaping over the crest of the house.

"Whoa-ho!" he cried again as his feet went out from under him, and he landed with a grunt and a thud on his backside.

"What—? Gor!" cried the footman behind him.

Nathaniel's feet flew in a frenzy of activity meant to stop his gradual slide down the slant of the roof, scraping across the tiles until of a sudden he quit sliding. He did not stop to think, but scrambled to his feet, knowing he moved too quickly for safety, but the ladder was now only a few feet away, his only avenue of escape. He tried to slow his descent down the roof incline, not very successfully, bending to grab for the ladder. He gave a strangled cry—in fact, Simon's name taken in vain—as he swung his weight around, one arm reaching out to full length, slapping against the roof tiles, his fingers scrambling for a hold in a desperate attempt to steady the ladder. There was no hold to be had; the ladder rocked and tilted. He brought his hand back to the ladder, put his shoes on either side of the wooden structure, and willed his hands to unclench, allowing the splintery wood to slide past his flesh as he made the kind of shooting descent he had last done at the age of eleven. The wood bit at his hands as he slid down its length, causing him to grit his teeth against the pain, and he had not slid more than halfway down before the thing tipped away from the house.

Another strangled cry—perhaps a kind of prayer—escaped him just before he missed the solid structure of the stone fence, his feet striking the pavement of the road just beyond with a thump that made him gasp from the sudden sharp pain in his right heel. A weight crushed his arms, pushing him to the road, until it occurred to him that he yet clutched the ladder with both hands. He shrugged out from under the weight of the thing, and it clattered on the roadtop as he pushed its length aside.

Several of the Alexander hounds—fair sized hounds with long-toothed snarls and hungry-sounding howls—lunged at the ironwork gate, rattling it on its hinges.

"Bravo!" came a laughing cry, and Nathaniel looked up to see Simon back at the front window, his arms lifted in salute. "Well done! Bravo!"

Nathaniel lifted his arms—now a bit shaky—in an answering salute.

Suddenly Joan appeared once again at Simon's side, thrusting him out of her way unceremoniously, and even from this distance Nathaniel could not miss the light of alarm that crossed her face. It did not matter that a moment later it was replaced by consternation once she saw he was well and hale, for that glimpse of fervent dread had been enough to all but erase the pain in his heel. Joan could not know he was Lord Price and yet something had come of their brief meetings as Cavalier and Guardian, something that for a moment had left her worried for his well-being. How extraordinarily warming it was to know she minded that she might have seen him dead or dismembered!

Simon stuck his head back out the window, crowding Joan. "Cavalier! Away! Before they open the gates to the hounds!"

Nathaniel needed no further encouragement. He limped as rapidly as he could to where, three streets away, he had paid a young lad to mind his horse.

"If this pattern of never achieving my aim keeps up, I suppose I shall have to start renting you by the week rather than the day," he grumbled to the animal as he mounted. His hands stung where slivers of wood had imbedded themselves, his right thumb throbbing and bleeding.

"Shoulda worn gloves, guv'nor," the lad advised him.

"I would like to see you work a pair of small scissors while wearing gloves!" Nathaniel retorted, putting heel to horse.

It might have been more prudent to ride the opposite direction, but it was closer to home—and a good hot soak for his bruised heel and some salve for his thumb—to ride back past the Alexander house.

Thankfully the footman had descended from the roof to retreat inside, along with the Alexander hounds, and everyone else had gone from the windows—everyone but Joan. She leaned there, her chin in her hands, a frown upon her brow. Nathaniel had only a moment to gaze up at her before she saw him in return, and although he expected the frown to deepen, instead it lightened upon sight of him. He surprised himself by gathering in the reins, slowing his horse before the house.

"You are bleeding!" Joan cried down to him, and now there was again concern upon her face.

"This little scratch?" It seemed to throb in response to his blithe dismissal. "It is your fault, you know," he pointed out, softening the criticism with a smile.

Joan planted one hand on her hip. "I do not think so, Sir Cavalier. *I* never said you ought to climb the ladder to the roof." She surprised him further when, instead of glowering at him, she actually smiled down at him. Even from this distance, he could see there was a definite gleam in her eye. "Do you know," she said, "I have thought of a way you may be done with all this."

"I presume you mean you will at once parade the girls out the front door to my side?" he countered, only belatedly remembering to alter his voice. In a deeper timbre, he added, "How good of you."

"No." She disappeared from the window for a moment, returning at once, holding something aloft for him to view. "The twins' hair," she informed him. "You may have these strands for your tokens. I will even bring them to the gate for you, if you will but take them and tell whoever cares that the wager is done, and leave us be."

Nathaniel narrowed his eyes. "I cannot believe you snipped a lock from each of the girls' heads."

"I did not," she replied, and, yes, there was certainly a gleam of mischief in her brown eyes. "I combed these for you from their hairbrushes."

"Oh, you are too good to me," he said dryly, smothering a laugh at her impudence.

"What? Do you say they will not serve?" she asked, her manner the epitome of feigned innocence.

"Someday, Miss Galloway, I shall repay you for making sport of me," he said, deliberately making his tone too light to be a threat, but not so light as to be dismissed.

Her response showed her lack of concern, however, for she only laughed and tossed forth the tufts of hair. They both watched as the wind carried the golden strands farther up the street, nowhere near where he sat upon his horse.

"You had better go, sir, if you are to avoid another encounter with the footman and the hounds," she advised him.

It was good advice, and yet he felt no need to hurry away just yet, despite his throbbing thumb, despite the fact that curtains were stirring at the windows of some neighboring houses.

"Oh, dear, you linger," she said, not looking in truth upset by this revelation. "Can this mean you are not yet daunted?"

"Never daunted," he assured her, grinning.

"But, sirrah, one of these days I shall have to let a coachman shoot you, or a dog chew upon you, or a footman strike you on the top of your tight hat. It is only a matter of time."

"Only a matter of time until I have my kisses, you mean."

"I do not mean that at all—"

"But you argue the point so vociferously! Can it be I have put a fear of my eventual success in you?"

"No," she said, yet there was something in her gaze that had lost its playfulness.

He started to ask why that aspect of concern had crept into her voice, across the planes of her face, but she spoke before he could. "A month. If only it were possible you could delay your attempts for a month."

"Never so long as that," he answered at once, and then regretted his quick words, for the defiant hand slipped from its posture at her hip, her shoulders drooped, her mouth turned down. "I am sorry," he continued at once, "but I am under a time limitation. I have not a month to spare."

"I know. You were given but two weeks," she said, unable to hide from him the bleakness in her voice.

"With only eight days remaining. Seven, if you count today a loss, which I am forced to admit I do."

Her mouth did not turn up again. "Seven days?" she repeated, her eyes round with dismay.

"Why is seven days so poor a thing? I should think you would be pleased to have my time restricted," Nathaniel said, reaching to pat his restless mount's neck. How long would it be before a footman noticed him or a constable was summoned to the street? he wondered idly, putting that concern aside, interested in her answer.

"If I had a month, or even three weeks," she spoke softly, so that he hardly heard her words, as if she spoke more to herself than to him, "A few weeks where I need not concern myself with anything but my own affairs—" She cut herself off abruptly, her chin raising. "It does not matter. I cannot imagine you would care a groat for anything beyond your seven days. Well, go on then! Go ahead and make your best attempts. I am afraid it will be to no avail, Sir Cavalier. Good day to you, sir!" she said firmly, retreating within the window frame, bringing down the window pane with a thud, and an audible snap as she secured the window lock.

Nathaniel lifted his eyebrows at the now empty window-frame, disconcerted by the sudden antagonism that had been in her voice. Was she truly that angry with him? How could she be, when but a few minutes earlier it could almost have been said that she flirted with him? Perhaps the events of the past few days had been a bit overwhelming—certainly they had for him.

Would Joan be at the Monclester ball tonight? Simon had informed him that the twins would be there, so it was logical to assume their watchman—watchwoman—would go with them. Not that Nathaniel would attempt to appear there as the Cavalier—his wounded thumb and heel told him it was better not to make the attempt—but perhaps in his own guise he could learn something of why seven days was so disappointingly short a time to her.

It occurred to him that her concerns were her own and no matter of his, so he dismissed his eagerness to see her at the ball tonight as merely a convenient way to avoid dancing. After all, these days Joan was usually to be found seated among the matrons and chaperones. How convenient for him if he could avoid dancing by sitting at her side.

Even though his thumb throbbed and his heel ached—not to mention the pain of a dozen other splinters stinging in his fingers—he also told himself he considered going to the ball because he might learn something of the twins' future activities that would finally put him in a place to win his wager. He would learn more if only he were not so battered as to prevent dancing, for it would be a simple thing to waltz one of the twins at least briefly away from her guardian, but the members of the Alexander household would see he was the Cavalier the minute he limped on to the dance floor. No, he assured himself, it must be an evening at Joan's side to lead to some kind of useful revelation.

It was irrelevant that the idea of sitting with Joan gratified him ever so much more than the idea of dancing with one of the twins.

Thirteen

Nathaniel wore the loosest pair of dancing shoes he owned, and still they pinched his swollen heel. He had found, however, that he could walk without limping too visibly if he moved slowly, in a dandified fashion that was never his usual manner, but served his purpose well enough otherwise. His thumb bore a sticking plaster, as did several other deep splinter injuries on his fingers, all hidden beneath a pair of buff-colored gloves.

A hand touched him on either sleeve as he stepped into the Monclester ballroom, and he looked to find Miss Gabrielle had taken one arm, Miss Eleanor the other.

"Simon said you might come tonight," Eleanor trilled, smiling up at him with a bright smile.

"Do you know, I have just arrived, and so no one has bespoke a single dance of me," Gabrielle told him, moving her hand so that their arms became firmly entwined.

"Ladies," Nathaniel greeted them, looking from one to the other, hoping his tenuous smile gave the impression he had missed Gabrielle's blatant solicitation that he secure a dance from her. Why so transparent an invitation? Why the scowl cast at her by Eleanor? Why in heaven's name this newborn desire for his attention from the two of them?

Simon, with Joan on his arm, sauntered before Nathaniel. His friend grinned, an echo of amusement left over from this afternoon's rooftop adventure, but when he spoke it was to

Joan. "See? I told you the girls had not been spirited away. In fact, could they be safer than with my good friend Nate?"

Nathaniel pretended to skewer Simon with a look, twisting his mouth upward to put a note of humor in the glance. "Do you say I am harmless?"

"Utterly," Simon answered.

Nathaniel chose to ignore this remark in favor of greeting Joan. "Miss Joan, how do you do this evening?"

"Well enough," she answered, her expression unreadable. "And yourself?"

"Joan," Eleanor bubbled, interrupting his response, "you have come just as Lord Price was on the point of asking if he might share the first waltz with me."

"Indeed?" Joan asked, one eyebrow rising.

Nathaniel could have easily echoed the questioning response. He looked to Eleanor smiling up at him on his right, thought of his aching heel with trepidation, and gave a thin smile of capitulation. "And what is your answer to be, Miss Eleanor? Am I to have the first waltz?"

"Of course!" she replied with another smile for him, and a very quick superior glance for her twin.

"Then I must have the second waltz," Gabrielle announced, her smile as bright as Eleanor's, if slightly less triumphant.

"And I must have a drink," Nathaniel said, quickly adding, "So, what may I fetch for you ladies? Miss Joan?"

One eyebrow still raised—though its inquiry was aimed at the girls now, rather than himself—Joan replied, "Ratafia, please, Lord Price."

"Miss Gabrielle? Miss Eleanor?"

The twins allowed as how ratafia would be fine for them as well, and Gabrielle added, "But four glasses is too many for you to see to by yourself, Lord Price. I shall assist you, shall I not?"

She did not wait for his response, her arm entwined with his pulling him forward.

"I shall come, too," Eleanor announced, adding a giggle

that seemed to imply it would be the greatest sport to fetch a glass of ratafia.

"An excellent suggestion," Joan said, putting out her hand to Nathaniel. "Simon and these two will procure a glass for each of us, and you, Lord Price, will have the honor of taking me in for my first dance, even though it will not be a waltz."

He did not gainsay her, especially as at her words and gesture, the twins released his arms, pretty pouts already in place. He immediately offered his arm to Joan, smiled fleetingly in Simon's general direction, and swept Joan forward, toward the part of the room dedicated to dancers, doing his best not to limp.

A country dance, a progressive longways set, had been ongoing. It was a simple matter to join the end of the line, exchange nods with the couple just before them, and weave their way into the pattern. As Nathaniel stepped forward to take up Joan's offered hand in the movement of the dance, he said quietly, "I cannot thank you enough for rescuing me from your cousins."

Joan laughed. "They are scapegraces, both of them."

"Whatever got into them tonight?"

"Girlishness, I should think. Actually, to that point, at some time we must take a quiet moment to speak about them."

"Ah yes," he said, recalling her interrupted attempt to speak with him just this morning.

"Tonight, if we may. After this dance?"

"My pleasure. But for now, let me ask again how it is you thought to rescue me from your cousins?" he asked. He leaned forward a little, hoping the motion would force her to look up into his face, rather than at his left shoulder as she seemed wont to do.

"How is it that you are limping?" she returned.

His gaze steadied on her face, but she betrayed no deeper knowledge with the expression—or rather, lack thereof—by her calm and collected features. Besides, when they had talked, he mounted and she at her window, he had not spoken of his bruised heel, and she could have no way of knowing the Cavalier had the very same injury as Lord Price. He had rather thought he was moving with a kind of fluidity tonight, but perhaps she noted the slight hesitations when he was forced to shift his weight onto his bruised heel. "But how unkind of you to point out my infirmities."

She had the grace to blush, but her sensibilities did not keep her from responding, "So, you admit to possessing an infirmity."

"Yes, I admit to being old and broken and scarcely any use for dancing anymore," he replied, sighing dramatically.

They exchanged places, and as she backed away from him in time to the music, she asked, "But you are not seriously injured, are you?"

"Not at all. A mere bruising." He could have teased her about asking such personal questions, but he did not care to make her blush again. His reluctance also had to do with the trace of actual concern that flickered across her face.

"Then I will plague you no more about your infirmity, Lord Price."

"Come, surely now we have met these two years past, and with me all these years a friend to your cousin Simon, you may call me Nathaniel?"

He had made her blush before, but now he was startled to see he had actually flustered her as she stammered out a sound that was not quite a word, blushed a deep red, and made a noise rather like a relieved sigh when the music came to a conclusion. She swallowed, and said in a too-rapid manner, "I am promised to dance next with Mr. Irving!" She dropped him a curtsy and hurried away, leaving him alone on the dance floor.

Her departure was so abrupt, so unlike Joan, he almost went after her. He might well have if it were not for Simon, who came up behind him, startling Nathaniel by clapping him on the shoulder.

"Run, my friend," Simon advised.

"What?"

"I said 'run.' Gabby and Elly have decided to court you. I heard 'em say as much. You would be exceedingly wise to flee before they can reattach their claws on you."

"Court me?"

"I know it sounds backward of the way the rest of the world does it—you know, boy pursues girl—but it *is* the twins we speak of here. So flee, flee while your life is yet your own."

"You grinning idiot," Nathaniel said with no real hostility. "Cease with your nonsense and tell me something I can really use, such as *why* of a sudden your cousins have decided I am the very air they need to breathe."

"Oh, lovely turn of phrase, that! But to answer your question: who knows? They are the Alexander twins. The workings of their minds are incomprehensible." Simon took a deep drink from a glass of champagne he carried.

Nathaniel tilted his head to one side, a thought occurring to him. "Decided to 'court' me, eh? Could that be what Miss Joan has in mind to speak with me about? Can it be one half of the Alexander family seeks to warn me away from the other half?" It made sense, but it still did not explain why Joan had dashed away so suddenly.

He shook his head, and then his swelling foot. "My heel aches abominably," he complained.

"It will if you insist upon dancing."

Nathaniel sighed, at last turning his gaze away from where Joan had disappeared into the crowd. "Simon, the world has run mad."

"Only just waking up to that truth, are you?"

"What do you say to going abroad? Australia or America. I vow I will talk your uncle into allowing it."

"Good luck, fellow. And while you are at it, why not see if you can talk him into providing me with a thousand pounds to see I am properly financed for a complete education in foreign dissipation!" Simon scoffed, swirling his champagne in his glass. He took a sip, then took on a more solemn look. "But why this old tune? Does the thought of being pursued by my lovely cousins fill you with such dread that you must leave the country to escape them?" He lowered his voice, "Or do you seek to abandon your vow to kiss them and snip their locks, and therefore must flee to avoid the scorn of our fellows?"

"You must imbibe no more, Simon. You are becoming loquacious, and you only do that when you are in your cups," Nathaniel said, sounding rather sour even to himself.

"And I cannot remain so cast away that you must help me home again. No, that would never do, for Gabby or Elly would surely abduct you should you put so much as one foot in the house. Or they would see to placing you in a compromising position, and then it would be the altar—horrors!—for you, my friend."

"You read too many books from the Minerva Press." Nathaniel almost smiled.

"Only the ones you have recommended."

Nathaniel laughed despite himself, and the thought of the gothic novels—all dashing knights or swaggering sea captains, and besieged maidens—made him think of Joan. Joan, whom he had once thought of—when he thought of her at all—as a bookworm. But there was more to the woman, he had seen it for himself these past few days. Certainly she had proved herself to be a staunch guardian, but, too, she had a sense of humor, a wit about her to which he had never been exposed before.

That woman, the one he had kissed at the masquerade . . . there had been a wit there, clearly realized despite the brevity of their encounter. He had been moved by a sensibility that had stayed with him for days and weeks after.

What had it felt like when he had kissed Joan in her bed, mistaking her for one of the twins? But no, that peck had been too quick, too surreptitious to judge anything by. Were

Joan's lips capable of returning a kiss as thoroughly as had those of the woman of the masquerade?

But Joan had denied she had kissed anyone, ever.

And just what manner of woman *would* admit to a deep and shattering midnight kiss with a stranger! If that woman had been Joan . . . proper, penniless Joan . . .

Nathaniel shook his head, unable to reconcile the thought of Joan being the woman of the masquerade, and yet also unable to dismiss the thought entirely, either. Of course, there was one way to find out for a certainty: all he had to do was kiss her.

"Whyever are you smiling?" Simon asked at his side.

"Was I? I must learn to school my expressions not to reflect my thoughts."

Simon lowered his glass from where he had been about to sip at his champagne. "What manner of thoughts?"

"That the Cavalier has some avenging to do."

"Against the twins?" Simon frowned.

Nathaniel shook his head briefly, distracted by the sight of Joan moving through a Scottish reel, partnered by Lord Crowell. "What the deuce is she doing dancing with *him?*" he demanded in a puzzled tone.

Simon followed his gaze. "Crowell?" He shrugged. "Hard to fathom, but, only look at Joan! She is smiling. I must admit I never thought to see her smile in his company, she seemed that disenchanted with him."

"How peculiar," Nathaniel said, shaking his head. "You saw how she denounced any association with him to her father."

"Too true. And it is not like Joan to equivocate, so I cannot think she was putting on some form of performance for Uncle Eugene, nor think of a reason why she would bother to do so. *I* certainly believed her when she said she would have naught to do with Crowell—but, Nate, only look at her! She does not play the coquette for him, but she does not shun his company either." Simon put down his champagne glass, a tenseness coming into the line of his shoulders. "I find this very odd. And look at his hand on her elbow. Rather . . . possessive," he growled. He took a step forward, toward the couple. "I think it may be time for Cousin Joan to come dance with me instead."

Nathaniel put a restraining hand on Simon's arm. "With me, not her cousin," he said, already moving across the dance floor to where the couple moved together in the reel.

The music ended just as Nathaniel approached, Joan making her curtsy to Crowell and he a bow to her.

"Are you engaged for the next dance?" asked Nathaniel, speaking before Crowell or any of the other nearby gentlemen who might have a chance to seek her company, just as she turned to face him.

"Oh," she said, looking to the floor, apparently still upset with him. "Well, no."

"My dear, how much you dance tonight!" Crowell said, a sting in his voice.

Nathaniel watched as Joan gave a quick glance between Lord Crowell and himself, knowing she could not have missed that both men had snubbed the other by not offering a greeting.

"And now a second dance with Lord Price?" Crowell went on. "How intriguing. I vow it makes me quite jealous. Miss Galloway, will you spare poor me another dance? Perhaps the first waltz, dear lady?"

Joan smoothed a ridge on her glove, her gaze still downcast. Belatedly breaking a long silence, she answered, "Of course."

"Splendid! I only wish all your dances might be mine."

"A remarkable thought," she said, and the corners of her mouth tilted up for the briefest moment, in a fashion that might be called complimentary, although Nathaniel would have treated it with suspicion were it aimed at him.

"But you have not said whether you would dance this dance with me, Miss Joan," Nathaniel said even as he offered her his arm.

She put her hand there, and if she saw Crowell's scowl—because she accepted Nathaniel or because he called her by her Christian name?—she ignored it. "I will dance while I may," she said.

Nathaniel moved them into a set for a country dance, pondering her rather enigmatic statement. Dance while she may? Did she plan to leave London? Is that what she meant? Yet she would not have longed for a month's respite from the Cavalier if she meant to leave. She would presumably prefer a mere seven days in which to guard her cousins, so what else could she mean?

They did not speak as they wound their way through the steps, for she let it be known by her few brief replies to his questions about her plans for the immediate future that she was disinclined to chat. Here was the Joan he was more familiar with, the quiet Joan with a mildly uneasy set to her mouth, silent cares hidden deep in the depths of her eyes, not to be coaxed out. How odd to know there was more to her than this, more than the woman who until only recently had been pushed among the dowagers and wallflowers, to know this quiet side was only a small portion of who she was.

The dance ended, they made their bows, and when she placed her hand on his arm to be led from the floor, instead he led her to the open doors that spilled light out into a garden. "You wished to talk," he explained at her questioning glance. "Not to fear, I shall have you restored to the ballroom before the waltz is called."

She sighed, seemingly pleased to be out in the evening breeze, and allowed him to lead her down a cobbled pathway, well lit by lanterns posted every ten feet or so. Others strolled past them, and they would pause a moment to exchange greetings or a snippet of gossip, then stroll on. Nathaniel did his best to ignore his wretched heel as they walked.

"You seemed to enjoy Lord Crowell's company tonight," he stated.

She made a noise that was perilously close to being un-ladylike. "Is it possible to enjoy Lord Crowell's company?"

"But—!" he said in surprise, coming to a sudden halt, staring down at her. "But I thought . . . I mean to say, you were smiling, and you seemed to find him acceptable enough—"

"Acceptable, I suppose. Enjoyable, no."

"God's teeth, Miss Joan, you nonplus me! If you were a man I should be tempted to accuse you of being a fortune-hunter!"

Her face flushed, but she did not lower her gaze from his. "An ugly word, but true enough, I suppose."

"You think of marrying him?!"

"I spoke out of turn. Never mind my ramblings. It is just that I grow weary—!" She sighed. "Tell me, Lord Price, what do you think of Lord Avonleigh? Is he as creditable a whip as they say?"

"Yes, yes," he said absently, remembering her distress that she could not have a month's relief from her duties as duenna. She wanted more time free of worries—time in which, it seemed, to pursue a betrothal. A betrothal to just anyone, even Lord Crowell? Even though she obviously disliked him? Was her life with her Uncle Newland so unpleasant as to drive her to find a way out of his home, any way possible?

"I am cool enough now," Joan informed him. "And your limp does not improve. We should return to the house."

He shook off his ruminations, finding more questions than answers for each moment he pondered her words, and turned back toward the house. It was only when he saw a branching path—one ill lit and obviously designed to provide more seclusion to a wandering couple—that he recalled the real reason he had brought her out to the garden in the first place. He had determined that he wished to know a kiss from the lady. Perhaps tonight he could settle at least one mystery about her.

"Return to the crush? So soon?" he asked, stalling. It was one thing to wish to kiss a lady, another to go about the

business of doing so, he suddenly realized. It seemed she had
forgot the issue of her cousins she had meant to discuss with
him, for she was silent at his side. He did not mention the
girls himself, for he had not brought her outside to speak of
her cousins, but to learn something of this lady herself. He
fumbled for a moment of inspiration, finding none. "Do you
know," he said, leading her to a bench to one side of the dim
path, "Ah . . . I . . . ."

"You?" she urged quietly.

"I have been quite inspired," he said, rushing on with the
first words that came to mind, "by the Kissing Cavalier."

"Oh, have you?" she asked archly.

"I have. It seems to me he has brought a measure of excitement to London this year. Who will be kissed? Who will
not? I vow I could thank the man for providing us with such
interesting *bon mots* as we have enjoyed this Season. Only
look to Lady Bostwicke-Martin! Now that is a tale to tell, is
it not?" Did he sound as ridiculous to her as he did to himself?

Joan gazed at him, silent, watching his expressions, perhaps a hint of a smile playing about her mouth. He waited
for her to bat her lashes, or simper an agreement, or join in
telling one of the tales of the Cavalier, but she simply gazed
at him. She was so unlike her cousins, who were nicely predictable creatures who would have encouraged this talk of
kisses with a display of feminine tricks and charms. This
woman, this reader of novels, only looked at him with the
patient tolerance he recalled sometimes being exhibited by
university masters who had found his statements wanting.

"The thing of it is . . ." he said, running a hand through
his hair, all at once not terribly pleased with his meandering,
contrived words. He cast them aside. "The thing of it is that
I wish to kiss you!" he said baldly.

"Great Heavens, why?" Joan cried, her eyes widening.

"Well," he stuttered, once again at a loss. How could he
explain, especially if she were not the woman of the mas-

querade, just as she claimed not to be? "I . . . well, I just do."

"To what advantage?"

"Advantage? I do not understand—"

"I do not . . . I think I do not understand either," she said, standing from the bench, shaking her head. She backed away from him until she ran into a hedge, gave a strangled cry, and for the second time this night, fled from his company.

Fourteen

"He asked to kiss me," Joan whispered at the face she saw in the mirror, as though watching her lips form the words would somehow cause her to comprehend their meaning. Instead of insight, all she got reflected back at her was her own tired visage. It was nearly three in the morning, and she had yet to sleep.

Why had he asked to kiss her? Was he so baseborn as to kiss whomever, whenever possible? But how was that possible when he was the one man she had thought to possess some insight into the nature of those around him, who displayed a capacity to be sensitive to other people's feelings?

Joan rose from her seat before the mirror, giving up on finding any answers there. What a night it had been! Once she would have danced every dance, and tonight's busy turns around the floor had reminded her of easier, more congenial days. Ah, but in past days she had never danced with Lord Price!

She shied away from that thought, recalling with a momentary pang of guilt that she had never gone to Lord Crowell to withdraw from the waltz she had promised him, instead merely persuading Simon she had the headache and must return home at once. She could not have stayed at the ball a moment longer, not once Lord Price had said he wished to kiss her.

But *why?*

It was too late to puzzle it out tonight, her head swam too

much with weariness and confusion. Better to lie on the bed, to think of other things until sleep finally overtook her.

What of Lord Crowell? she asked herself as she slid under the already rumpled bedclothes. She realized the little guilty pang she'd known because of her social lapse of not excusing herself from her dance with him had already been dismissed from her list of concerns. What was one little *faux pas* compared with how she had allowed him to think she did not detest his company? Yes, she had not flirted, as she had promised herself she would never do again merely to engage a man's notice, but she had allowed herself to once again consider him as a potential mate. Was one action so very different from the other? And had she not been in some way pleased to see the interested gaze he turned her way, even if she suspected it had been her exaggeration of her soon-to-be-income that put the speculative gleam in his eyes? Was she any better than he? Had she not been attempting to find something about him to admire, to make the idea of encouraging a courtship with him somehow palatable? Desperation had allowed her to look in his direction, but was that a good enough excuse?

She had determined his smile was still his best feature, but could a woman build a life upon a smile? The only happy news to come of her flirtation tonight was that now she knew for a certainty there was yet one more thing she would not do to secure her future, and that was to seek marriage to a man she had come to loathe.

She sat up in bed, glaring at the covers as though they were the culprits keeping her from sleep. And what of her determination to inform Lord Price of her cousins' wager to see that one of them wed him? Opportunity had presented itself, but she had forgotten her intent once he led her into that garden, and certainly once he had asked to kiss her.

Joan tossed back the covers with an irritable sigh. She supposed if she were ever to find rest this night, she had best go to the kitchens and prepare herself a spot of warmed milk.

She rose from the bed, took up a copper candlestick—the twins had silver candlesticks in their chambers, she recalled testily—and made her way belowstairs.

She had just placed the toe of her house slipper on the carpet that ran the length of the downstairs hallway, when an "Oof!" came from the green salon to her left. Joan froze in place, listening.

There was a thumping, and a hissed, "Devil take it!"

Joan, candle not quite steady in her hand, crept to the salon's doorframe, peering around its edge cautiously. Either the servants had left the draperies open, or else they had been opened deliberately, for moonlight provided ample light by which to see all but the murky corners of the room. There was a large clothes press in the room, and one of the cabinet doors was open. Even in the muted light, Joan could see that a person attempted to disentangle his legs from some hanging table linens, folded as he was—and undoubtedly severely cramped—inside the cabinet space. "Seymour?" she questioned, unable to think why the butler would crawl inside her aunt's linen cabinet.

There was an immediate silence. Joan almost retreated, alarmed, but then her gaze found, lying on the room's floor, a large and floppy-brimmed hat. Her gaze flew back up to the man in the cabinet, seeing what had not made sense to her eyes before, but which she now realized were two eyeholes cut in a dark mask.

Joan's fear melted away at once, instantly replaced with chagrin. Was she to have no peace for any hour of the day from this man?

She marched into the room, ignored the muttered "Good evening . . . er, morning" Lord Price offered her where he poised ensnared by cloth, and shut the cabinet door on him. It was a moment's work to place her candle on the nearby table, turn her back to the press, plant her feet squarely on the carpet, and lean with all her weight where the two doors met. "Ha!" she cried. "You thought you were so clever, waiting here until everyone was surely asleep! But I have caught you, my lord!"

The door rattled at her back, but she would not budge from her position. Stillness came again, and she wondered if he could sense her triumphant smile even through the wood of the door. If she had not known he was in truth Lord Price, she would have questioned how it was that he managed to get in the house—by Simon's hand certainly—but no, Simon was out, so by taking advantage of his familiarity to the servants, no doubt—but also how he had avoided discovery by a footman. As it was, she wondered how he had smuggled his disguise inside the house, but she supposed that could be concealed under a coat or some such trick.

"Miss Galloway?" came his voice at length.

She felt a moment's disappointment that he did not call her "Miss Joan" but then that was what Lord Price called her, not the Cavalier.

"Yes?"

"What happens now?"

Her mouth twitched at the plaintive, logical question. "I am afraid I shall have to shout until some footmen come to cast you out."

"Ah. Yes." He cleared his throat, and spoke softly, "Uh, Miss Galloway, may we lower our voices a bit, please?" He must have taken her compliance for granted, for he went on, "I understand that I must needs be cast out from the house, but I would like to ask that you not insist upon removing my mask or in any other wise revealing my true identity."

"You feel you are in a position to demand terms?" she questioned, her voice lowered, indulging his request.

"Not for myself, mind you. It is just that should my identity be revealed tonight, it might prove extremely unfortunate for someone in this house."

"Yes, *you*," she said dryly.

He moved in the cabinet, grunting, and she resettled her feet, the better to counter the outward pressure of the doors at her back. The pressure eased, but she was not so foolish as to think he was done attempting an escape. But who could he mean would suffer if his identity were known? The twins? Uncle Newland was set in his determination to protect their virtue to the highest degree possible, but surely even he could not blame the girls themselves for an *attempted* kiss? Well, he might if his staff informed him of how the girls had acted earlier today, beckoning the Cavalier to climb the ladder. But, more likely, Lord Price meant Simon—for Lord Price had undertaken this entire farce for Simon's sake in the first place, she was still convinced of that.

And anyway, she had no intention of revealing his identity—she could have done that long ago were it not for the stubborn streak that still wanted to best him at his own game—but she need not let him know that.

He went on, "I know it sounds as if I speak only in hopes of tempering my own punishment, Miss Galloway, but I assure you it is not so. Is not evicting my presence from the house punishment enough? I assure you, it stings my pride to walk away, again, without the tokens taken."

"But if you are revealed, then I shall know the peace of having this folly finished," she argued against her own inclination.

"A peace bought at what cost?"

She frowned, his words summoning an image of Simon on some smoke-filled battlefield somewhere.

He continued, "I have something to lose in all this, true, but I give you my word that it is nothing compared with what this household stands to lose. Your cousins will be well-served, but what of . . . your uncle? Yes, your uncle! What if he learns my name? Will he not feel honor-bound to call me out? Do you really want to see him fight a duel?"

She had not thought of that! It would be just like Uncle Newland to demand "satisfaction" when in truth nothing untoward had occurred. How clever of Lord Price to think of such an argument! For he dare not mention Simon, dare not imply that Simon had anything to do with the Cavalier, not if the whole aim was to keep Simon free of his uncle's censure, and hence the army.

"I cannot have that, not a duel," she admitted. She stepped away from the doors, turning to pull them open. Lord Price must have been using the door as a support, for now he teetered, his flailing hands reaching out and only finding one of Aunt Hannah's long hanging linens, which immediately slid from its rod at his pull, sending him head-first to the floor. He gave another "oof!" as his right shoulder hit the carpeted floor, the linen sliding down to cover his face as the cloth that had ensnared his leg gave a loud rip just as it pulled his shoe free of his foot. Slowly, accompanied by a grunt, the rest of his length slid free of the press, until he lay supine before the piece of furniture that had so recently housed him.

"Gracious! Are you hurt?" Joan cried, moving to lift the cloth from his face. "First your foot and now this!"

He looked up at her with an outraged expression, his face a reddish color obvious even in the gloom. How fierce he looked, but then he began to laugh, big, large guffaws that swept her along with him, until she found she was laughing as uproariously as he.

A footman, the youngest one, Denny, appeared at the door with a candle in his hand and a suspicious look fixed on his face. He paused, his expression clearing as though he had assured himself nothing untoward was happening, only to do a double-take that showed he tardily realized the opposite might be true, given there was a masked man lying on the carpet. Joan laughed all the harder, pressing a hand to her stomach as if it might relieve the ache she created there by her mirth.

"Miss Galloway?" Denny questioned.

"You must . . . must show the . . ." she got caught by another wave of hilarity, but finally managed to gasp out, "Show my lord out, please!"

Lord Price sat up and moved to his feet, still chuckling.

He nodded at Joan. "I thank you for your indulgence, madam."

"Only once," she warned with a grin, waggling a finger of admonition at him.

He looked at her oddly. Not in an unfavorable fashion, but a curious one, and he took a step nearer her.

"Were only all ladies so gracious, clever, and kind-hearted as yourself," he said, his breath disturbing the pincurl at her temple, sending a shiver down her spine.

"Well, I . . . flatterer! Oh, go!" she stammered, moving her hands as if to shoo him from the room.

The footman cleared his throat, and Lord Price scooped up his hat and missing shoe, and turned to follow Denny out of the salon, Joan trailing.

"You, boy! What is happening down there?" came a bellow from the head of the stairs as they stepped into the hallway.

Joan turned quickly to Lord Price, who had ducked his head to hide his face with the hat's brim. "Go, go!" she instructed in a whisper, putting her hand on the footman's arm. The fellow gave an uncertain look from her to Lord Price, and back again. Lord Price needed no further opportunity, offering her a small, quick bow before dashing for the front door, his limp not impeding his speed, nor the fact he held one of his shoes in his hand.

"Joan? What in hades is going on? What was all that laughter about? Is Simon drunk again?"

"Indeed not!" she called back, and to the footman she firmly said in an undertone, "You will see the door is secured behind our visitor, and I will inform Mr. Alexander of what has transpired."

Denny looked relieved, putting his hands to the curled forelock of his powdered wig in a gesture of acknowledgment, taking his candle with him as he retreated.

"Joan?" her uncle bellowed.

" 'Twas merely some silly business caused by one of Simon's friends having remained too long in the house," she called up to where a flickering brace of candles illuminated her uncle's face beneath his sleeping cap.

"Too long? Do you tell me some lout dozed on one of my sofas? And no servants noted him ere this time of night?"

"Apparently so," she said. "Excuse me, Uncle. I have left a candle burning in the green salon. I must bid you a good night so I may go fetch it."

"Hmmph!" he said, and added, "See that you do!" He turned away from the railing, muttering something about importunate relations who are so careless as to burn a body out of house and home.

Joan stepped into the salon only to discover her candle had become extinguished some time since she had set it down. *How apropos!* she thought, for it did feel as though all light had gone from the room the moment Lord Price— Nathaniel, he had said she ought to call him Nathaniel—had gone from it.

Thank God I thought to mention the possibility of a duel! Nathaniel thought as he bent to retrieve his roughly tied parcel from the bushes below the Alexanders' salon window. He hoisted the bundled clothing, knowing he could not change before he got home, but that the late hour provided the invisibility his costume did not. He hurried from the yard, climbing the locked gate. No dog growls had issued forth, leaving him to wonder if the creatures were too well asleep at this hour or else confined to the kitchens or the pen Mr. Alexander paid to keep at the mews. Either way, he was grateful for someone's ineptitude or what was quite possibly Simon's intervention.

He shook his head, remembering how he had feared Joan had quite caught him, that all this nonsense was about to explode into disaster—for what could have been more disastrous than that Simon's best friend had been shown to be the

Cavalier? Nathaniel had no doubt Newland Alexander would leap to the conclusion that Simon was a co-conspirator.

This "game" became as volatile as the actions that had brought the game about in the first place! Still, how could Nathaniel desist? Was it more dangerous to take these risks and hope for completion of the wager with Crowell, or to surrender and allow Crowell to win? If beaten, would the man slink away as once Nathaniel had hoped, or would he strike back, like a cornered rat? More importantly, was Simon the more likely to be threatened by a triumphant Lord Crowell or a vanquished one?

Nathaniel kicked at a clump of dirt on the road, put his shoe on, then pulled free his mask, burying it and his hands in the pockets of his trousers. His heel still hurt, but that was hardly to be wondered at since he had danced on it, and now he had a long walk home to bruise it further. He had not wanted to make a horse stand while he waited all the while for the house to settle, so he had at last confessed his secret to his valet, Millard, and instructed that fellow to accompany him in a gig, the Cavalier costume tied in a bundle at their feet. A stiffly silent and disapproving Millard had left him one block from the Alexander home, a tidy arrangement that now left Nathaniel with a long tramp ahead.

It had been no problem entering the house. The Alexander servants, long used to Simon's friend coming and going at the odd hours the twosome were used to keeping, had admitted him without surprise, accepting at face value when he implied Simon was already at home and awaiting his friend. If they had noted the bundle Nathaniel carried, they had evinced no curiosity or recognition as to why he might be carrying it about.

After changing into his disguise and stashing his new bundle out the window, Nathaniel had spent over two hours in that cabinet. "Two hours too long," he grumbled to himself, putting a hand to the tense muscles in his lower back. Those pangs were joined by the bruise his shoulder had taken when he fell from the clothes press. He was a mass of pains. Would Joan evince any sympathy if she but knew? He thought she might. She pretended to be heartless, but she wasn't very good at it, he thought with a grin.

Ah Joan! The one who made sure the Cavalier was defeated at every turn. The one who kept her cousins from flirting too outrageously with him. She who had leaned over him, alarm in her eyes, asking if he were hurt. He had meant to reassure her, for she did look so very distraught, but the absurdity of the situation had got the better of him. Ah well, their shared laughter had served to soothe her concern as well as any spoken words would have done.

"Joanie," he mouthed the nickname, trying it on for size.

Miss Joan, Joan, Joanie—he could almost hear her voice, and now that he was free of the danger of discovery, he at last perceived what she had said. Suddenly the words leaped at him, and he could only wonder why it had taken so long to take stock of her words. Why, she had twice called him "my lord" not "sir" or "Cavalier," as she always had before! Moreover, she had inquired as to his injured foot. She was only supposed to know of his injury as it pertained to the dance floor, as it pertained to Lord Price, not the Cavalier.

Confound it! Joan knew he was the Cavalier!

Fifteen

"I tell you, she knows!"

Simon shook his head, running a hand through his already disordered hair. "It does not mean anything that last night she chose to say 'lord' instead of 'sir.' When you do not know someone's identity, you might call them a lot of things."

"Not 'my lord.' And she knew about my bruised foot," Nathaniel whispered fiercely, keeping his voice so low it would not carry outside of the Alexanders' box. The theatre was not crowded, so even normal speaking voices might carry through the air tonight.

"She saw you limp—"

"Not until *after* I left the room. No, Simon, I tell you your cousin knows I am the Cavalier."

"But it makes no sense! Why did she not say something, to me if to no one else?"

Nathaniel sat back, hand to chin. "I do not know."

Simon's eyes grew round. "And knowing this, you still plan for 'the Cavalier' to take action tonight?"

"What else can I do?"

Simon slumped in his seat. "Well, that's a true enough question. Although I suppose you could abandon the wager?" His upper lip curled in derision at the thought.

Nathaniel made no reply, for the curtain at the rear of the box billowed forward, admitting Joan, Mr. and Mrs. Alexander, and in their wake, Lord Crowell with Miss Eleanor and Miss Gabrielle on either arm.

"Egad!" Simon muttered under his breath.

Upon spying Nathaniel, the twins each gave a little squeal, abandoning Lord Crowell to slide into a chair on either side of Nathaniel. Their hands at once twined around his arms.

Mr. Alexander made certain everyone was introduced, and although he looked at Lord Price with a sniff of mild disapproval, he did not reprimand his daughters for their forwardness, much to Nathaniel's consternation.

Crowell took a seat next to Joan, who looked away from him without so much as a small smile, leaving Crowell to turn back to Nathaniel. "Lord Price," Crowell greeted him coolly, eyeing the twins.

"Crowell."

"But how singularly disappointing! I thought I should have this box of lovely ladies to myself, and instead I find a cousin and a courtier have proceeded me."

Nathaniel felt his jaw tighten at the word "courtier." He did not think Crowell would break his word by revealing Nathaniel was the Cavalier—at least, not directly—but Crowell would take an opportunity to taunt, given any chance.

It would be best to say little and respond even less to any goads the man issued. Nathaniel looked away, turning to tell Miss Eleanor, "That lavender feather in your hair matches your gown perfectly and to charming effect, Miss Alexander."

He almost regretted his decision to concentrate on the ladies, for he spent the next half hour captured betwixt the twins, his conversation divided between them as though with a blade, so that one should not have a moment's attention more than the other. One girl could not have a compliment without the other pouting until she had one, too. One could not tell an amusing *bon mot* without the other telling one as well. One could not smile, or bat her lashes, or flash her eyes at him from behind her fan without a similar demonstration from her sister. In short order, Nathaniel began to pity all the shuttlecocks he had ever hit with his battledore paddle, for this business of being bounced back and forth was tedious

beyond words. It also left him no room in which to speak
with Joan, except for the occasional times she turned in his
direction to quietly suggest how the girls might amend their
behavior to a more ladylike demeanor. The girls only listened
when Mr. Alexander cleared his throat, apparently a signal
that he agreed with Joan's admonition.

Their general behavior, however, remained extraordinarily
cloying, for Mr. and Mrs. Alexander seemed to feel that public homage was their daughters' due, and so took few steps
to correct their coy behavior or alleviate Nathaniel's entrapment by them. It would not be so terrible a thing if only
Nathaniel could turn their impetuous behavior to advantage,
but he could not see how the person of the "Cavalier" could
profit from this demonstration given to "Lord Price" while
sitting in the Alexanders' box.

"Does anyone care to stroll?" Joan asked as the curtain
lowered between acts, her tone droll as she now gazed directly
at Nathaniel.

"Certainly!" Nathaniel declared, leaping to his feet. The
twins did not respond to his movement quite rapidly enough,
for he slipped his arms free of their grasping hands, stepped
quickly around the seats, and grabbed Joan's elbow to propel
her from the box. "Do please walk with me," he belatedly
invited her, even as the curtain fluttered to behind them.

"It seems I do so already." There was that droll tone again.

"Miss Joan, you seem to be enjoying yourself at my expense." He released her elbow to offer his arm instead.

She accepted, placing her gloved hand on his sleeve, and
they began to walk. "You are so very kind as to provide the
evening's entertainment, and therefore it behooves me to enjoy
it."

"Why, you minx! What have I done to deserve such a tart
reply?" he retorted quietly, so that his words would not carry
beyond her ear.

His mock-outrage amused her enough to cause her to smile
openly. "Why, my lord, you have been foolish enough to

begin a flirtation with my cousins! I should feel more pity for the fawning you just endured if it were not a result of your own making." She put her head to one side, still smiling. "Although, I must admit, perhaps my cousins contributed a pinch to your adversity."

"A pinch? Remind me never to have you salt my food for me, Miss Joan—it would be wholly unpalatable if that is your notion of 'a pinch.' "

She looked away, but not before he saw her repress a laugh.

"And what of your Uncle Newland?" he went on. "Why the deuce did he not save me from my own folly? I mean to say, he is ever the sentinel, frowning at any man who would dance twice with one of his daughters, or challenging a fellow to a duel if that fellow so much as dares to wink at one of the fair Misses Alexander!"

"Do you mean why did he not chase you from the box with the point of his walking stick?" Now she laughed. "Surely you could not have wanted that?"

"I would have welcomed it, I tell you, instead of sitting there waiting for judgment to rain down upon my head! I was trembling from fear that I would be dead of a pistol shot on some dueling ground come morning, the way those two leaned into me, but your uncle said scarce a word to them! His forbearance was extraordinary, I tell you! And let me add, if the twins were not members of your family, I might have felt compelled to check whether or not one of them had chiseled me out of my purse or my watch, for I vow they had their hands all about my person!"

"How shocked you sound! But I tell you most men would not have complained overmuch if they could have exchanged places with you. And need I mention how vain you make yourself appear in these complaints to me? 'Oh my, they could not keep their hands from me!' " she mimicked, although her smile softened her words.

"I do not think it can be vain to state the truth," he said, putting on his best haughty tone.

She looked up at him, their gazes locking, and then they were laughing together. After a moment it occurred to him that he ought to have altered his laughter, for this sound might be familiar to an ear that had heard it just the night before, but it was too late a thought now. He had laughed, and she had heard it. Although, there did not seem to be any dawning light of comprehension in her eyes, and when her laughter faded to a smile, her gaze remained amused and unconcerned.

Miss Eleanor walked past on Simon's arm, giving Nathaniel a long, lingering look and an audible sigh. Joan turned away from her cousin, her mouth twitching with suppressed amusement, but then a troubled look came into her eyes.

"Do you know, my lord, I do not quite know how to interpret what you say."

"What do you mean?" he asked.

"I cannot help but think of the old saying about protesting too much. Can it be one of my cousins has in truth captured your heart, but you do not care to admit to it?"

"It is not so—but how concerned you look! Do you find my actions in any way objectionable? I vow, all I did was compliment one of them—Miss Eleanor, I believe—on her choice of a feather, and before I knew it I felt like a comfit over which too greedy pups were fighting! Is it vanity to feel so?"

"I said it was, but perhaps I was harsh," she allowed. "But I do not ask idly . . . ." The usually forthright Joan ducked her head, looking away, exchanging nods with other acquaintances, perhaps that she might not have to look back to Nathaniel.

"You may not leave me hanging upon such a statement," he chided gently.

She sighed. "No, I suppose not, for I have already twice neglected to tell you something of import. It is only this, Lord Price," she said, still not looking at him, "I am torn between loyalty to my family, and the need to do what is right. By you. For you."

"For me?" he said, unable to speak for a moment because a kind of warmth, thick and warm as honey on toast, spread through him. The feeling reached through him, softening his humor, disarming his caution. "Tell me what you mean. And call me Nathaniel. Please."

Now she looked back to him, flustered, unhappy. "It is the girls, my lord . . . Nathaniel."

A curious feeling, like the shiver of pleasure that goes through one when an errant sunbeam touches one's skin, threatened to distract him. He had never given much thought to his name—it was just his name—and yet how well it sounded shaped by her lips.

He blinked and ever so slightly shook his head, forcing his thoughts back to the conversation. "The girls? Are they ill? Or has your uncle threatened to disavow them for some offense?"

"No," she said with a slight smile, "Nothing so terrible as all that. But it could be terrible, for you see, they have concocted a scheme between them. They are doing their best to see if either of them may attract your attention, to engage your affections. It is just that . . . I have been thinking that you ought to know, that you ought to be aware their interest is as much in winning a wager as it is in yourself."

A lightening bolt, striking invisibly, caught him in his very center. That simple word of "wager" held so much power in it, now that he was certain she was aware he was the Cavalier. Did she use the word to accuse him? To strike at him in a way that might shame him into leaving her cousins be?

"Oh dear!" she cried, flustered. "That came out all wrong! I did not mean to imply you are anything less than the prize of the Season . . . or, well, it seems I cannot speak at all well this evening! But I hope you understand what it is I try to say."

She stopped, bringing their strolling to an end. When he pulled her toward a quiet alcove with hands that were not quite steady, she did not resist.

"Miss Joan—!"

"You see," she overrode his words, speaking rapidly, "I have been thinking how ignoble it is of them to wager on such an important matter. And although they are harmless creatures, and mean no cruelty, I feel certain, I worry that one or the other might pledge a troth to you for reasons less than you deserve—less than you might wish."

She held her hands folded together before her, and he could see she was earnest, all mirth now erased, no anger or censure in the set of her shoulders. He gathered her folded hands between his own, gazing down into her upturned face.

She had not spoken to condemn him; she was simply attempting to warn him of schoolgirl schemes.

"Your uncle would not allow either of them to accept me, should I be so foolish as to make one of them an offer," he assured her, and looked down at her seriously. "I am aware you know that, so I also know you are not just still trying to maintain your uncle's dictates."

"His dictates!" she shook her head, looking alarmed. "I never even thought of them! I only wanted to warn you—!"

"Warn me? Why?" he asked, pulling her hands so that she had to step a little closer to him. Why indeed? If she were not attempting to lash out at him for being the Cavalier, nor just to retain her cousins' flawless reputations, then why warn him of their plans at all? Of a sudden he remembered how he had hoped to have a kiss from her last night. A hope unrealized.

"Because . . . because wagers are a very silly reason to do anything so important as to marry."

So, she did not want him to marry one of her cousins. There, that thought brought on that feeling again, that warmth, so different from the tingling he had experienced with the woman of the masquerade, and yet it inspired the same response: he wanted to kiss her.

He pulled her closer yet, so that the toes of their shoes met, eliciting a small sound from her. Not a sound of denial, but the kind of noise that meant both surprise and reluctant pleasure. "Joan," he said, looking down into her face, "Say you will not run away again, not just yet."

"Why would I run?" she asked, but the idea of flight leapt in her eyes. Still, he almost smiled to note that she did not pull away, did not put any distance between them.

He held her gaze a moment longer, and then slowly, very slowly, he lowered his face toward hers. She did not step back, did not turn her face away, and even in the dim light that came into the alcove from the corridor, he would swear she lifted her chin, just a little, as though to offer her mouth to his.

"Joan!" came a shrill cry.

She spun away from Nathaniel, one hand springing to her cheek, which he saw, even in the gloom, darken with a blush.

Gabrielle and Lord Crowell stood before them, each eyeing the occupants of the alcove with disapproving gazes. "I think it time we returned to our box," Gabrielle declared, turning her scowl for Joan into a pout for Nathaniel's benefit. "Come, Lord Price, you must lead me back." She took his arm before he could accept or decline.

Nathaniel cast Joan a quick glance that he hoped said "sorry" and more, and frowned when he saw Crowell offer Joan his arm. She placed her hand there, although not with any show of eagerness.

The rest of the night's performance passed with Nathaniel once again trapped between the twins, who monopolized his time and conversation. Mr. Alexander gave him his only respite, in the form of asking Nathaniel if he knew of any recent émigrés with titles, the sort eligible to marry Miss Eleanor and Miss Gabrielle? Having no response to that vulgar question, Nathaniel allowed the girls to sweep him back into their discourse.

As soon as the ballet that followed the play was over, Mr. Alexander announced he would stroll again, now before the second play of the evening commenced. This apparently was taken as a sign that all others would stroll as well, for the members of his household all rose, excluding Simon, who earned a frown for his temerity.

"Pray allow me to escort you, Miss Galloway," Lord Crowell offered at once.

Joan looked up, once, briefly, to Nathaniel.

He stood, wishing he might offer to escort her instead, thinking that perhaps she hoped he might. Something in his chest twisted, but he had to make his excuses to Mr. Alexander. "I am sorry, but I must leave you now. I am to meet a friend for a late dinner. I thank you for your hospitality."

"Oh no!" Gabrielle cried. "Say you will not go already."

"I am sorry, but I must."

Joan looked to the floor, then lifted her chin again, and gave a very fleeting smile of acceptance to Lord Crowell, putting her hand on his offered arm.

Crowell shot Nathaniel a superior glance, and escorted Joan from the box.

"I say," drifted back Mr. Alexander's question of Lord Crowell as he followed that fellow out, "Do you have the direction of any recent émigrés? The titled sort, of course?"

The twins swept away with the others, leaving only Nathaniel and Simon in the now roomy box.

Simon turned in his chair. "I presume you slip away now to become the Cavalier?"

Nathaniel nodded absently, blindly looking down toward the curtained stage below.

"Well then, hurry to it, my good man, or else you will miss your chance to surprise the girls." Simon leaned forward, peering into Nathaniel's face. "What is it?" he demanded, at once serious.

"What do you mean?" Nathaniel asked, crossing his arms and sliding down in his chair.

"I mean, why do you yet sit here, and why is there a ferocious frown on your face? Did Gabrielle propose?"

Nathaniel waved the silly question aside.

"Then, what?"

"I cannot like your cousin being dragged into Crowell's company," Nathaniel admitted reluctantly.

"Oh, Joan can handle him," came Simon's confident reply.

He was right, of course. After all, she had certainly "handled" the Cavalier to great effect, but that was not what really had him disgruntled. What really struck him was the notion that for a moment, out there in the alcove, he had forgot all about the woman of the masquerade, had forgot that was why he meant to kiss Joan, to discover if she might be that same woman. In the end he had meant to kiss Joan simply because he had wanted to, to know Joan's kiss for itself, her mouth to his.

Realization spread slowly over his face. He could feel its movement like a sticking plaster drying on skin. "Oh no!" he moaned, covering his face with his hands. "Oh . . . devil a bit!"

"What is it, fellow! Are you ill?" Simon cried in alarm.

"I am!" Nathaniel replied. "As ill as a man may be," he said from between his hands.

"Then we must away to a doctor, at once—"

"No," Nathaniel laughed, the action hurting his ribs, for they had tightened inside his chest. "Simon, I believe . . . I think I have just discovered what it is to be in love!"

"With Gabrielle? Or Eleanor?" Simon cried, a look of horror crossing his face.

"No. Joan!" Nathaniel said, and could only believe it was true when he said her name and it made his stomach do a jig just below his heart.

"Devil a bit!" Simon echoed, and whistled in astonishment.

Sixteen

Nathaniel stood in an alcove very much like the one he had taken Joan into only a short while ago. Only now he was dressed in his Cavalier's disguise, his own clothes borne away by a helpful Simon. His heart hammered in his chest in a painful, distracting fashion. He could not say if the thought of reappearing in the theatre box—this time garbed as the Cavalier—was what made his breathing shaky, or the knowledge that Joan would know it was he who dared to make the public storming of the Alexander twins.

It did not matter, either way. Even the indomitable Miss Joan would not be prepared to ward him off here at the theatre.

His mind shied away from thoughts of how Joan would look at him once he set foot in the box. Better to think of how this assault must be staged. It would be impossible to beat an unnoticed retreat from the depths of the theatre, and luck and timing would be necessary to allow him to flee successfully. He only hoped no enthusiastic swain or theatre employee thought to detain him.

Simon had taken Nathaniel's clothing below to a waiting coach, and now walked past the alcove, allowing Nathaniel to see that he returned to the box. That Simon not be accused of having any part to play in the scheme, it was agreed that Nathaniel was to wait a length before entering and swooping down upon the girls. He would take a kiss each from those lips that had proved so capable of meandering speech, and snip their locks before anyone in the box could do more than gasp in surprise. Then it was away with him, a quick flight down the stairs to the carriage that Simon supposedly had waiting, and with luck on his side, he would be home in bed in half an hour, content in the knowledge that all this folly was now behind him.

Nathaniel waited five minutes, at which time he noted the corridor was clear of strollers. He moved from his hiding spot, dashed across the corridor, threw aside the box curtain, and stepped into the box.

He ran directly into Mr. Alexander, who tottered backward and regained his balance just enough to manage to twist into a chair, thereby saving himself from a spill to the floor. "You!" he snarled, "Cavalier!" He said the word as though it defined something filthy.

"I beg your pardon!" Nathaniel cried just as Joan leapt to her feet and gave a cry of, "Oh!"

Nathaniel, out of long habit, put out his hand to the tripped man, an offer to help restore him to his feet.

Mr. Alexander swept his cane up, bringing it down in a sharp blow on Nathaniel's outstretched palm. "There's more to follow, sirrah, if you do not leave my box this very minute!"

Nathaniel cradled his hand under his arm, glaring at the man through his mask, aware of all the staring eyes and rounded mouths in the neighboring boxes. "That was rather unsporting," he accused, thinking he should be more careful of what he wished for in the future, for had he not but a short while ago told Joan he would rather be struck by Mr. Alexander's cane than languish in the company of the man's daughters?

"Unsporting! By Jove, you've some cheek!" Mr. Alexander replied, rising to his feet, brandishing the cane again.

"Oh, Uncle, no!" Joan cried out, dashing forward to put her hands on his arm, restraining him.

He tried to shake her off, unsuccessfully. "You silly chit! Whyever are you stopping me? This fellow has long deserved a thrashing, and by all that's holy, he shall have one!"

Nathaniel looked to the twins, their eyes wide and eager, and wondered if it were worth the blows he would receive to stride forward and be done with the whole pathetic circumstance.

The decision was taken from him, because just as he decided it might be worth a bruise or two more, a reticule struck him on the shoulder.

"Shoo!" cried Joan at him. She pulled back her arm, the reticule swinging, and gave him a long, speaking glance. When he simply stared back, she said from between her teeth, "Well then, *run,* you lobcock!" and proceeded to strike him with her beaded reticule again, this time catching him on his chest and a little on his neck, exposed because he had discarded his cravat to don the disguise.

He winced. "That beading will leave an impression, I hope you realize," he said directly to her.

"Oh," she replied, changing her posture to a less aggressive stance, and giving her reticule a quick perusal. "It might," she conceded, looking a trifle abashed.

"Do not concern yourself," he said gallantly.

The cane came down upon his shoulder, sending a sharp pain clear to his elbow. Nathaniel yelped, and stumbled backward rapidly. He fought off the tangling curtain, and needing no further encouragement, turned to run full out toward the stairs.

He heard Mr. Alexander shout down the corridor, "Stop that man!" but with the exception of one rather large fellow guarding the exit door—whom he kicked with all his might in the shin, successfully setting the fellow from his initial intention—Nathaniel's retreat was uninterrupted.

A hired hackney cab waited for him, and the driver was either impressed enough by his passenger's garb, or by the sight of the large man who limped out of the theatre directly behind him, as to whip his horse into instant action.

Nathaniel was home in his desired half an hour—his hand bruised and a little swollen where the cane had struck him across the knuckles, his shoulder throbbing worse than his heel ever had—and amongst it all, he experienced the emotional pain of knowing the wager still loomed.

He could not blame Joan for his lack of success this time however: only his own foolishness for not sneaking a peek through the curtain before he charged in. He should have thought of that. But no, all he had thought about was how would Joan react to his presence, to his continued pursuit of the twins' kisses? He had asked himself if Joan would, after all this was over, be amenable to a courtship by him? He had wondered if she were missing him as she sat there in the box without him in it. He had recalled how last night at the ball she had said his Christian name at last, how it had made him feel to hear his name upon her lips.

"I am in love," he said aloud, and grinned widely. No wonder his fellows had always acted such silly sots when they were caught in love's web! Could anyone have acted more a silly sot than Nathaniel himself tonight? Impossible! "Oh yes!" he said, the sound almost like a cheery bit of song despite the aching of his various wounds. "At last I am in love! With the penniless cousin. Simon's shy and quiet little cousin! Who would have ever thought it?" He sighed, happily, quite aware Joan was far less shy and quiet than he had once thought.

However, there was one fly in the ointment, for it was deuced difficult enough completing this wager, and now, because of all this "love" business clouding his brain, he had lost his ability to reason when it came to being anywhere near Joan Galloway. He could almost weep from this night's frustration, he thought as his valet entered bearing his nightclothes, if only he did not have a foolish, lovesick grin plastered across his face instead.

Joan sat awake in her bed, a book spread open beside her on the blanket, the tome unread and neglected. She could not read tonight, lost as she was to thoughts of how this beef-witted matter of the Kissing Cavalier could and must be put behind them all. Her uncle's use of his cane on Lord Price's person had so angered Joan she had refused to speak to her uncle as they climbed into their carriage. She had even refused him the satisfaction of seeing her reaction when he had forbade her to accompany the rest of the party to the midnight event to which they proposed to journey on. Following the debacle at the theatre, the twins had attracted so much attention with their retelling of the Cavalier's arrogant entrance to and subsequently ignominious exit from their box, that they had been invited as guests of honor to one Sir Vincent Ferrobee's impromptu midnight repasts at his town house.

"I do not know what you were about, holding me off from further striking that rogue," Uncle Newland had lectured at Joan, "but I find your behavior tonight less than satisfactory. You let the fellow get clean away!"

"But, Papa, she *did* strike him with her reticule," Gabrielle put in.

"And you *did* manage to strike him twice, Papa," Eleanor added, a tiny frown between her brows. "I thought Joan was merely being her soft-hearted self—"

"Hush, girls! That's as may be, but I am not so dull-witted as not to notice she gave him an opportunity to escape, even told him to run away!" He turned back to Joan, his gaze thunderous. "I daresay you have proven yourself to be less of a chaperone than is desired. Very well. From here forward, until the day you leave my house—"

"Papa? Is Joan leaving?" Eleanor cried, obviously alarmed by his tone.

"You will no longer accompany my daughters on their outings. I will hire a more competent companion to do that. You will keep your own company until such time as you leave us. I only pray you will not perform in some other disgraceful manner until then."

"Oh, Papa, no! We like to have Joan with us," Gabrielle said, turning to catch up Joan's hands, utterly surprising her cousin with the disclosure. "Joan?" she asked with a tremulous lower lip.

Joan shook her head, looking out the window at the night's shadows, blinking back tears. She squeezed her cousin's hands in gratitude for her sympathy. Gabrielle was not really a disagreeable girl, only a little spoilt, and even so she dared her father's anger to offer a little comfort. She was a sweeting at heart, and Eleanor, too. With the right men to help guide them away from their more selfish inclinations, both girls could grow away from childish pouts and fancies if they so chose.

"It is all right," Joan said to the girls. "I am going to join my father at the end of the month you see."

"Oh, but she need not leave, need she, Papa?" Eleanor pleaded.

Uncle Newland was not to be persuaded otherwise, and had let Joan out before the house without another word as he signaled the driver to continue on to the dinner at Sir Vincent's.

Now, hours later, with it closer to dawn than to midnight, Uncle Newland and the twins had yet to return—although their carriage had. The twins had obviously agreed to accept a return journey in some other carriage, and Uncle Newland could hardly leave them unattended and so presumably had been put in a position of having to stay into the late hours with them. Joan had yet to sleep.

So much had happened in so few days! She had been ordered to marry and move away. She had accepted the responsibility for seizing her future. She had thwarted Lord Price's "Cavalier" any number of times. As for Lord Price himself—well, much had happened there, too.

How worried she had been when he clambered about on Uncle's roof—why, he could have fallen and been killed! He nearly had been when that ladder had fallen away from the roofline. And then he had lifted his hands in a triumphant salute, and she had wanted to kill him herself, just for being such a saucebox. She had conquered the impulse by teasing him with the hair from the girls' brushes, only to then foolishly debate aloud her desire to have a month free of his attempts at stealing kisses from her cousins. A debate during which she had been unable to answer his bewildered questions.

Because of the way he had spoken to her, she had almost told him why, almost been tempted to confess that she would be leaving soon, going away from the city that held the one man she had ever wished to marry. Not that she and he ever would wed, of course. But that was the worst thing of all that had occurred recently: just when he began to note her presence, just when he claimed he wished to kiss her, her devotion must be given over to finding a husband. She could not indulge in a perhaps-might-be-if-only kind of courtship, not when her entire future had to be decided in the next handful of days.

Does it have to be that kind of courtship with Lord Price? a voice in her head whispered. After all, he *had* asked to kiss her. Did it matter that she was not sure why he had asked? Or why he almost had kissed her at the theatre this night? Did his actions not imply he found her in some way intriguing?

Was Lord Price so far above other men that she dare not hope he might find the value in one Miss Joan Galloway? He was not a frivolous sort—she knew that now. As much as she had pondered why he played the farcical part of Cavalier, she knew in her heart it was far more a burden than a lark for him. Did she stand in the way of her own happiness? Had the last few months made her unable to trust her instincts? After all, she had never known Papa was in such dire financial straits, proving her instincts could be ill-tuned. She had once thought her cousins to be only mean-spirited and empty-headed, and had once thought to attract Lord Crowell's attention, now much to her regret. Why *should* she trust her instincts? They had done naught but lead her astray.

But . . . Lord Price *had* wanted to kiss her.

Joan hugged her arms to her chest, indulging herself in a

brief flight of fancy. When she had danced in Lord Price's—Nathaniel's—arms at the Monclesters' ball, all thoughts of leaving London, of looking upon other men, had fled her head. She had somehow become again her cousins' social equal, perhaps even sparkled in a way that less than beautiful women could sparkle, all because Nathaniel wished to twice dance with her. It was at the ball, too, that he had first bid her call him "Nathaniel," an intimacy she had only before voiced to herself in very late night dreams. Even now, it made her skin tingle to say his name quietly to herself.

The clatter of small stones against window glass drew her from her ruminations. She recognized the sound for what it was at once. While attending Miss Harmaunckle's Seminary for Young Ladies, it had been the practice of the swain of an attendant young lady to cast pebbles at her window, thereby announcing the young man's forbidden presence in the court-yard below. At the familiar sound, Joan rose at once from her bed, moving to open the drapery and the sash.

She was not really surprised to see that the culprit, sitting on the top of the garden's brick wall, was the Cavalier. "The twins are not here," she greeted him in hushed tones.

"I know," he answered at once, equally as careful with his voice. Even though it was night and he at least fifteen feet below her, she saw his smile. "Why else would there be no footmen to molest me while I rest here? They are attendant on the party-goers."

"And the hounds are penned at the mews for the night."

"Exactly so."

Joan leaned out her windowsill in hopes that her whispered words might carry all the better to his ears below. "Bringing us back to my question: if you know the girls are gone, what brings you here in all your glory?"

"Oh, so you find my costume glorious?"

"Infinitely. An answer, if you please?"

"Miss Joan, Miss Joan, Miss Joan," he said, shaking his head, grinning all the while. "You have missed your calling in life. You ought to have been a schoolmistress, for you cannot be swayed from having answers."

She watched the light breeze play with the brim of his hat, making the angles of his face slip in and out of moonshadow. She knew he meant to answer her eventually, and although she could not imagine why Nathaniel wished to play at bantering with her when the dawn was less than an hour away, she knew she had only to wait to receive her explanation, which came a moment later.

"I am waiting for the girls to return. Should be anytime now."

Had he been at the midnight dinner with the twins? Had he hurried here before them when he saw them making motions as though they were ready to leave Sir Vincent's entertainment? Or perhaps Simon saw them there and sent word to Nathaniel's ear that they were preparing to leave. It did not matter how, of course, for here he was, and here he waited.

"You intrigue me," she admitted.

He stood, one hand to his ear as though the better to catch her words.

"I said, you intrigue me, for I cannot fathom why you would warn me of your presence here," she said, as loudly as she dared. It was true the footmen were far more lax with neither the twins nor Uncle Newland in the house, but she did not care to witness another scene such as earlier tonight, with Lord Price at the receiving end of any violence. "You have given up the advantage of surprise!" she exclaimed when he only grinned up at her.

"Have I? You, my Dragon Extraordinaire, are far up there. I, however, am clear down here, where the twins will be. I cannot help but think that distance will allow me to have my kisses at long last."

"It would take me but half a minute to come down. So why have you told me this, as well as alerting me with pebbles against my windowglass?" she asked, shaking her head at him.

"Well, dear lady, to put it rather simply, I was hoping you *would* come down, and thereby keep me company until they arrive." He grinned. "I see you are puzzled by my illogic." He lifted a hand, waving her down. "I have seen a light in your room for over half an hour now, not to mention the occasional shadow of a restless pacer. I know you are not resting up there, and I consider you would be at the window in a trice as soon as you heard carriage wheels. Knowing all this, what point is there in hoping against all logical hope that you would suddenly retire and leave me unnoted to complete my task? So, you see, you might as well join me at my vigil."

"Dear me," she said, half-flustered and half-laughing. "I was not pacing. Well, not just recently anyway. And it is evident you are deep into your cups, or perhaps my uncle struck you too hard, for you do not make the slightest sense! You rouse me to tell me I cannot come down in time to save my cousins from you, and then you invite me to come down and keep you company, to be there when they arrive! Your plan, if such it may be called, makes no sense!"

"It does to me. And you may slip away, unseen by uncle or cousin if you so desire, the moment we hear carriage wheels approaching the house, and need not be involved in any way or wise, if that is your wish. Come down, will you please? Then we shall not have to strain our voices with loudly hissed whispers." Again he summoned her with a wave of his fingers.

"Of course I would not 'slip away!' " she cried indignantly. "Do you think me a coward?"

"Does that mean you will come down?" He grinned again.

"You would not club me, or throw a blanket over my head, or something vile such as that to stop me from aiding my cousins, would you?"

"Great Heavens, no! I swear it," he said, his tone sincere. "Indeed, I swear it on my given name, not my borrowed title of Cavalier."

"I am a fool to take a masked man at his word, but somehow I find I might trust your vow," she conceded, unable to believe Lord Price would break his word, or for that matter do anything untoward with her person.

"You are bored. You are restless. As am I. Let us, please, pass the time while we both wait for the overdue young ladies to return."

"I should have to come down in my wrapper, for my uncle would cast me out immediately if he saw I was with you and that I was dressed."

He laughed, the sound a hundred times more delightful than any smile of Lord Crowell's ever was or ever could be. "The opposite logic of what most young ladies would say of an evening to a masked man in their garden, but I take your meaning: he would think you conspired with me, elsewise why would you be yet in your daytime attire?"

"Exactly."

"Then come as you please."

She did, with heart pounding and hands shaking in a fashion that had nothing to do with daring to unlock the door that led out from the library—the front door was "guarded" by a dozing footman—and slipped out into the night. It was not the daring to go, nor even the fact she did so in inappropriate attire—she had pulled a wrapper over her nightrail, and then for good measure, another woolen one over that— but rather that each step she took brought her closer to where Lord Price waited to pass some time in her company.

"You came," he greeted her from the top of the wall as she stepped across the grey and charcoal-tinted nighttime yard.

She said nothing in return, not knowing what to say. She risked much by coming at his bidding, and yet it was what she wanted to do, even more than she wanted to secure her future, even more than not wanting to burden Papa with her keeping. Tonight, this dawning, she would do as she wanted. When the carriage approached, then she could become Joan the Dragon Extraordinaire again, but right now, right here was for no purpose, for no one other than herself.

He leapt down from the wall, making an effort to take most of the weight on his uninjured foot, and extended a hand to her. "Shall we wait here on this bench? It is slightly more accessible than my prior seat, you see."

She smiled and accepted his hand, walking the three paces needed to bring them to the bench. It was not entirely sheltered, but the arrangement of ivy on an arch behind it provided some cover from any eyes that might be watching from inside the house.

"I was glad to see your light tonight," he said, sitting beside her on the narrow bench. He did not release her hand, although she could have withdrawn it if she had tried even just a little.

"To keep you company," she affirmed.

He tilted his head—perhaps an agreement. "But how is it that you did not go with the rest of the party to Sir Vincent's?"

"I was ordered to remain home."

"Really? Why?" He seemed honestly perplexed.

She was glad of the pre-dawn darkness, for he would not be able to witness any blushes his well-meant questions brought to her cheeks. "My uncle thought I tried to help you get away. In the theatre."

"Ah! When you told me to run."

"Yes."

"So you are being punished by being made to remain home tonight."

"And every night." Perhaps it was wrong to share her woes, but she had no heart for half-truths tonight. With dawn just beginning to stretch a thin hint of silvery grey at the horizon, with Nathaniel's ungloved hands warm against the gloveless skin of her own hands, there was no room, no need for prideful silence. Not this one night, this one time she was to have him all to herself.

"Every night?" he echoed, his tone puzzled, the concerned gaze of his eyes like a warm caress across her face.

"Uncle says I am not a fit chaperone. I am not to accompany the twins anymore," she explained. To her own ears, her voice was soft, unaccusing. What was done, was done. There was no place for bitterness, not anymore. Perhaps everything was even for the best.

"You are forbidden a place in society?" Nathaniel frowned.

"Oh no," she assured him at once. "It just will not be beside my cousins. I may come and go as I please. Until the end of the month, and then I go to join my papa in Kent."

"Kent?" The frown deepened.

"Unless," Joan smiled at her own words, "Unless someone offers for me in the next two weeks or so. Then it might be possible to marry by special license without my ever having to leave London." She gave a soft laugh. "But I do not make plans for such a precipitous day, I assure you."

"What fustian is this?" he asked.

"Exactly that: fustian." She looked away from his masked face. Where hearing her own explanations only served to calm her, to begin to accept what the future held, the steady look from his eyes and the down-turned set of his mouth beneath the mask made her want to tremble, even though she was not cool from the night breeze. "There is only one thing I regret in leaving London," she said, proud her voice did not shake. An hour ago she would not have said what she now meant to say, but an hour ago she had not yet been invited to sit at the Kissing Cavalier's side in the middle of the night in a garden.

"And that is?" he asked, and she smiled to note he had forgot all about disguising his voice.

"That I never had something returned to me."

"Name it. I should be pleased to see it is sent to you," he offered at once. "If it is in any wise within my power to see that it is returned, of course."

She turned back to gaze at him, directly into the eyes behind the mask. "I left a simple black velvet mask with a man I kissed two months ago at a masquerade. I once told him I would ask to have it back, and I regret to this day I never made the request."

He sat very still, so still that if she did not know better, Joan would have believed entirely that she was mistaken in the Cavalier's identity, for this was the stillness of incomprehension . . . or anger that she had lied about kisses that day in the mantua-maker's shop, or perhaps it was the shock of learning it was "only Joan" who had kissed him over two months ago.

But that was what she had feared, was it not? That on learning the woman he had shared a wondrous kiss with was only "Simon's cousin," that he would turn away, disappointed, disillusioned. Now he sat still as stone—and she wished her heart were made of that same substance, for then perhaps it would not pulsate with agony each time it beat under his quiet, still gaze.

His hands came up, and she flinched. She did not expect a blow, that was not it, but she felt she might in truth shatter if he made a motion of denial. She could not bear to see it. She turned her face away.

A hand touched her shoulder, and she shuddered. Another touched her chin, pulling her reluctant visage back to face him, even though she could not raise her eyes to meet his.

"I thought, once or twice, it could be you," he said quietly. Two silent heartbeats passed, heavy and painful. "Joan," he demanded, his voice gentle, "Look at me."

She did, because he asked it of her. She did not see revulsion in his eyes, but then her own vision was swimming with unshed tears.

"I have already twice tried to kiss you. They say three times is the charm. May I, finally, do so?"

She could have asked "why," or demanded he let her go back to the house, or any number of other things, but the tenor of his voice was so persuasive, the gentle humor of his question so finely couched, that she could give no answer at all but a nod.

He lowered his mouth to hers, giving her no time to think or change her mind, and at first the touch of lip to lip was so light that she kept her eyes open just to be sure she did not dream the moment. But then he pulled his floppy-brimmed hat from his head, brought his arms around her, and kissed her deeply, in a manner she had never imagined could be so thorough and exhilarating. There had been their first kiss—wonderful, memorable, filled with the excitement of anonymity and sport. And now there was a second, and it was the same mad, spinning moment of connection, of unrestrained sparks, but, too, something even greater, even more extraordinary.

As surely as she knew her own name, Joan knew Nathaniel recognized it had truly been her that night, without doubt, now that he had kissed her again.

At length he pulled his mouth from hers, his arms tightening around her, closing the space between their two seated bodies, and she scarce knew what to think, what to feel when he held her head to the shoulder of his coat in a gesture of tenderness, or perhaps high emotion of another kind. And she was humiliated to find she then began to sniff back tears, tears of uncertainty and feelings too strong to be entirely contained.

"Oh my, I am very close to being quite the watering pot!" she cried, her voice up and down and all uneven. She struggled against him until his hands released her, at least enough to slide to her elbows and hold her at arm's length. She brought her hands to her cheeks, elbows still held by his warm hands, dashing at the two big, fat tears that rolled down her cheeks as though she might erase the emotional display from her face.

"It is quite all right. I think I could almost care to join you," he said, laughing unsteadily, and her heart leapt into her emotion-crowded throat at the dancing moonlight in his dark eyes. "Joan, I—"

He got no further, for the sound of carriage wheels interrupted.

"My uncle!" Joan cried, coming to her feet, glad for Nathaniel's hands still at her elbows, steadying her over her trembling knees.

"What will you do?" she asked.

"You cannot be seen as you are," was his reply. "Hurry! Into the house!"

She knew it to be true—how could she ever explain her tears, her strangely layered wrappers, her undoubtedly ruffled hair free of a bonnet or nightcap, her very presence in the garden? She could not make it seem the "Cavalier" had attacked her, or frightened her so badly as her disheveled appearance would make it appear, for then the Cavalier's courtly ways would be deemed to have become something more than harmless. Nathaniel would look to be a ruffian. Uncle Newland's patience with the Cavalier was already exhausted, and he would give such a hue and cry against the man that the *ton's* tolerance might very well turn against the Cavalier, too. One way or another, tonight, the game must surely end.

Suddenly, perversely, she wished it need not. This could very well be the last time she would speak with Nathaniel. In fairy stories it was right for a tale to end on a kiss such as they had shared, but in real life such an ending was dreadfully inadequate, an act needing words and explanations to complete it. Words that might never have the chance to be said, words that might be needed for her to forget, to put him finally in a place just in her memories, to go on with life without Nathaniel's presence in it.

"Go on!" he whispered fiercely at her.

A sob caught in her throat, but she obeyed, turning from him, blindly finding the library door, securing the catch with shaking hands as she closed it behind her. She pressed her forehead against the painted wood for a moment, taking a deep, steadying breath that chased a shiver from her nape to her toes, and then turned to move with quiet haste past the sentry dozing near the front door. Once the first set of stairs was safely conquered, she flew up the rest to her room.

She ran to the still open window, locating the carriage, with its lighted exterior lamps, almost directly below. Uncle Newland handed down one twin, the other, and then his wife from the carriage. He fumbled at his waistcoat pocket for the key to the garden gate. That creaked open, the party entered the garden area between the gate and the front door, and Uncle Newland took another minute to lock the gate behind him once again and call a thank you to whoever else was in the carriage. He then turned to pound upon the front door, to stir the footman from his nap. The door was unlatched and opened within a matter of moments, and the party below entered the house, undisturbed.

Where was Nathaniel? Why had the Cavalier not swept down upon the girls? Their entry had taken five minutes if it had taken one, so why had he not surprised them?

Joan surveyed the yard below, now made a uniform dusty light grey by dawn's spreading influence, but saw nothing, not until a shape atop the garden wall moved. Nathaniel, who must have been reclining there, more than hidden from the casual glance, now stood. He looked up toward her window, nodding when gaze met gaze, and lifted a hand in salute just before he leapt down to the far side of the wall, disappearing from her field of vision.

It was only then that Joan became aware that the carriage yet waited in the road, the carriage that had brought Uncle and the twins home. Dawn's light was grown enough now that it was no trick to see the crest painted in gold upon the door panel: the carriage belonged to Lord Crowell.

Seventeen

"No, thank you very much, Lord Crowell, but I must refuse your kind offer of marriage," Joan said the following morning, staring fixedly across the room at where Aunt Hannah's gilded clock read eleven o'clock.

Silence fell between the only two occupants of the morning parlor, until he said in a thick, amazed voice, "I beg your pardon?"

"I said I could not accept your kind offer," Joan repeated, still staring away from him.

"But your uncle gave me to understand—"

"My uncle was mistaken."

"Why, this is preposterous!" Lord Crowell said, then gave a disbelieving laugh.

Joan stood still. "Perhaps. Do please excuse me—"

"I think not! Not until you offer me some explanation."

At last she looked at him, allowing her own disbelief to show. "Is it so difficult to think someone might not wish to marry you, Lord Crowell?"

"Frankly, yes. You stand to gain everything by marrying me—"

"Not wealth."

That stung him, she could see.

"What do you mean?"

"I mean, in every matter that has had to do with the two of us, the only item that has ever sparked your interest has been the matter of money. You insisted you must be paid back every penny of the money you paid for my father's debt—"

"And what is wrong in that?"

"And how warm your courtship of me was when you thought my father was wealthy, only to cool to the point of nonexistence for two long months when you saw he was not. Then, suddenly my cousins needed to be kept from being kissed, and by being so kept you would win some manner of wager, would profit somehow. And then I was so foolish as to imply that I would be getting an inheritance of size, and now here you are again, with scarcely an effort at courtship, asking that I marry you. I am not so great a fool, my lord, that I cannot see you are a man hoping to better the condition of his purse!" she cried warmly.

He stood up, his face going rigid except for the working of his disapproving mouth. "You baggage! You, with your airs of being a viscount's daughter and your empty pockets, dare to say I am a fortune-hunter?"

She blushed but refused to look away. "I am certain of it."

He lifted his chin and curled his lip. "Very well. I not only accept your refusal, but I consider it a severing of any relations between your family and mine. I therefore demand full payment of the outstanding debt your father owes me. That means three hundred pounds are payable to me, today, by no later than five o'clock this evening. Good day, Miss Galloway."

He turned in one sharp movement, marching from the room to loudly demand his hat and cane be brought.

Joan stared after him, numb to everything except her roiling stomach. Three hundred pounds! Papa had owed three hundred pounds to a pastry chef? She'd had no idea! And the sum of it was due tonight, or else . . . or else what would Lord Crowell do? Why, pay the fee for Papa to be re-arrested, of course. Crowell was so angry, Joan had every reason to fear he would send a Bow Street Runner all the way to Kent to see the arrest went forward.

It was a little more than three weeks until Joan reached her majority, and so Grandmama's funds served her no purpose tonight. It was only to be two hundred pounds anyway—not enough to satisfy Lord Crowell's demand.

What can I do? she thought as she paced out of the room, down the hall, and up the stairs . . . only to be halted at the second story by the sound of her cousins' voices. Perhaps the girls could lend her the money? It was *possible* they *might* have saved their pin money . . . *and I am the Archbishop of Canterbury,* Joan concluded.

The sound of weeping caught her ear, and she moved to the door that led into the twins' joined chambers.

"Lord Price prefers you," Gabrielle said around a sniff.

"I could wish it!" Eleanor said, looking up as Joan stepped over the threshold. "Joan!" she said, rising to take her cousin's hand and draw her over to the bed, where Gabrielle sat amidst a pile of used and discarded handkerchiefs. "This has been an awful week!" Eleanor went on, explaining, "First we learn that you will be leaving us soon, and now Gabrielle is quite determined to believe I shall marry before she does."

"Oh, I do not care that you might marry first!" Gabrielle replied, stopping to make a lady-like dab at either eye. "I only care that you will marry an Englishman, and get to live in London, and see all our friends, and go to wonderful parties such as Sir Vincent threw last night. And I shall have to move to Russia, to freeze and weep my days away."

"Has a Russian gentleman proposed?" Joan asked, confused, sitting down in a flurry of skirts to put her arm around Gabrielle.

"No, but he will. Or a Prussian. Or a Frenchman. Oh, but can you imagine if Papa should accept a Frenchman!" Gabrielle cried in real horror. "I should not be able to come home until the war is over, and a war with France has been going forward ever since I was born!" She sniffed, and brightened for a moment, "Although it is possible we might not be able to even travel *to* France for many more years. Do you think it might be so, Joan?"

"I think you ought not wish a war might continue so that you need not move to France," Joan said, her voice a trifle ascerbic, but she softened the comment with a smile and by adding, "And I think you worry unnecessarily."

"I do not think so. Ever since I was born, I have heard that I am to marry a foreign man—

" 'Of title and position,' " Eleanor quoted their father.

" 'Of title and position,' " Gabrielle reiterated with a nod. "I do not see how I might escape my fate."

"Eleanor does not seem unduly concerned about such a fate," Joan pointed out.

"Well, I am! It is just that Gabrielle has it in her head that I have attracted Lord Price, and that he will make an offer for me."

"That's as may be," Joan said, unable to tell how those words affected her heart, for she had left that organ in the garden last night. Just as well, she supposed, for now she could think with her head. The girls must be given the happy lives they so desired, and she must save Papa from Lord Crowell's wrath. "But there is a way to be sure you both have your hearts' desire."

"There is?" both girls said at once, with hope gleaming in their identical sets of blue eyes.

"There is. And for the first step, I shall have to talk with Uncle Newland."

"Oh, pooh! You will never change his mind! There is no point in talking to him about what we wish."

Joan squeezed Gabrielle's shoulders, and said, "I quite agree."

Joan sent the money—all three hundred pounds of it—to Lord Crowell in a sealed box carried by Uncle Newland's very own valet.

She had accosted her uncle in his library, startling him by closing the door and telling him she had much to reveal, and that at the end of her tale he would lend her three hundred pounds, and she would leave his house forever.

"Blast it! You are the second person to assault me here in my study this morning! Have all the young people of the world run mad of a sudden?" Uncle Newland growled at her.

"The twins . . . ?" Joan queried in confusion, frowning.

" 'Twas that ramshackle friend of Simon's!" Uncle explained, also frowning as he rapped his knuckles on the top of his desk. "He came in here, told me he was done with my 'controlling of Simon' and that he meant to support the fellow himself. Said 'tell his father to take his money and his pride, and have joy of them!' The presumption! He said with a little faith in him and a little capital, Simon would do quite well, thank you very much."

Joan stared, and then cried fiercely, "Good! I am glad for it."

Uncle Newland looked up from under heavy brows. "You would be. Well, missy, I will have you know that was not an end to the matter. I said I would not have my nephew roaming about with no pride or purpose—"

"Which you have never allowed Simon to have," Joan interrupted to say.

"Even as Lord Price said. You two are of the same pernicious mind. He said to talk to the boy—"

"He is not a boy."

"And let the boy tell me what would please him, rather than telling him to do as would please me. And so I shall, and be done with the conflict in my household! His father should have raised him better if he wanted better for him. I'll have no more to do with the fellow's future! Even as you and I shall be quit of one another soon, Miss Joan. That is what you said you will exchange for these three hundred pounds you demand, is it not?"

"It is, and it is a fair price to be sure I leave you and

your family alone, and for being so stingy as to not loan it
directly to my father in the first place. In return, I will pack
my things and be gone to Kent in no more than three days'
time, never to darken your door again, and never to ask for
another single penny, so help me God."

He stared at her, frowning terribly, until slowly a sheepish
look began to creep over his features. "Well, I daresay you
will come to call if your father ever returns to London, or
comes to visit," he mumbled. "I mean to say, a man may not
expect much of his family, but they still remain his family.
And the twins would scold my ears from my head if they
were never to see you again." He had the grace to seem embarrassed at how he was all but turning his back on family.

She had received the money from him with a kind of satisfaction, knowing it would never occur to Lord Crowell that she
could get the funds by so simple a method as telling her uncle
why she needed them. A man such as Lord Crowell would
never admit to a perfidious act, but Joan would not act the
slave to pride when it would prove so foolish. She explained
to Uncle Newland without a blink that the money had been
loaned by Lord Crowell, not freely given of him, and that he
had demanded it be paid in full tonight. And it was all Uncle's
fault, for she ought never to have had to borrow from a stranger
to save her Papa from the horrors of prison.

"I would never have let Eugene *die* in there," Uncle Newland had murmured, too abashed to meet her steady gaze.

Next she had written a note to Nathaniel. She had frowned
down the footman's obvious disapproval when she had given
him Lord Price's direction, not caring what he thought of a
young woman sending a note around to a bachelor's residence.

Joan had been equally direct in her note to Nathaniel as
she had been with her uncle, writing:

Dear Lord Price:
    *My cousins and I shall be found riding in an open
landau in Hyde Park today at the hour of five o'clock.*

Please join us in your Cavalier garb, and it will be my pleasure to allow you to take their kisses and their locks as required for your wager. There will be no footmen or guards in attendance, and, I promise, no hounds. It is my wish that you do this in as public a fashion as possible, for my cousins and I have determined that Continental marriages are not the thing to make them happy in life, and are convinced my uncle will not listen to reason, and therefore must be made to see that not all things of this world are his to decide, especially matters of the heart.

We will consider your cooperation to be a great favor, and look forward to helping you achieve your aims.

Thank you. Ever yours,

Joan Galloway

She had blushed over the "ever yours," but had written it all the same. He would dismiss it as a mere polite phrase, while she would have the lasting satisfaction of knowing she had only written the truth.

And she felt no guilt at what she planned for her cousins, although perhaps she ought. For even though she was no longer obligated to see that she carried through with the duty for which Lord Crowell had paid—that is, to keep the twins free of the Cavalier's kisses—it was true it was Uncle Newland who had settled that account in the end. Uncle would not wish her to do anything but what she had been doing all along. She ought to feel atrociously ungrateful that he had freed her to do the very opposite of what he would desire, but the twins' desire, this time, came first. She planned the event without a backward glance, for after all she could not be more in her uncle's bad books anyway.

"What are you reading?" Simon asked, momentarily distracted from his own enthusiasm. He had been rambling on, and only belatedly realized Nathaniel was unusually quiet as they sat together in the slanting late afternoon sunlight coming through the tavern window. "You must have read it twelve times since I walked in."

Nathaniel looked up at his friend, saw they sat alone at their table despite the noisy crowd of their driving club fellows debating the likeliness of Nathaniel's completing the ongoing wager with Crowell, and silently handed over Joan's missive.

Simon read and whistled. "How peculiar! This is not like Joan." Simon put his head on one side, and added, "But, as I have said, your interview with my uncle left the man not quite himself. I was never so pleased, so delighted, so relieved as when he agreed that I should be allowed to study law. 'A perfectly respectable occupation for an eldest son,' he said, and I thought I would fall from my chair to hear it from his lips! 'I have had plenty of difficulties with those of the law myself,' says I, half silly from the hope he meant what he said, and he agreed I would know how best to provide a defense, as I have been offering them by the score since boyhood.

"All these years of demanding I be my own man, and yet it took only a direct charge from you, from someone outside the family, for the man to finally concede there was another way for me to go on! Can you believe it, Nate?" Simon crowed, his giddy enthusiasm rising again.

"It is all your doing, you realize," he went on. "I *liked* the way I felt when I set up your escape at the theatre. I liked planning it, I liked executing it, I liked seeing it completed. I felt I had saved you, my good man. That is when it struck me how I must spend my days: in the law! Not against it, so much, but using it to help other unfortunate souls." Simon leaned forward, the light of satisfaction filling his face. "I vow I shall learn the profession in the shortest time possible, that I might at last be able to afford to bring Anthony and Wallace to live with me. And Father may even come to approve such a thing, if I show my determination and diligence with my studies! He would want such an example for his youngest sons, I know it. Ah, Nate, you must know how happy I am! . . . but, oh, I can see that you are not. And I digress from this note."

"Something is wrong," Nathaniel said, rubbing his upper lip in thought. Why this sudden change of heart with Joan? Why was she now willing to allow her cousins to be kissed? Why this reversal of stance? It surely had something to do with what she had revealed, how Joan and her uncle had come to difficulties, that Mr. Alexander had forbidden her her cousins' society.

"There is a tone to this note," Simon said, waving the paper. "It sounds, I do not know . . . final somehow. It reads rather like a farewell."

Nathaniel sat up, his vision now sharply focused on the note in Simon's hand. "That is because it is. She means to leave as soon as may be. I would bet my last ha'penny on it."

Simon frowned. "Leave?"

"By Jove, Simon, you really do have a knack for this lawyering business. My friend, you have chosen wisely, and if I was a part of that decision, I can only be pleased."

"Joan is leaving?"

Nathaniel leapt to his feet, pulling out his pocketwatch. "Four o'clock," he announced with satisfaction. "Time to go home to my scandalized valet and have him help me change into the clothes of the Cavalier one last time."

"So there is some good to come from this note of Joan's: you will not have to lose the wager with Lord Crowell. I vow I look forward to seeing his face when you show him Gabby and Elly's locks."

"Hang the wager!" Nathaniel stated, pulling up on Simon's elbow to guide him to his feet as he announced, "You, my dear soon-to-be-a-barrister friend, are going to come with me."

"Wouldn't miss the denouement for love or money," Simon assured him. "I *will* miss drink, though, but I shall have to all but give it up if I am be a legal fellow."

"I promise I will not raise a toast to you the day you earn your silks," Nathaniel said with a smile. "But as for now, you are going to help me earn something even more wondrous and more important."

"Am I? It seems a fair exchange, since you helped me. But what is this business of Joan leaving, Nate?"

"I shall tell you on the way."

Eighteen

"A little scandal can be a good thing," Eleanor said to Gabrielle, who giggled.

"I daresay it will prove so for us," Gabrielle agreed.

"Papa will be furious."

"At first," Joan agreed, surveying the park with watchful eyes.

"But you think Papa will see we are determined?" Eleanor asked.

"I think you will be able to convince him you are beyond the blush once the Cavalier kisses you, and so publicly, too. It should be simple enough to persuade him to look to his native land for impecunious, titled young men once he believes his first preference has disappeared."

"Perhaps certain British gentlemen are not so high in the instep as a count or a marquis," Gabrielle said knowingly, "but at least they will speak English so that I might understand it!"

"There are plenty of foreigners who speak English perfectly well, but that is never the point. The point is you two do not want foreign husbands, and so you must convince your father you will not accept or be acceptable to them," Joan advised.

"I wish you could stay. You could convince Papa if no one else could!" Eleanor cried.

"Tush! You are halfway to convincing him already. Just

remind him often of how you wish it to be, and soon enough it will be so."

The twins put their heads together, giggling, leaving Joan to watch for the Cavalier.

He did not come. It was ten past five o'clock, and still he was not to be seen in the park. It was impossible to miss Nathaniel in his disguise, and the few closed carriages that had chosen to wander through the park had not stopped to set anyone down.

Aside from the tension of waiting and watching, and wondering if her missive would be taken seriously or neglected, Joan stiffened at seeing Lord Crowell at the ribbons of his favorite driving team.

He drove past, slowly, but did not bother to turn his head or in any other way acknowledge Joan's presence, and for that she was grateful. The twins might have enjoyed a scene, since they knew nothing of Lord Crowell's offer of marriage that morning, but Joan preferred to have them remain ignorant of that fact.

Where was Lord Price?

She saw Simon instead. Simon, pushing a bath chair, upon which sat an old man, hunched over and covered by lap blankets. Simon spoke in a low voice to the old man, whose felt hat obscured his face, and then pushed the chair directly toward the landau where Joan sat and stared.

She was not quite surprised when the old man pushed aside his blankets, tossed off his hat, revealed a masked face, and leapt from the chair. "The Cavalier," she said softly, allowing a tiny, painful smile to flirt with the corners of her mouth.

"The Cavalier!" Gabrielle repeated with a shriek, pointing vulgarly at where he pulled open the small landau door.

"The Cavalier!" Eleanor repeated, drawing the last bit of attention that had not already come their way.

Nathaniel looked to the twins, sketching them each a bow before he settled on the seat next to Joan. "Ladies."

"But you should not have involved Simon," Joan chided

ever so gently. "It might well be unpleasant should Uncle Newland learn of his part in this."

"Simon and your uncle have agreed Simon is to study to become a barrister. Today's event will cause only a ripple in their agreement, at worst, for they are both well pleased to have the fellow settle his heart and mind to a task at last," he replied, looking only at her.

"What are you doing?" Joan gasped as he reached up to untie the mask from about his face.

He brought the fabric away, turning to the twins, who both stared open-mouthed.

"Lord Price?" Gabrielle ventured as if she could not believe her own vision.

He inclined his head, smiling ever so slightly.

"But you need not have revealed your face, my lord," Eleanor said. "We were quite willing to kiss 'the Cavalier.'"

"Thank you," he said. "I will treasure that knowledge. But it is not the two of you I have come to kiss."

All three women in the landau gasped, as did not a few of the ones who strolled or rode nearer to overhear this revelation of the Kissing Cavalier.

"I came to kiss Joan," he said, turning back to her, taking up her suddenly trembling hands. He laughed kindly. "How startled you look, my dear Joan. Did you think I could kiss anyone but you after last night's kiss in the garden? Oh dear me, it seems I have compromised you in front of all these witnesses!" He clucked his tongue. "You know what that means, do you not? Now I have to ask if you will have me. Joan, will you do me the honor of becoming my wife?"

"Why, I," she sputtered, the trembling reaching to the very last hair on her head, only to subside of a sudden into a calm, a calm so right and good and wonderful that now she laughed. "Why, yes, Nathaniel, I should care for nothing more than to become your wife, but only if you really wish it so."

He did not answer her with words, but by shockingly reaching for her face with both hands and kissing her in broad daylight in the center of Hyde Park with dozens of witnesses at hand to testify as to not only *who* the Cavalier was, but what he had done to the plain and plainly delighted Miss Joan Galloway.

"Captain Nate?" came a voice from the crowd, causing Nathaniel to at last pull his mouth from hers with a reluctance she could only share.

"Sir Francis," Nathaniel said to the man staring over the edge of the landau's side.

"Good gad, man, do you know you have kissed a woman in Hyde Park, in broad daylight?"

"I do." Nathaniel grinned.

"But, you nodcock, do you forget you are to kiss *them!*" Francis cried, nodding to the twins.

"I shan't. Sorry, Francis. I will not complete the wager, and so I fear your twenty quid are lost."

Joan, a hand pressed to her lips, blushed a little when the gathering crowd broke into laughter at Sir Francis's dismayed stare.

"Why, you puppy! I shall deduct that twenty quid from the cost of your wedding gift, I hope you know!" Francis cried, raising another laugh from the crowd. Then he put out his hand, which Nathaniel shook as Francis added, "Guess I wish you happy all the same."

Others pressed forward to add their own congratulations, but Nathaniel turned away from them. "We are not done here," he said.

She watched as Nathaniel's hand went to his waistcoat pocket, stared as a pair of tiny scissors were brought forth, and gasped a little when he reached to snip a narrow lock of hair from near her temple. "That," he told her, his eyes dancing, "is the last lock of hair I shall ever clip in my life."

And Joan shocked and amused the crowd further by leaning into him for another kiss.

A horse snorted nearby and the sound of wheels on the path brought the two apart yet again. Joan looked up with dismay to see Lord Crowell pulling his coach to a halt next to them, looking down in disdain from his seat. "Do you say you have forfeited, and therefore now lose the wager?" he coldly asked Nathaniel.

"Gladly so," was Nathaniel's response, looking at the man situated higher up on his driving box. "For I have gained a far greater treasure by doing so." He looked back to Joan with a smile that made her head believe what her heart had already accepted.

"I shall claim the coach-and-four tomorrow morning at eleven," Crowell stated coldly.

"You do not mean to make it a wedding gift to us?" Nathaniel laughed.

"What is it?" came a voice from the crowd. "What does he want? What wager?"

"Simon!" Nathaniel cautioned, but he spoke under his breath so that only Joan heard him.

The cry was caught up and carried around the circle of gathered onlookers, becoming something of a chant.

"Make it a wedding gift!" came the same leader's voice, and Joan, too, this time thought it might be Simon who roused the crowd.

"A gift! A gift! For the couple! A wedding gift!" came the cries, accompanied by smiles and clapped hands.

Lord Crowell looked about himself, and snarled loud enough to be heard, "I earned that coach! It is from a wager fairly won!"

"Be a brick," came a cry, followed by others of similar intent: "You've lots of blunt, Crowell. Give 'em the coach!" and "Price is a romantic and a gallant. Least you can do, to follow suit," and "Sour grapes, looks to me!"

The cries turned insistent, so that Nathaniel stood, hands outstretched to signal the crowd to listen. "He may have the coach and my bays as well, with my blessing," he told the crowd.

A large cry of protest went up, and Lord Crowell's face

began to darken and twitch. He looked from side to side, to the urging faces of his peers, and stood up himself, raising a fist. "By all that's holy, Price, how do you get the crowd ever on your side? Keep the dratted coach then! Keep it, damn you! And may you both have merry of it. I would not care to own it, as it comes to it, not knowing you had ever set foot in it!"

"What, do I take it you do not wish an invitation to our wedding?" Nathaniel replied with a lift of his brows.

"I shall be traveling at that time, whenever it is to be," Lord Crowell ground out from between gritted teeth. "I find I cannot bear the stench of London and its people a day longer."

He gave a savage flick of the reins over the horses' backs, and they leapt forward, knocking Lord Crowell back to his seat with a lack of grace that nearly set him sprawling from the coach before he recovered.

"Well!" Gabrielle sniffed in disgust.

"I pray he really does go abroad," said Joan, her hand now pressed to her throat.

"Australia would be too close," Eleanor sniffed.

"I doubt he will show his face for a good while to come," Nathaniel said, his hands reaching for hers again. "I think his pride is at last broken, poor creature. But perhaps it will eventually serve for the best. I would have gladly let him have my coach, although I admit I was concerned for how he would have treated my cattle," Nathaniel said soberly. "I had hoped to purchase them back."

"You planned this all out."

"All but Crowell's unfortunate—or perhaps not so unfortunate—part in the day. But, Joan, did I hear you right? Tell me again, did you say you would marry me?"

Gabrielle and Eleanor sighed from across the carriage, but their sighs were tinged with romantic appreciation rather than envy.

"Perhaps. But before I remind you of my answer, it occurs

to me that I should have asked you a question, Nathaniel."
She blinked back sudden unbidden tears, tears of happiness,
managing to smile around them nonetheless.

"Yes, Joan?"

She reached up to where he had snipped her hair. "Despite
this mark, I am aware I am not the most beautiful woman
in—"

She got no further, for he pressed his fingers to her mouth.
"My dear lady," he said, entirely serious, "I assure you, the
Kissing Cavalier knows true beauty when he finds it."

She smiled, the motion making a kiss against his fingers,
and two fat, happy tears rolled down her cheeks. He moved
his fingers to take her in his arms.

"Then," she said, smiling up into his loving dark eyes, "on
that happy thought, let us gladly and forever retire the Kissing
Cavalier."

He again ignored convention and the crowd of onlookers,
to agree with her pronouncement by yet again kissing her
with a thoroughness that was as scandalous as it was irresistible.

It was such a kiss that for years to come it would amuse
its participants into a warmly exchanged glance whenever
they heard of it in its retelling. The Hyde Park kiss became
a part of the legend of the Kissing Cavalier, no less important
to the story than were the less true and far more exaggerated
tales of derring-do such as might be found between the pages
of a Minerva Press novel.

I enjoy hearing from readers!
You may write to me at:
Teresa DesJardien
P. O. Box 5845
Bellevue, WA 98006
If you would like a response,
please be sure to enclose a
self-addressed, stamped envelope.

ZEBRA REGENCIES ARE THE TALK OF THE TON!

A REFORMED RAKE   (4499, $3.99)
by Jeanne Savery

After governess Harriet Cole helped her young charge flee to France—and the designs of a despicable suitor, more trouble soon arrived in the person of a London rake. Sir Frederick Carrington insisted on providing safe escort back to England. Harriet deemed Carrington more dangerous than any band of brigands, but secretly relished matching wits with him. But after being taken in his arms for a tender kiss, she found herself wondering—*could* a lady find love with an irresistible rogue?

A SCANDALOUS PROPOSAL   (4504, $4.99)
by Teresa DesJardien

After only two weeks into the London season, Lady Pamela Premington has already received her first offer of marriage. If only it hadn't come from the *ton's* most notorious rake, Lord Marchmont. Pamela had already set her sights on the distinguished Lieutenant Penford, who had the heroism and honor that made him the ideal match. Now she had to keep from falling under the spell of the seductive Lord so she could pursue the man more worthy of her love. Or was he?

A LADY'S CHAMPION   (4535, $3.99)
by Janice Bennett

Miss Daphne, art mistress of the Selwood Academy for Young Ladies, greeted the notion of ghosts haunting the academy with skepticism. However, to avoid rumors frightening off students, she found herself turning to Mr. Adrian Carstairs, sent by her uncle to be her "protector" against the "ghosts." Although, Daphne would accept no interference in her life, she *would* accept aid in exposing any spectral spirits. What she never expected was for Adrian to expose the secret wishes of her hidden heart . . .

CHARITY'S GAMBIT   (4537, $3.99)
by Marcy Stewart

Charity Abercrombie reluctantly embarks on a London season in hopes of making a suitable match. However she cannot forget the mysterious Dominic Castille—and the kiss they shared—when he fell from a tree as she strolled through the woods. Charity does not know that the dark and dashing captain harbors a dangerous secret that will ensnare them both in its web—leaving Charity to risk certain ruin and losing the man she so passionately loves . . .

Available wherever paperbacks are sold, or order direct from the Publisher. Send cover price plus 50¢ per copy for mailing and handling to Penguin USA, P.O. Box 999, c/o Dept. 17109, Bergenfield, NJ 07621. Residents of New York and Tennessee must include sales tax. DO NOT SEND CASH.